CAMP
QUILTBAG

CAMP QUILTBAG

NICOLE MELLEBY

AND

A. J. SASS

ALGONQUIN YOUNG READERS   2023

Published by
Algonquin Young Readers
an imprint of Workman Publishing Co., Inc.
a subsidiary of Hachette Book Group, Inc.
1290 Avenue of the Americas
New York, New York 10104

Printed in the United States of America
Design by Carla Weise

LIBRARY OF CONGRESS CATALOGING-IN-PUBLICATION DATA

Names: Melleby, Nicole, author. | Sass, A. J., author.
Title: Camp QUILTBAG / Nicole Melleby and A. J. Sass.
Description: New York, New York : Algonquin Young Readers, [2023] |
Audience: Ages 8–12. | Audience: Grades 4–6. | Summary: "After a bit
of a rocky start at Camp QUILTBAG, an inclusive retreat for queer and
trans kids, Abigail and Kai make a pact to help each other find t
heir footing, all while navigating crushes, their queer identities, and
a competition pitting cabin against cabin"—Provided by publisher.
Identifiers: LCCN 2022040497 | ISBN 9781643752662 (hardcover) |
ISBN 9781643753669 (ebook)
Subjects: CYAC: LGBTQ+ people—Fiction. |
Friendship—Fiction. | Camps—Fiction.
Classification: LCC PZ7.1.M46934 Cam 2023 | DDC [Fic]—dc23
LC record available at https://lccn.loc.gov/2022040497

ISBN 978-1-64375-266-2 (hardcover)
ISBN 978-1-5235-2402-0 (paperback)

10 9 8 7 6 5 4 3 2 1
First Paperback Edition

TO EVERY READER WHO HAS
BEEN LOOKING FOR THEIR PLACE:
CAMP QUILTBAG HAS A SPOT FOR YOU.

ABIGAIL

(SHE/HER/HERS)

ABIGAIL FOUND THE WEBSITE HERSELF.

It was a very un-Abigail-like thing to do. She'd had a bad day at school (weren't they all bad days ever since Stacy had stopped being her friend?) and came home, traded her school uniform skirt for sweatpants, and did what she always did on bad days: took out her laptop to watch interviews of her celebrity favorites on YouTube.

Mostly Laura Dern. Or Teri Polo. Or some other older actress, usually at *least* over forty, who was pretty enough to steal Abigail's heart that week. She sort of had a thing for older ladies. It sort of got her into all this trouble in the first place.

She couldn't enjoy the YouTube interviews that day, though. She tried. She pulled up an old *Jurassic Park* interview, and Laura Dern said something silly, and Abigail blushed at the sound of her laughter, and she'd had such a bad day at school that even just blushing in the privacy of her bedroom was, well, embarrassing.

Really embarrassing. Abigail couldn't explain it, but she felt the tips of her ears get warm, and her shoulders tensed and inched up her neck, and she couldn't enjoy Laura Dern anymore. Not when all the kids at school had been making fun of her for weeks for having stupidly admitted to having a crush on Stacy's mom.

Nice job, Abigail. No one needed to know about that.

But now they all *did* know. Stacy had stopped inviting Abigail to hang out because she said it was now super weird, and honestly, Abigail didn't blame her. It *was* super weird.

It was even weirder when Abigail realized that she not only missed hanging out with Stacy, she also missed seeing Stacy's mom.

You're hopeless, Abigail. And now you have no friends.

It was kind of a double-edged sword that summer break was nearly here. Because, *Yay, no more school where she could have bad days!* But also, *Oh no, no friends to make summer plans with.* Stacy and the other girls would all go to the beach and the boardwalk without inviting her, and they would post pictures all over social media, and Abigail would not be in a single shot.

That was what Abigail was thinking about when she closed YouTube and pulled up Google and typed, *How do I find LGBTQ friends?*

That, too, felt kind of embarrassing. Who used Google to find friends? Abigail was definitely hopeless, was definitely alone, and definitely had no real people skills whatsoever.

She was seriously considering asking her mom to send her to a convent or something to escape being such an awkward excuse of a human in such a cruel, cruel world, when she saw it (on the third O page of the Goooooogle results): *Camp QUILTBAG.*

She clicked the link.

Camp QUILTBAG, according to its website, was a two-week camp for LGBTQ+ youth in Minnesota—which was delightfully far, far away from Abigail's friends (ex-friends?) in New Jersey. The very top of the page had a quote from a former camper that said, "Camp QUILTBAG felt like more than just a summer camp, it felt like coming home." There were pictures of kids in rainbow-colored shirts, smiling, arms around each other. The descriptions said it had activities just like any other camp—obstacle courses, swimming, kayaking, archery—and ones specifically for LGBTQ+ kids—workshops on gender identity and expression, body image and self-esteem, LGBTQ+ history, and drag makeup.

It sounded terrifying. Abigail was just . . . *Abigail*, and the kids in these pictures were all smiles and dyed hair and cool colorful clothes. The kids in these pictures looked totally *out*, and totally proud, and probably never got embarrassed.

But it also sounded perfect *because* those kids probably never got embarrassed and probably *were* totally out and proud, and maybe Abigail could somehow learn to be, too. Maybe they'd understand her crush on Stacy's mom and Laura Dern and Teri Polo and all the other beautiful women in the world.

So she clicked the *More Information* link and filled out her mom's email address, and then hit send before she could stop herself.

She had a minor panic attack and major regret immediately afterwards. It wasn't that her parents didn't know, but there was knowing, and there was *knowing*. There was a difference between *Oh, Abigail has crushes on actresses* and *Abigail wants to go to gay camp*.

Not to mention the fact that she wouldn't exactly be able to tell a single soul at school she'd be spending her summer at gay camp, of all things.

Though, in fairness, it wasn't like she had anyone to tell right now, anyway.

But it wasn't like she could take it back now, either. She sped out of her room and down the stairs to where her mom was sitting in the living room, but all she could do was stand there, eyes wide, watching it all unfold, like realizing the Jell-O was wiggling and knowing a T. rex was about to show up but really, how well could you run from it now?

Abigail's mom was basically glued to her cell phone, and Abigail had the pleasure of making it to the room just in time to hear it buzz with the notification of an incoming email. Abigail pressed her lips tightly together, holding her breath.

"Is this something you're interested in?" her mom asked.

"No. Maybe. Yes," Abigail replied.

"It's over two thousand dollars to attend," her mom responded.

Which was a lot of money. Abigail knew that from how intensely she'd studied the website in the first place. But her mom and dad paid for Catholic school every year because they wanted Abigail to have a foundation in faith, or whatever. If they could spend the money on something they wanted, they could spend it on something Abigail needed.

Right?

Don't be selfish, Abigail.

"If it's too much, I don't have to . . . ," she said.

"You clearly want to," her mom said. "I don't know that I understand all this, and I'd need to look into this camp a bit more. But if this is important to you, you need to let us know."

Abigail took a deep breath, and in her second very un-Abigail-like move, she admitted, "It's important to me."

Three weeks later, she (fortunately) wasn't packing to be sent away to a convent. She was packing for a long plane ride to Minnesota to spend two weeks at Camp QUILTBAG. She packed her favorite Laura Dern poster and her favorite *Jurassic Park* shirt. She searched her clothes for something colorful to bring but came up empty. She hoped she'd come home wearing rainbows. She hoped she'd come home feeling out and proud and not even a little bit embarrassed.

Even though, right now, she was still kind of embarrassed. She hadn't told anyone at school where she'd be going this summer. She'd lied and said she was spending the summer at her family's lake house in upstate New York. Stacy, who had been Abigail's best friend basically her entire life, who knew full well that Abigail's family didn't have a lake house—nor did she have any family that lived in upstate New York in general—had stopped giving Abigail the cold shoulder solely to ask her a million questions about it.

Abigail just kept lying.

"Well, I'm sure you'll post a lot of pictures for us to see," Stacy had said.

"Yeah, of course. It's so beautiful there," Abigail had lied.

But she'd worry about the lies later. She hoped it would all sort itself out.

Abigail—as she zipped up her suitcase and headed downstairs, ready for her parents to drive her to the airport—hoped most of all that she'd make at least one friend who would understand her.

2

KAI
(E/EM/EIR)

KAI STARED OUT THE CAR WINDOW FROM BEHIND THE driver's seat, frowning. E studied the skyscrapers of downtown Minneapolis, then the older brick buildings along the outskirts of the city as they traveled north. Here, the homes were newer, more uniform, and looked a lot like the one Kai's family lived in farther south.

In the front of the car, Kai's parents chatted about the weather (humid for this early in June), about some work project eir mom had that was due soon (she was a marketer, whatever that meant), and when they should start looking for the highway exit (in half an hour, give or take, between the 221 and 222 mile markers).

8

". . . don't you think?" Mom asked.

"Absolutely," Dad replied, his voice superficially bright. "Seems like a sign, if ever there was one."

Kai kept quiet, only half listening as e stared at the trees, homing in on the occasional movement of a bird or squirrel—looking anywhere except the seat to eir right. There, an orientation packet lay open to a glossy spread, featuring grinning kids. It felt like they were mocking em.

"Kai, sweetie?"

Kai jerked at the sound of Mom's voice, and a dull ache prickled down eir shoulder. E shot a quick glare at the sling holding eir arm in place, then looked up. "Sorry, what?"

"Your father and I were just saying how nifty it is that this camp is on *Shakopee* Lake Road."

Kai could imagine a bare minimum of fifty things niftier than some road in Middle of Nowhere, Minnesota, sharing a name with their hometown. But eir mom was giving em such a hopeful look.

"Okay."

Kai chewed on eir lip. Normally eir younger sister, Lexi, would chatter with eir parents on road trips, but she'd left for swim camp last week. Now it was just Kai and the orientation packet, with all its happy kids and rainbow colors.

CAMP QUILTBAG:

A safe space to be yourself!

Kai didn't see why e couldn't just be emself back at home. Instead, eir parents were sending em someplace where e wouldn't know anyone, all because a few kids at school last year had a problem with Kai and eir pronouns.

So. Dumb.

"It feels like a sign," Dad said again. "Don't you think, Kai?"

"I guess."

Kai knew e was being difficult, that eir parents were just trying to be supportive. But e was fine. E definitely didn't need to attend Camp QUILTBAG to figure out eir identity, because e already knew it. Kai Lindquist: Former gymnast-turned-parkour wizard. Almost-eighth-grader.

Pronouns and identity were only a small part of em. It wasn't Kai's fault that's what everyone focused on.

E slouched in eir seat and let Mom and Dad continue talking. Kai couldn't help wishing e was back in the real Shakopee as they passed mile marker 204. E slipped eir phone out of eir pocket, eyeing the notifications.

Nothing from Cie-Cie, or any of eir old gymnastics teammates, but that wasn't a shocker. They'd all been pretty quiet since The Incident that started this whole "let's send Kai to a camp e doesn't want to be at" business.

There was a group text from Leo, last year's parkour team captain. Loneliness washed over Kai as e read the reminder about next week's practice, plus an upcoming event two weekends from now. Most of eir teammates lived a few towns away from Kai and attended a different school, so practice and events were the only times e got to see them. Kai wouldn't have been able to participate in the event due to eir shoulder, but e still could've gone to the gym and spent time with eir friends between now and then.

E wouldn't know anyone at Camp QUILTBAG, so it felt a lot like e'd be starting from scratch. Kai had already started over when e'd quit gymnastics and e wasn't eager to do it again, now that e'd already found a group of supportive friends.

The second text was from another parkour friend.

Queen Aziza:
Hey, King Kai!
Are we (you) there yet??

The corners of Kai's mouth twitched up.

Kai:
In like ten miles
Have you figured out how to teleport and save me yet?

"Sweetie?"

Eir mom was looking back at em again.

"You promise you'll give this a try? For your dad and me?"

The entire drive, both Mom and Dad had been acting all bright and positive. It reminded Kai of the smiles e used to practice with Cie-Cie before gymnastics meets. E'd eventually gotten so good at looking confident, it was impossible to tell what was real or faked.

Eir mom's and dad's forced expressions were a lot more obvious.

But now, Mom's tone was less upbeat, more pleading. Her brows pinched toward the bridge of her nose and a worry line wrinkled her forehead beneath blond hair that matched Kai's own. As much as this camp felt like a punishment, Kai knew eir parents were just trying to find a "good balance" between letting em do eir own thing and showing they supported em. That's what Kai's therapist kept saying, anyway.

Kai had learned to visualize positive outcomes with eir therapist since coming out last year, but e still couldn't imagine meeting anyone like Aziza at camp. Two weeks just wasn't enough time to build that kind of trust.

It was too late to turn back, though.

Throat tight, Kai nodded. "Plus, you said I could leave

early, right? Next Friday instead of Sunday. So I can go to Aziza's parkour event?"

Mom sighed. "We said we'd think about it. Let's see how you settle in at camp first, all right?"

Kai didn't reply.

"We will definitely make a decision before the beginning of the second week," Dad promised. "Try not to worry about it until then. Besides, you might realize you're having so much fun that you'll want to stay through to the end."

Not likely. But Kai stayed quiet as Dad kept talking.

"Just give it a chance. If you really don't want to stay, you can let us know at the end of next weekend and we'll get you early. How's that sound?"

It sounded like Kai and eir parents weren't on the same page—that they were reading completely different books, actually. Still, there was no point in arguing, now that they were almost there.

"Okay."

Mom's worry line disappeared. She sat back in her seat just as they drove past mile marker 220.

"Not long now, pal," Dad said, and Kai's chest clenched a little.

The car slowed after mile 221. Beyond it, another sign came into view.

It said, *Shakopee*, just like back home. Except not even close, because of the added *Lake Road*.

"I really do think this will be a great experience," Mom said as Dad turned off the highway and onto a gravel road. "Maybe you'll even meet other parkour fans."

"As long as you don't actually *do* any parkour," Dad chimed in.

The car bumped along the gravel road, jerking them all against their seatbelts. Kai's shoulder twinged again.

"I get to take this off in like three days though, right?"

"Hopefully," Dad said. "We'll see what the camp nurse thinks."

"And that doesn't mean you'll be able to do all the tricks you used to before those awful boys"—Kai's stomach twisted as Mom paused—"before you got injured."

A wooden arch appeared, painted like a rainbow. Dad drove under it, then parked at the end of a row of cars.

Mom hopped out first and hurried around the car to open the door for Kai.

"My other arm's fine, you know," Kai said. "I can open doors myself."

"I know." Mom smiled. "I just wanted to give you your first goodbye hug."

Kai leaned into her, cheeks hot. Last year, eir face would've been buried in Mom's shoulder, breathing in the perfume she always wore: vanilla lavender. Now, eir chin almost cleared it, giving em a clear view past her.

Kids hopped out of their cars. Some were hugging their parents, just like Kai. A few waved or called to campers they seemed to already know. Others headed out of the parking lot, toward a group of kids and adults who'd formed a line in front of a sign-in table.

Dad patted Kai's back, and eir stomach performed a flip that would've made half eir parkour team jealous. "Ready, pal?"

Kai didn't honestly know. But e'd promised to try, so e forced a smile and nodded as Mom handed over eir suitcase.

3

ABIGAIL

(SHE/HER/HERS)

ABIGAIL HAD BEEN AT CAMP FOR EXACTLY TWENTY-THREE minutes before she fell in love. And that, of course, was a problem.

Or maybe it wasn't a problem? Abigail was still unclear on the particulars, but maybe falling in love was okay here, at Camp QUILTBAG, where there were a ton of other kids who maybe also got inappropriate crushes on members of the same sex who were old enough (older, even!) to be their parents. That was why Abigail wanted to come here in the first place.

Right?

As they all arrived at the campgrounds, the kids were swiftly shuffled away from their parents and into the large building near the center of camp. It was made of wood like all the other smaller cabins scattered about, but it also looked much sturdier, like the wood was for show and it was actually held together by concrete. Inside, there were rows and rows of tables. Abigail chose one in the back, clutching her suitcase and backpack tightly, using the bulk of both to keep herself mostly hidden.

Her own goodbye with her mom had happened at the airport, and with very little fanfare, which was quite all right with Abigail. Her mom was doing that thing, that capital-s Supportive thing she did, where her smile was much wider than normal and her eyes were kind of bugged out. Though being an unaccompanied minor gave Abigail *Jurassic Park*-style pterodactyls in her stomach, she was kind of relieved. She had breathed a lot easier once her mom was gone.

The rest of the kids filed into the big building, taking up the empty seats all around her in what, to Abigail, felt like a blur of literal rainbows. She reached into her pocket to pull out the brochure the camp had sent after her parents had signed her up for it. The one that had all the rules and all the information necessary to survive the two weeks at camp. Abigail had it memorized.

She would still pay perfectly rapt attention during this orientation, though, just in case something changed, or if there was more to learn, or for anything new that didn't fit into a four-page brochure. Abigail knew that right after this, they would be separated into their cabins—which made the pterodactyls in her stomach fly around like crazy. Until then, she would focus on the familiar. She would focus on orientation, and on the camp leader whom she had yet to meet. The rest would sort itself out. Hopefully.

She wasn't really sure why there was so much art of white squirrels along the walls, though. A bunch of finger paintings, with the fingers all bunched together to make it look like a big squirrel tail. Collages of a bunch of photos of white items—milk jugs and clouds and sneakers—ripped up and pasted together to look like a giant squirrel, too. There definitely wasn't anything on the website about squirrels, and she didn't think a squirrel was a gay symbol. She was pretty sure, anyway. *Though, wait, what if it was?*

Abigail just had to cross her fingers that she'd understand the squirrels soon enough.

The kid sitting beside Abigail was practically vibrating. "Oh, tell us which cabins we're in already! I really want a good color. I want a shirt that brings out my eyes," the other camper said. It took Abigail a couple of seconds of weird silence before she realized the camper was talking to *her*. Abigail turned to look fully at the kid next to her. She (*They?* Abigail paused; she shouldn't assume anything about anyone here, and she needed to remember that) had brown skin, was dressed in feminine clothes, and had long, long hair. They were leaning against the table, close to Abigail, though they weren't looking at her, so Abigail wasn't sure if they were talking to *her* or not. "My first year here I wrote like three emails expressing my concern that they'd have the cabins separated by gender. Don't worry, if you're new. They don't. I'm Juliana, by the way."

So they *were* talking to her.

Abigail actually *had* been worried about the cabins. Mostly because some of her friends—her girl friends— didn't want her at sleepovers anymore. The thought still made her neck feel super warm, a blush spreading up into her cheeks. She didn't think kids at an LGBTQ+ camp would be as cruel, but it worried her anyway, so she researched. A lot. "I know. It's part of the camp's mission statement. My parents had to sign a form saying it was okay when they signed me up."

Juliana blinked at her for a moment, before immediately dropping her gaze.

Abigail blushed. Again.

Nice job, doofus.

"I've read the mission statement, too, of course." Juliana shrugged. "I've combed through a lot of their so-called mission statements, actually. I've been trying to get them to change the name of the camp, because—"

Juliana didn't get to finish their thought. As quickly as their conversation started, it stopped, as a tall woman stepped up to the podium in the very front of the room.

Twenty-three minutes after Abigail had arrived.

"Okay, everyone, settle down!" The woman's voice was stern enough that everyone did settle down, but she was smiling so big and wide (all teeth and dimples) that there was a kind sound mixed in with it, too. Almost like laughter, even though she wasn't laughing. She was Black, and had sharp cheekbones and big dark eyes. Her hair was extra curly and long, surrounding her head like a cloud. She wore one of the Camp QUILTBAG T-shirts that some of the older teens (counselors, probably) had on—white, with the camp name surrounded by a big bright rainbow over a tent and campfire. It was partially tucked into skinny jeans, and she wore a big brown belt with a buckle that caught the light of the fluorescents that spanned the ceiling.

"My name is Lena, my pronouns are she/her, and I'm in charge here at Camp QUILTBAG," she said, and seemed to look directly at Abigail, even though she was all the way in the back and Lena probably couldn't see her anyway. Still, it made Abigail smile, and bite her lip, and want to die.

"I'm so happy you're all here," Lena said.

Abigail, heartbeat in her throat, was so, so happy, too.

It was a good thing Abigail had the rules and regulations and all the information she could possibly get her hands on fully memorized beforehand because, well, she barely processed anything Lena had said.

She almost missed her name being called by one of the counselors as they divided the camp into age levels and cabins. Camp QUILTBAG, in an attempt to be funny—and, honestly, Abigail did enjoy a good pun— had separated the camp into three age groups:

KNITTERS: the little kids, ages six to eight;
WEAVERS: the middle ones, nine to eleven; and
CROCHETERS: Abigail's age group, the twelve- to fourteen-year-olds.

Each age group was then separated into cabins, and each cabin was designated by, of course, a color of the rainbow.

Abigail was a Yellow Crocheter.

Suddenly, they were all being funneled back out of the main building, and Abigail wasn't ready to leave. Juliana, the only person Abigail had spoken to—not that it made them friends, exactly, but at least it was something—was shuffled into the Purple Crocheters cabin, and Lena was still up at the podium, and Abigail really, really didn't want to leave.

The pterodactyls came back, and Abigail could only hope that she would see Lena again come dinner.

She found the Yellow cabin pretty easily. Besides the pride flag, which all the cabins hung—the one with the black and brown stripes as well as the trans flag colors—it was draped in yellow flags, too. The only relief in getting to the cabin was that she could finally put down her suitcase and backpack, which was starting to hurt her shoulders. She took a deep breath as she approached the counselor standing at the front of the Yellow cabin door.

"Hi!" the counselor said. He was wearing the same Camp QUILTBAG shirt as Lena, except his was yellow. "I'm MJ!" He pointed to the name tag he was wearing, which did indeed say, *MJ: he/him.* "I'm the counselor for Yellow, here. Are you one of mine? What's your name, sweets?"

MJ was tall and lanky, with windblown shock-white hair full of glitter. He wore short jean shorts and tall knee-high rainbow-striped socks. He was the type of guy who clearly knew exactly who he was and exactly how he wanted to look. He terrified Abigail, who felt exceptionally inadequate. There was no way someone like MJ ever got embarrassed about who *he* was.

"Um, yes. I'm Abigail. Abigail Rabb."

"Great!" MJ chirped. He took the cap off a Sharpie with his teeth. "I've got a name tag here for you, and your very own aggressively yellow shirt. What size do you think? I'm guessing small, you're super teeny. And what're your pronouns?"

That feeling crept up again. "Small's fine. And, uh . . ." Abigail paused. She shouldn't have to think about this. She should be able to just say it, like everyone else in this camp probably did. "She, um. And her," Abigail said. It wasn't that she didn't know—it was just . . . she'd never really thought about it before. Was it something all these kids had thought about before?

She couldn't imagine asking any of her friends back home what their pronouns were. She *could* imagine the look on their faces if she did, though.

"Here you go," MJ said, handing her the name tag and the world's brightest yellow shirt. At least she wouldn't be getting lost in the woods here. "There will be new name tags for y'all every morning, so you don't have to worry about memorizing everyone's pronouns, and so y'all can change your pronouns from day to day if you want. But for now, here you are, Abigail, she/her! Go right on in."

Abigail stared at the door for a moment. Would all her bunkmates be wearing rainbow-colored socks and totally know their pronouns and sexualities and have glitter-crazy hair? Abigail had wanted to come here, she wanted to find people who would understand her crushes . . .

But what if she didn't fit in? What if she wasn't enough here, either?

"Hey." MJ interrupted her thoughts. "I've always got the best of the best in my cabin. Trust. You'll like them."

Abigail nodded. It was now or never. Even if the pterodactyls were acting up again.

She took a deep breath and pushed open the cabin door.

It was small. And unlike the big main building, this one looked like the wood really was the only thing holding it up. There were two sets of bunk beds along two walls, and four little dressers with drawers were scattered against the others. One set of bunk beds was already taken: a Black girl (Abigail paused to scold herself; she needed to stop assuming the gender of the other campers here) was on the top bunk, hanging a poster of a player from the US women's soccer team.

"Oh hey!" she said when she saw Abigail standing in the doorway. Her hair was slicked back into a high ponytail, and she had on basketball shorts and a tank top. She pointed at her name tag. "I'm Cassidy! She/her. Below me is Bryn, he/him!"

Abigail looked down at Bryn. He was a white kid, shorter than Abigail, and had long shaggy hair. He wore a black beanie and a black baggy sweatshirt to match. "Hi."

"I'm a lesbian!" Cassidy exclaimed, which absolutely took Abigail by surprise. Her face must have shown it. "Sorry! I'm just super excited. Pick a bed! Our fourth roomie isn't here yet, so you can choose top or bottom!"

The door suddenly slammed open and a beanpole of a kid, with brown skin and all arms and legs, came running in. Abigail quickly looked at the name tag they were wearing. *Stick: they/them.* "Am I the last? Oh man, I didn't want to be the last! I sprinted and everything!"

"Where the heck did you sprint from? You're dead last!" Cassidy said. "She hasn't picked her bunk yet, though, so start begging for your preference now before she does. I'm Cassidy, by the way. She/her."

"I'm Bryn," Bryn said. His voice was quiet and gentle. "Oh! He/him. Please."

Stick turned to look at Abigail, and she realized it was her turn. "Abigail. She's fine."

Stick's teeth were just like the rest of them: big. Everything about them seemed incredibly long. They looked like someone had stretched them all out, making them as long as humanly possible. They made both Abigail and Bryn look like velociraptors standing next to a *Tyrannosaurus rex.*

"I'm E—Stick! Call me Stick!" Stick practically screamed their correction at the group. "Stick, Stick, Stick. I've never gotten to introduce myself by Stick before. So cool. It's new. Do you like it?"

Cassidy looked them up and down. "Well, it suits you."

That was absolutely the truth.

And Abigail was completely overwhelmed.

"Can I have the bottom bunk?" Stick said. "I'm afraid I'll roll off the top and die."

Well, now that they brought it up, Abigail was kind of afraid of that, too. "Oh. Sure."

Stick and Cassidy started talking about which of them should get which dresser—"Why do you get that one? It's closer to my bed!" "Uh, no, it's literally right below my bed"—and Abigail just kind of stood in the center of the room, her backpack still hung over her shoulder, her suitcase pulled close in front of her like a shield.

"Is this your first time?" Bryn asked.

Abigail almost didn't hear him. She nodded, and Bryn gave her a small smile.

"Me too. I didn't think my dad was going to let me come. I don't really know what to do now that I'm here, though. This is all kind of . . ."

"Yeah," Abigail said, because even though Bryn didn't finish his thought, Abigail knew exactly what he meant.

There was a sharp knock on the cabin door. Abigail jumped at the sound.

Cassidy called out, "Come in!"

MJ poked his head in. "Just wanted to hurry you chickens up! Use this time to unpack, and you can wash up in the communal bathroom out here to the left, if you want. Some of y'all are rank!" He paused to give them a wink so they knew he was (mostly, probably) kidding. "I'll show you where it is, but a quick reminder that we use the buddy system here for bathroom trips. We've got about twenty minutes before we need to get this show on the road."

The show wasn't even on the road yet? Abigail's head was spinning enough. *You wanted this*, she tried to remind herself. *You want this. You've got three potential friends right here, right now. Don't screw this up.*

"Hey! You're wearing a *Jurassic Park* shirt! That's awesome," Cassidy said, dangling off her top bunk to get closer to Abigail.

Tell her how much you love Laura Dern, Abigail told herself. *Cassidy already said she was a lesbian, too. She'd totally get it. She would.*

"I was obsessed with dinosaurs when I was little," Stick said.

The pterodactyls were back. Abigail was starting to think they'd be hanging around for the next two weeks. Cassidy, Stick, and Bryn were all looking at her, waiting for her to say something about *Jurassic Park*, and this was her chance! This was why she had combed through the camp website for hours and sent it to her mom in the first place! This was the opportunity she'd been missing back home, the chance to meet kids just like her who could understand.

But thinking of home, thinking of Stacy, and Abigail's crush on her mom, and the way her friends had all looked at her when they found out . . . she just couldn't get herself to say it out loud.

"I really like dinosaurs, too," she said. Her cheeks felt really, really hot.

Stick nodded like they understood, and Cassidy lost interest, and Bryn was putting his clothes in the dresser, and they weren't focused on her at all anymore.

Abigail was really disappointed in herself.

No one else in her cabin seemed ashamed at all about who they were and what they liked. Abigail's embarrassment was feeling an awful lot like failure.

As she continued to unpack, she kept her Laura Dern poster rolled up and tucked away in her suitcase.

KAI

(E/EM/EIR)

THE CELL RECEPTION HERE TOTALLY SUCKED. KAI HOPED it was something odd about this one specific building and not the entire camp.

Kai checked eir phone every few seconds during Lena's speech, ignoring the undercurrent of whispers. E just needed to hear back from Aziza.

E only looked up when Lena started calling names. First, it was the Knitters: all little kids. Then the Weavers and Crocheters. This sounded like a camp for grandmas.

Only two Purple Crocheters got called, and they had been informed there was a flight delay for their other two cabinmates. For now, it was just Kai and a kid with brown skin and long, dark brown hair whose name sounded like Hoo-lee-anna; Kai couldn't even begin to guess how it was spelled.

Kai didn't approach eir cabinmate when everyone got dismissed. E found eir own way to the assigned building with purple flags.

A counselor waited at the front door, with a name tag that said, *Leticia: she/her/hers.* Leticia's skin was as richly dark as Aziza's. But where Aziza's hair was a sea of tight braids that danced with her every movement, Leticia's was free. It swayed like a friendly wave.

Kai hovered behind Hoo-lee-anna, who stepped toward Leticia.

"Hey there!" Leticia handed out purple T-shirts to each of them, then name tags and Sharpies. "Your other cabinmates should be here any minute. In the meantime, go ahead and unpack. Get to know each other."

That was honestly the last thing Kai wanted to do. If there was one thing e'd learned since coming out, it was that even the kids you'd known a super long time could turn on you. Even the friends you trusted most.

Hoo-lee-anna claimed the bottom bunk on the far side of the cabin. Kai quickly scribbled eir name on the tag, along with *e/em/eir*, then stuck it to eir old gymnastics academy T-shirt.

Eir cabinmate was done by the time e looked up.

JULIANA: she/her/hers

Kai stared at the name tag.

"The pronunciation is Spanish," Juliana said.

"Oh." Kai swallowed. "I take Spanish in school. I feel like I should've known that."

"I take French."

Juliana's expression didn't change, so Kai couldn't tell if she was joking.

She grabbed her purple T-shirt and made her way to the back of the room. She reached for a curtain that was attached to a wire on the ceiling and pulled it until it concealed her from view. A moment later she reappeared, then peeled off the back of her name tag and stuck it to her purple shirt.

"Want to share my bunk?"

She pointed up.

"Okay."

Kai tossed eir duffel bag onto the top mattress, wondering if e should unstick the name tag from eir shirt and change behind the curtain too. Aziza also should've responded by now—if this cabin had any signal. Kai slid eir hand into eir pocket to check.

"So you use neopronouns?" Juliana asked.

Kai froze. "What?"

"That's what those are." She nodded toward eir name tag. "I've never used them with anyone before."

Kai waited for Juliana to say things e'd heard a million times: *Those aren't real words. They're too hard to remember. Why can't you just pick* him *or* her, *or even* they?

"Is *eir* pronounced like *air*?"

"Yes . . ."

Juliana's gaze grew distant. She mouthed the word silently to herself, then looked back over at Kai. "So, what do you think of the camp's name?"

Kai hadn't been ready for the change of topic. "I—"

The cabin door flew open and two kids rushed in. One was Black, with hair shaved short. The other had dark hair that fell around their face in wild, messy waves, plus a pale complexion.

"Hey, Juli," the first kid said. "What's up?"

The kid looked over at their fourth cabinmate before Juliana could answer. "Cool if I grab the top bunk again this year?"

"Sure." The other kid nodded, then turned toward the closest dresser to fill out their name tag.

That's when Kai spotted the kippah. Silver hair clips secured it to their head. Mostly navy, it had white accents around the rim, with a Star of David at its center.

"Oren, Jax, this is Kai," Juliana said.

"Hey." Jax nodded.

Kai made emself say hi back to Jax (Jaxon, actually, according to the name tag; he/him/his). But then eir eyes darted back to the other kid—Oren—who pressed the name tag in place, then waved.

OREN: he/him/his

If Kai had to guess, Oren was Jewish.

Kai's family was too, kind of: Dad was Lutheran, Mom Reform. The Lindquist family bounced between churches and temples, depending on the holiday and any invitations they received from relatives. Kai hadn't been baptized or confirmed in eir dad's church, and e hadn't had a mitzvah ceremony at the temple eir mom's family attended, either.

"How'd school go for you this year?"

Jax's question pulled Kai from eir thoughts.

Juliana shrugged. "Better than last year. My teachers are all cool. Most of my classmates got used to my new name and pronouns fast, too."

Their conversation reminded Kai of the moments before parkour practice, or gymnastics further back, that comfortable chatter because they were all friends.

Everyone already seemed to know each other here, too.

"Awesome." Jax shifted his gaze to Kai. But he wasn't looking at Kai's face, or even eir name tag. Jax's gaze was aimed at the sling supporting eir arm.

Kai tensed. Jax looked like he was about to say something, but Leticia reappeared first.

"Hey! Everyone ready? We're meeting at the Benches in five."

"Give us a sec," Jax called, turning away from Kai. "Some of us still gotta switch shirts."

Kai's body went hot and then cold as Jax stripped off his shirt and Oren followed. Even if eir sling didn't make changing clothes tricky, there was no way e was taking eir shirt off in front of other people.

"Want to use the curtain?"

Juliana looked up at em without any noticeable judgment, but Kai still shook eir head. E tore off eir name tag, then carefully unclipped the sling, pulling the purple T-shirt on over eir gymnastics shirt.

By the time eir sling was back in place, the others were already changed. Juliana slid a book into a canvas bag, then swung the bag over her shoulder and stood. Oren and Jax followed her out of the cabin, with Kai trailing behind.

As Leticia led the way, Oren slowed to match Kai's pace. "Keep an eye out for the squirrel."

"The . . . what?"

"That's just a myth." Juliana scoffed without slowing down. "A camp legend no one's ever actually seen."

"Whose name is Mx. Nutsford," Jax called after her.

"Well," Oren said, "maybe this will be the year we spot him. Or her or them. Maybe em?"

"It's zem," Juliana said. When the other three looked over at her, she shrugged. "That's what I've heard the counselors and other campers use: *zie*, *zem*, and *zir*." She glanced briefly at Kai. "Also neopronouns."

"Noted." Oren looked over at Kai with a grin that made Kai's breath catch. "So, where are you from?"

"Um." Kai hadn't been expecting the sudden change of topic. E was still thinking about what made a squirrel mythical.

"I'm from here." Kai watched Oren brush his hair away from his blue eyes and lost eir train of thought for a second. "I mean not here, here. Just Minnesota. A few hours south."

That should've been that. Kai didn't want to make friends.

Except, e also had manners. And honestly, there was something about the way Oren had so easily accepted the concept of neopronouns, even if they were for an imaginary squirrel. He seemed kind, as well as comfortable around all sorts of people. It made Kai's chest flutter.

"What about you?" e asked as they made their way past the cabins and down a dirt path. Trees rose up on both sides, casting shadows on everyone's faces.

"New York. Jax and me both," Oren said.

"Except I'm upstate, in Ithaca," Jax jumped in. "Oren lives in Brooklyn."

"I'm from Oakland, California," Juliana said.

"And you've all been to this camp before?" It was the only logical explanation for how much they already seemed to know about each other.

"Yeah." Jax's head bobbed up and down but he didn't turn around. "Last year was my first time here. My parents found the camp's website right after I came out to them when I was thirteen."

"Same here," Oren said. "Basically."

So that made Jax and Oren a year older than em— they were almost high schoolers, while Kai still had a year of middle school left. Kai really wanted to know if Oren was out to everyone, or just his parents, or what, but e didn't know how to ask. Maybe this was something Juliana and Jax already knew. Maybe it was private.

"This is my third year," Juliana said. "I came out when I was eleven, but it's my first being out as pansexual."

Kai couldn't remember what *pansexual* meant off the top of eir head, but e also didn't want to admit it.

"Congrats, by the way." Jax threw her a thumbs-up.

"Thanks."

Kai could hear the smile in Juliana's voice.

Ahead of them, the trees opened to a clearing that overlooked a lake Kai remembered seeing on the front of the camp's brochure. A few groups of kids already sat at picnic tables.

"I'm going to check in with some of the other counselors," Leticia told them. "Be back in a sec."

As soon as she headed off, Juliana claimed an empty table. Jax sat beside her, with Kai and Oren across from them. Beads of sweat formed along Kai's back now that they were sitting in direct sunlight. E definitely had regrets about doubling up on T-shirts.

Juliana resumed the conversation right where she'd left off. "Figuring out that I'm pansexual is also why I hecka think they need to change the camp's name. It's totally *not* inclusive."

Jax and Oren nodded.

Another thing Kai was in the dark about. Awesome.

"All right, everyone." In the center of the clearing, Lena stood with the camp counselors. "Get yourselves seated and turn your listening ears on so I only have to say this once."

Juliana pulled out a notebook and pen from her bag. Kai glanced at Oren and Jax, relieved to see neither of them taking notes.

"Welcome again. Glad to see everyone's made it." Lena nodded in the general direction of Kai's table. "As most of you know from the orientation materials, we have some scheduled content like movies and group discussions, plus many fun activities to keep you busy over the next two weeks."

Kai scanned the other tables. Four kids were sitting in a group to eir left. They looked about the same age as Kai. To eir right, the kids seemed younger, probably Weavers. The camp counselors were all gathered behind Lena, sitting on longer benches at the clearing's center.

"But wait. There's more." Lena raised her eyebrows and smiled wider. "This year, we decided to add an element of competition to the mix to encourage camaraderie and build leadership skills."

A competition? Kai's ears perked up.

"Each day, a list of activity options that your cabin can choose from will be posted on the cafeteria bulletin board. Each camper will receive one point per activity they complete. There'll be some games where cabins face off, but you can also earn points in other ways if these activities aren't your thing," Lena explained, "like winning a competition, helping out around the camp, creating art, and working on advocacy projects. There will be a winning cabin from each age group, Knitters, Weavers, and Crocheters."

Across the table, Juliana scribbled furiously in her notebook.

"What does the winner get?" a younger kid shouted, which led to some giggles.

"Well." Lena didn't miss a beat. "I'm actually thrilled to tell you that the winning cabin in each age group will get to suggest a new name for our camp. I'll bring your proposed names to the camp's board of directors later this summer, and then we'll make a decision on what this place will be called going forward."

A murmur of disappointment. Across the table, Juliana's pen froze. She sat up straighter, totally focused on Lena.

"Hey now. This is a wonderful opportunity to get a say in choosing a more inclusive name. The QUILTBAG acronym encompasses many identities, but it doesn't have a letter for every single one."

Out of the corner of eir eye, Kai saw Jax nudge Juliana.

"We wouldn't be living up to our mission of being a safe space to be yourself if we left people out. Now you have a chance to make even more campers feel welcome," Lena continued. "We'll tally up the cabins' points at the end of each day and post them in the cafeteria."

Lena clapped her hands. "Now, dinner's in about half

an hour. Until then, you're free to stay here and get to know more of your fellow campers."

At the mention of dinner, Kai stole a glance at Oren. If he wore a kippah outside his temple, then he probably also kept kosher and observed Shabbat from Friday night to Saturday night. Kai wondered how that worked at a camp like this.

"This is going to be amazing." Juliana's voice pulled Kai out of eir thoughts.

"Yeah," Jax said. "Usually, the counselors just give cabins a daily schedule of what we'll be doing, but it sounds like we get a choice this year."

Oren nodded. "Of course, we'll want to be strategic and choose things we're good at so we can get the most points possible. And pick some of the competition events so we can get points for participating *and* winning them."

Oren sounded like he was as competitive as Kai. Kai's chest fluttered again.

Jax's gaze dropped back to Kai's sling. "No offense, but are you going to be able to do sports with that thing?"

"I'm fine." Kai's throat tightened. "I get it off in a few days."

Jax didn't look convinced. Shame flooded Kai's chest as a memory formed. Eir former gymnastics teammate,

Cie-Cie, stood behind a pair of boys in a school hallway. Watching. Saying nothing, while—

Kai pushed the memory away.

Before Jax could say anything else, a kid in a yellow shirt whose name tag read, *Cassidy: she/her/hers*, stepped up to their table. "Hi! Pretty sure we're in the cabin next to yours."

As Cassidy talked to the rest of eir cabinmates, Kai reached for another memory: something, anything, that'd made em feel strong. This time, e saw Aziza, phone up, recording eir tumbling pass to post online for a virtual parkour tournament. E'd nailed that sequence.

Kai felt eir anger at being forced to come here start to dissolve, replaced by a surge of determination.

Eir sling was coming off soon, then memories of why e'd needed it would be gone, too. Kai may not have wanted to attend this camp, and e was still planning to get out of here as early as eir parents would let em, but e'd never backed down from a challenge. There was nothing e loved more than the rush of winning.

Now e had a plan: Kai would help eir cabin earn top points on every activity, at least until e proved to eir parents that e was fine and could leave early. No need to come back to Camp QUILTBAG—or whatever it was going to be called—next year, either. In just under two weeks, Kai could move on with eir life.

This place would become just another memory e could push away.

ABIGAIL

(SHE/HER/HERS)

CASSIDY DID EVERYTHING SO *EASILY*. IT MADE ABIGAIL'S head spin with both whiplash and jealousy every time Cassidy disappeared and came back with more information. They'd been here for barely half a day and Cassidy already seemed to know *everyone*'s names and pronouns and assigned cabins.

Meanwhile, Abigail was having trouble just remembering her own cabin's pronouns. She kept messing up Bryn's, and she was terrified eventually Bryn might hear her. Everyone back home in her small Catholic school used the pronouns they were assigned at birth, and her school had rules about haircuts, and everyone had to dress in the same uniform. The Catholic Church sometimes had *things* to say about being gay, and when Abigail's friends made fun of her, she sometimes thought those *things* about herself, too.

Everyone here acted like rainbows had barfed all over them, while back home, at school, they weren't even allowed to paint their nails.

Abigail wasn't equipped for this. She felt wrong back home and she was feeling wrong here, too. Not to mention she'd barely seen the lake yet, just glimpsed it between the trees that were draped in rainbow flags so bright Abigail thought she'd be able to see them from Pluto. How on earth was she supposed to post photos for Stacy and them that made it look like she was at her lake house?

"We're sitting with the Purples for dinner!" Cassidy said.

Stick was tugging at their camp shirtsleeves, as if pulling them might magically make them fit better on their long limbs. "Is that Jax and Oren's cabin? We were Blues together last year. I'm gonna have to ask them to call me Stick now."

"Don't ask, *tell* them to," Cassidy said.

They continued talking, but Abigail tuned them out. They were walking toward the big main cabin, where they would eat dinner. Abigail swatted at a mosquito. She'd been swatting at them every time they stepped outside. Her mom always said it was because her blood was sweet, just like her, but Abigail wasn't exactly in the mood for the mosquito's attentions. She'd forgotten to pack bug spray; she hadn't considered there would be so many mosquitos. Being itchy was just the icing on the spilled milk that Abigail was trying not to cry over.

Maybe she could just bypass dinner altogether and hide in her cabin. She had nothing in common with these kids. *And* she was terrible at competitions. *And* every time Lena spoke, Abigail thought she was going to explode inside, which was exactly what she was trying to avoid. This was a mistake. This camp was a mistake.

Abigail herself felt like a pretty big mistake, too.

I'm Abigail, my pronouns are she/her, and I'm a lesbian. It should be so easy to say. It *was* so easy to say for Cassidy and Stick and everyone else, apparently.

Abigail didn't think she had ever even said the word *lesbian* out loud. It sounded too personal. It sounded too adult. She wanted to be able to say it, to tell everyone, *This is who I am.* But every time she tried, it seemed so crude. It made her feel too much like a little kid playing dress-up in clothes that didn't fit.

She used to fit just fine at school. Her small Catholic grade school was for kindergarten all the way through eighth grade, and because of that, at twelve, she was still in school with the same kids she'd been going to school with ever since she was five. Abigail loved that at first. She didn't need to meet new people; she didn't need to make new friends.

That all changed when Abigail herself started changing. Right around the time she realized she wasn't a tomboy who loved dinosaurs, like she and everyone else had assumed, but a little queer girl who loved *Jurassic Park* because Laura Dern was pretty, and Abigail liked pretty women.

Her best friend Stacy's mom was very pretty. Mrs. Mackenzie gave Abigail pterodactyl-sized butterflies in her stomach every time she smiled. The back of Abigail's neck would grow so warm anytime Mrs. Mackenzie gave her any attention. Stacy's mom hummed while she brushed her teeth (which Abigail noticed during sleepovers) and she had a collection of fuzzy, funny socks (Abigail's favorite were the dinosaur ones) and she didn't like pizza crust (Abigail stopped eating her pizza crust, too).

Abigail loved noticing things about Mrs. Mackenzie, but the more things she noticed, the more everyone else started noticing, too. Her friends—and most importantly Stacy—realized that Abigail acted weird around Mrs. Mackenzie. When they confronted her about it, Abigail was too flustered to lie.

That was how, after all the years of being in school with the same kids, after having the same group of friends since kindergarten, Abigail suddenly wasn't being invited to Stacy's anymore. She suddenly felt awkward sitting with her friends in the school cafeteria.

It was humiliating, hovering at the end of a long cafeteria table, her friends all chatting together, Abigail on the outside. Everybody knew that good friends didn't have crushes on their best friend's mom. Everybody also now knew that Abigail was gay.

Since then, Abigail had spent a lot of days in that cafeteria wishing she wasn't gay.

That wasn't supposed to matter here, now, at camp. Everyone knew that Abigail was gay because *everyone* here was queer, and she didn't have to wish otherwise anymore. That was the point of being here.

But if that was true, why, as she stood in the doorway of the big cabin, with its long cafeteria-style wooden tables and filled with the happy chatter of campers and the smell of dinner, did she feel like she shouldn't be here? Cassidy and Stick walked into the room as if they belonged there, heading toward the buffet. Bryn followed them, then turned around and glanced at Abigail.

"You coming?" Bryn asked.

I want to go home, Abigail thought.

When Abigail didn't respond and hadn't yet moved, Bryn gave her a small smile. Abigail took a deep breath.

"Yes," she said, and followed Bryn, who followed Stick and Cassidy, to the buffet line.

It was warm and stuffy inside. Abigail tugged at the collar of her camp shirt, feeling the fabric clinging to the sweat on her back. She wasn't a particularly picky eater—she was too polite not to eat whatever was put in front of her—but as she glanced at the mac and cheese and chicken fingers and french fries, she felt queasy. Stick and Cassidy were piling food onto their plates—Stick had two plates, even—and Bryn was shoveling mac and cheese onto his own. Abigail took a couple chicken fingers, a dinner roll, and some garden salad, hoping if she picked at it enough no one would question her lack of appetite. In a daze, she followed Cassidy to a table of campers wearing purple shirts. She sat at the very end.

"Scoot in, chicken!" MJ said, suddenly right beside her. Abigail had wanted to sit on the edge so she could make an escape if she needed to, but now she was sandwiched between her counselor and Bryn. Across from her, the counselor in the purple shirt—a really pretty Black girl—sat down. "Hey, MJ, how's it going?" the Black girl said.

"Leticia, my love! My cabin is gearing up to kick your cabin's behind!" MJ said, bumping his shoulder into Abigail's. She managed a wonky smile.

"I love your earrings," Leticia said, and Abigail blinked at her for a moment before she realized she was talking to *her*.

Abigail reached up to touch the dangling silver T. rex earrings. "Thanks," she croaked.

Leticia smiled, all teeth and dimples, and Abigail felt her face get even warmer in the heat of the crowded room. "I'm not a dinosaur pro or anything, but my mom loves *Jurassic Park*. She makes us watch it every single time it's on TV."

Me too! Abigail wanted to say. She bit her lip to keep herself from smiling too big.

"That doesn't surprise me about your mom," MJ said, throwing a french fry at Leticia.

"Don't throw things. You're such a bad example," Leticia said, dodging it.

"What're you gonna do? Tell your mom on me?"

The two of them fell into easy, teasing laughter, Abigail and her earrings now forgotten. She was both disappointed and completely relieved to be out of Leticia's spotlight.

Abigail should probably focus on the rest of her table anyway, especially since she'd clearly missed something. Cassidy was gesturing wildly toward a kid wearing a purple shirt, and Stick was shrinking in their seat, looking unnaturally small for such a long kid.

"I didn't mean it!" The kid in the purple shirt looked a mix of exasperated and upset. Abigail quickly glanced at his name tag for his pronouns. Jaxon, he/him, was clearly arguing with Cassidy.

"Well, now you know," the kid next to Jaxon said, and Abigail felt a pang in her stomach at the recognition. It was Juliana from earlier that day. She tried to smile at Juliana, but Juliana didn't seem to notice.

"It's just an adjustment because we knew you last year," a third kid—Oren, he/him/his—said. He was wearing one of those Jewish hats she didn't know the name of. She didn't really know much about being Jewish.

"It's fine," Stick mumbled. "But my name is Stick now."

"We'll definitely try to remember that," Oren said.

"You *will* remember that," Cassidy snapped.

"Would you stop?" Jaxon practically yelled. "It was a mistake! Cut us some slack!"

Bryn glanced at Abigail, and Abigail was grateful that Bryn seemed just as eager to keep quiet and stay out of it as she did.

"Just say you're sorry," the kid at the very end of the table said. Abigail had to lean over to see them. She couldn't read their pronouns because they were too far. She tried squinting. It didn't help. They were white and blond, their hair shaved short on the sides with a longer tuft on top.

Stick smiled when the last kid spoke up, and smiled even bigger when Jaxon looked them in the eyes, his face serious as he said, "Yeah, Kai's right. I'm sorry."

"I'm sorry, too," Oren said earnestly, his cheeks flushing.

Stick was smiling now, sitting up straight, suddenly the tallest kid at the table again. Even taller than MJ. "It's okay. Thanks. I'm still trying to get used to it myself."

Crisis averted. The Purple cabin boys and Stick began talking about videogames as if nothing had happened, and Cassidy and Juliana were excitedly talking over each other about some equality campaign, and Abigail didn't understand what had just happened.

Or she did. The kids messed up Stick's name, and everyone got upset, but then everyone apologized and felt better.

That was exactly why Abigail had wanted to come to this camp. She wanted to be with kids who understood. No one at home ever apologized. No one at home ever made her feel better.

No one at home ever tried. They carried on in the school cafeteria as if Abigail wasn't there at all.

Though, everyone here was kind of doing that, too.

Try, Abigail, she told herself. She swallowed back the pterodactyl in her throat. It fluttered all the way to her gut.

She just had to join in the conversation. These kids weren't going to hurt her. They'd accidentally hurt Stick, but everyone apologized. Everyone was okay.

It was going to be okay. She just had to open her mouth and try.

She could start with Bryn, who was sitting just as quietly as she was.

She could just say something simple. *These chicken fingers aren't bad.* Or, *Did you know there were gonna be so many mosquitos?* Or, *What's up with all the squirrel pictures everywhere?*

Do you have friends at home or do you feel alone, too?

Abigail scratched her legs and took a deep breath. She would ask about the mosquitos. Maybe Bryn even had some bug spray she could borrow, and they could bond back at the cabin.

Abigail opened her mouth to do this—and immediately closed it tight when she felt a presence step up behind her. She looked up to see Lena smiling down at her.

Oh my God.

Abigail's cheeks felt like they were on fire. The room was hot and stuffy to begin with, but now it felt as if someone had turned on the heat.

"How's everyone doing over here?" Lena said. Everyone stopped talking to turn their attention to her.

"We're good here, Mom," Leticia said, and, *oh my God*, Leticia was Lena's daughter! *Lena* was her mom who loved *Jurassic Park* and made them watch it every time it was on TV!

"It's a little overwhelming at first, huh?" Lena said to Abigail.

Abigail couldn't respond. Beside her, Bryn was nodding.

"Lena! I'm so excited you're changing the camp name!" Juliana practically screeched across the table.

Lena winked—she actually *winked*—and Abigail pretty much stopped breathing. "I thought you'd be pleased. You should be proud of yourself for sticking up for what you believe in. I'm sorry it took us so long to catch up."

Juliana beamed. Abigail didn't blame her.

She sat as still as she possibly could so that Lena wouldn't move.

Like she was in *Jurassic Park*, and Lena was a T. rex. *Stay still; she won't even realize you're here.*

The conversation was picking up around her again, but Abigail couldn't hear it. Her cheeks felt like they might melt right off her.

She glanced up, looking across the table, and accidentally met Leticia's gaze.

Leticia was smiling at her.

"Well, I'll leave you all to it," Lena said. Lena walked
to another table. Leticia was still looking at Abigail
with that smile.

"Lena's your mom?" Bryn asked. "That's cool, she's
so nice."

Abigail wished she could will her cheeks back to their
normal color. Damn her pale skin. It showed every emo-
tion she ever had, and right now, she was feeling mighty
embarrassed.

Though that seemed to be her natural setting, lately.
"Yeah. She's really nice," Abigail said.

"Yeah, Leticia. Your mom is *so* nice and *so* pretty," MJ
said, batting his eyes dramatically.

"Oh, knock it off," Leticia said, throwing a handful of
french fries back at him. And then she winked at Abigail,
just like her mom did.

Leticia knew. She *knew*.

MJ started laughing.

And Leticia and Bryn started laughing, too.

And Cassidy was leaning over, saying, "What's so
funny?"

The dining hall was so, so stuffy. It was so, so hot.

Abigail was having déjà vu. Another cafeteria, another group of friends. A different crush on a different mom.

"N-no, no. It's not . . . I mean, I don't think she's—I mean, she *is* pretty, but—wait, that came out wrong . . ."

Maybe I came out wrong.

"Relax, my new friend," Leticia said. "Your secret is safe with me."

But it wasn't. It *wasn't*. Because MJ was sitting right there, popping french fries into his mouth, still chuckling. Bryn was sitting right there, too, and he was watching Abigail carefully, too carefully. Cassidy was still trying to get their attention, because she didn't want to be left out of whatever was so funny, but it *wasn't* funny and it wasn't Cassidy's business, and Abigail did not want to do this here.

She was supposed to feel better here.

It wasn't supposed to feel like school all over again.

I can't breathe. It felt like a stegosaurus was standing on her chest.

"Where's the bathroom?" Abigail said, standing so quickly and abruptly, she almost knocked her dinner tray off the table. "I have to go to the bathroom."

Leticia wasn't smirking anymore. Abigail could not read the look on her face. She didn't want to know what it meant, anyway. "Down the hall to the right," she said, but Abigail was already leaving the main hall before she'd even finished.

Abigail didn't go down the hall to the right. She went out the main doors and into the cool evening air. She had to swat a mosquito almost immediately, and it was enough to make her start crying. She pressed her back against the hard brick wall, skidding down to sit on the damp ground. She tried to breathe the heat on her cheeks away.

Why did she think coming here would be the answer? That she would feel okay again? She was still Abigail. She was still the queer girl who crushed on people's moms.

What was worse, she would go home at the end of this two-week camp and nothing would be different. The girls at school wouldn't talk to her, and if they did, it'd be to ask her how she'd actually spent her summer, and they would laugh, and Abigail would be alone.

6

KAI
(E/EM/EIR)

KAI'S PHONE VIBRATED WITH A SERIES OF TEXTS somewhere between the Benches and the cafeteria. As eir cabinmates filed into the buffet line, Kai snuck a peek at eir messages.

> **Queen Aziza:**
> My teleportation skills are most lacking
>
> But hey, by the time you're back, you'll have your sling off, right?
>
> Asking for a friend who has a sick idea for a new tumbling pass!

While Oren, Jax, and Juliana chatted with the kids

from the Blue and Red cabins and the food line crept forward, Kai typed a response.

> **Kai:**
> It's supposed to be off in like three days. FINALLY
>
> Tell me about the pass!

Except neither text went through.

Kai piled food onto eir plate, then tried to send the messages again once they'd all settled down at a table beside the campers from the Yellow cabin.

Same error. No signal.

It was official. This camp was The Worst.

Maybe that was why eir words had been so sharp when the conversation turned to the Yellow Crocheter who wanted to be called Stick. Irritation prickled down Kai's arms. It wasn't like learning a new name was hard. Jax's response reminded Kai of every single time e'd had to correct eir gymnastics teammates when they called em by the wrong pronouns before e'd decided to quit the team.

Furrowed brows. Crossed arms. Like Kai was the one making things difficult.

But neither boy had complained about Stick's new name, or their pronouns. Jax had only really gotten annoyed at Cassidy, who *had* been pretty intense, in Kai's opinion.

Jax hadn't put up any sort of fight when Kai had told him to apologize. Then Oren said he was sorry too, even without being asked.

This was different. An improvement.

The conversation shifted from Stick to Lena's announcement about the competition, but Kai couldn't help remembering that some people in eir life had never needed to be corrected in the first place. Aziza and the rest of eir parkour friends just seemed to understand em, from the moment they'd met.

And that made Kai miss Aziza all over again.

E ate while half listening to the conversation, unable to keep eir eyes from traveling to Oren. Unlike all the other kids' plates that were piled high with chicken fingers and cheeseburgers, Oren was eating a salad with sides of steamed cauliflower and broccoli. His plate reminded Kai of dinners at home whenever eir mom got into one of her healthy-meal-making moods.

Except unlike Kai's mom, Oren's food choices were probably because he was trying to keep kosher.

Kai knew what kosher meant but not exactly. Like, e knew it was a word for food that was acceptable for Jewish people to eat, just not what those foods were and why some stuff was okay to eat while other things weren't.

E wanted to ask Oren more about it, but Lena appeared first. Kai listened to the conversation between Lena and Juliana, whose voice rose and fell as unpredictably as Aziza's freestyle flips and turns.

The moment Lena moved on to the next table, Juliana turned to Cassidy. "I've been sending letters asking them to change the camp's name since last fall. Literally nine months of telling them there's no letter in the QUILTBAG acronym for pansexual kids, plus a lot of others."

"I never thought of that before, but you're right," Cassidy said. "There's queer and questioning, unsure, intersex, lesbian, transgender, bisexual—"

"The T is for transgender *and* two-spirit," Juliana cut in. "Then there's bisexual, asexual *and* aromantic, gay *and* genderqueer. But nothing for pansexual, demisexual, and so many more." She sat a little straighter. "I still can't believe we get to propose a new name. This is so huge."

"The winning cabin gets to anyway," Cassidy said. "But yeah, Lena seems cool."

Jax, Oren, and Stick all nodded. Kai wondered if Cassidy had been a camper last year too, just like all eir cabinmates and Stick. Regardless, the Purples and Yellows seemed to be settling in. Kids from both cabins looked like they were already getting comfortable with one another.

Well, Kai thought. *Not everyone.*

A few campers down, a white kid with a short brown ponytail stood up and excused themself to the bathroom. Kai polished off eir last chicken finger and watched them go. E wondered if the bathrooms here were separated into boys and girls like they were at eir school or if they were all gender neutral.

This was probably something e'd have known if e had read through the brochure on the drive up instead of moping and texting Aziza.

Kai glanced down at eir phone and tried to resend the two messages. Same error.

But there had to be a signal *someplace* at this camp or else Aziza's texts wouldn't have come through. Kai just needed to figure out where. E already knew the parking lot was a dead zone. Same for this cafeteria. Maybe e'd have better luck in eir cabin, but e didn't want to wait hours to find out.

Kai pushed away from the table. Eir neck got hot as Oren looked up at em.

"I'm going to get more food," Kai said. "They're cool with that, right?"

"Yeah," Oren said. "They're basically cool with everything."

"Except, like, murder," Jax chimed in.

"I will make sure not to murder anything," Kai said. "Except more chicken fingers."

Oren laughed. It made Kai feel light, weightless, just like performing a perfect tumbling pass.

"Legit." Jax grinned. "Except I don't think it's murder if they're already dead."

Kai made eir way up to the buffet table, feeling better by the second. These kids wouldn't ever be as cool as eir parkour friends but at least they were better than the people at school. Kai figured e could live with that for a week and a half. Now, all that stood between em and a longer conversation with Aziza was a successful vanishing act.

As Kai pretended to reach for a clean plate, e surveyed the rest of the cafeteria. Everyone was seated except for Lena, who had her back to em, talking to some of the younger campers.

No one was looking Kai's way.

E pivoted toward a hallway to eir left. If anyone caught em, e would just tell them e'd gotten lost in search of the bathroom.

But no one stopped em. Kai made it outside.

E pulled out eir phone, upping the screen brightness in the dusk light, but froze at the sound of sniffles.

Kai turned, glancing down. The kid with the ponytail from the Yellow cabin sat up against the side of the building. Abigail, she/her pronouns, according to her name tag. Her knees were pulled into her chest, arms wrapped around them. She stared up at Kai, eyes wide and sparkling with tears.

"Sorry, I didn't mean to—" Kai started.

"It's fine. I'm fine. I was just—" Abigail went quiet as their words overlapped. She pressed her lips into a thin line.

Kai felt like e should leave. Whatever was going on here wasn't any of eir business. Abigail wasn't even in the same cabin as em.

Except, she reminded Kai of eir sister, Lexi. E wasn't sure what it was. They didn't look alike, and Lexi was usually bubbly and confident about everything—school, friends, swim meets. Kai was willing to bet that if confidence walked straight up to Abigail and offered her a hand, she'd flinch.

Kai looked down at her. "That bad, huh?"

"What?" She blinked at em.

"Camp. It looks like you don't want to be here either?"

"Yes. Maybe. No." A look passed across her face that Kai couldn't read. "Camp's fine."

"Okay." Kai leaned eir good shoulder against the building. "So you're homesick."

"No!"

Kai raised eir brows and Abigail seemed to shrink into herself, eyes darting around like she was worried someone inside might have heard her.

But it was just Kai and Abigail out here.

She swiped at her eyes, rubbing away streaks of tears with the back of her hand. Then she scratched her arm, brows scrunched up. Kai spotted a smattering of little red bumps.

"Are there always so many mosquitos here?" she asked.

"Well, yeah. My uncle Bill says the mosquito should be Minnesota's state bird." Kai tilted eir head. "Which would honestly be funnier if he didn't share the same joke like a thousand times every summer."

A small smile formed on Abigail's face, which disappeared fast as she swatted at another tiny pest. "I just wish I hadn't forgotten to bring bug spray."

"Do they not have mosquitos where you're from?" Kai asked.

"No, they do," Abigail said. "Just not so many. I live in New Jersey, by the shore. The ocean breeze keeps them away, usually. It's . . . very different from here. With the lake. And the bugs. Minnesota might as well be Isla Nublar, it's so foreign to me."

"Eye la what?"

"Isla Nublar," Abigail said. "The, uh, island from *Jurassic Park*."

"Oh." Kai hadn't seen that movie in years. "Hey, New Jersey's close to New York City, right?"

Abigail nodded.

"Which is also close to Brooklyn?"

"Yeah." Abigail studied em. "Why?"

This time when Kai thought of Oren, eir neck didn't get hot. Talking to Abigail felt safe and comfortable, like talking to Lexi.

"Just curious." Kai gave her a one-shouldered shrug. "One of my cabinmates, Oren, is from Brooklyn."

"Oh." Abigail seemed to think this over. "Do . . . you like him or something?"

"What? No, it's just, he's Jewish, and I am too. Except I don't know a lot of other Jewish kids . . ."

Now that e'd started talking, the words tumbled out like a confession.

"I don't wear a kippah or keep kosher. My family doesn't even go to temple except for the High Holidays like Rosh Hashanah and Yom Kippur. Sometimes not even then. And we never go for smaller stuff like Purim."

Abigail's face clouded with confusion.

"It just feels like we have something in common but don't at the same time, you know?" Kai tried again.

When Abigail didn't say anything, e looked down at eir feet. "Never mind."

E heard Abigail take a big breath.

"I think I get it. It feels like everyone in my cabin is way ahead of me, with everything. They know everything. They don't get embarrassed about anything. We haven't even been here a day yet, and it feels like I'm already way behind in class or something."

Kai looked over at Abigail, but she was staring off toward the cabins.

"Same here," Kai offered. "I mean, technically, they *do* know each other better, because some of them were here last summer, and this is Juliana's third year. The trick is to pretend it doesn't bother you."

"I don't know how to do that."

Abigail hugged her knees tighter. She looked so defeated, like Lexi after a really bad swim meet.

"Okay, well . . ." Kai picked at a thread on eir sling, thinking. "Do you play any sports?"

She shook her head.

"Dang. I was going to say, it's like performing in front of judges or a big crowd. Maybe you don't feel super confident but you have to believe that no one else can tell and just go for it. Except that probably won't help if you're not an athlete."

This time, Abigail didn't shake her head. She looked thoughtful.

"So . . . you were pretending to be confident when you told those kids to say they're sorry about using the wrong name for Stick?"

Actually, Kai had been too annoyed to guess how people might react, but e didn't think that'd be helpful to admit to Abigail.

"Yeah. Pretty much." E nodded, which sent a twinge down eir shoulder. A constant, annoying reminder. "Except it's gonna be hard for me to do this competition. I don't get this dumb thing off for another few days, but my cabin really needs to win."

"Why?"

"Because, you know the prize? Getting to come up with a new camp name?"

Kai waited until Abigail nodded.

"That's all Juliana's been talking about. And Oren and Jax seem super competitive, too." Kai thought of eir cabinmates and the way Stick and Cassidy seemed to get along with them so effortlessly at dinner. It felt just like the first day e had met Aziza and started parkour, when Kai had felt like e clicked with everyone so quickly. "They all know each other from last year, and I guess I want to help them win. You know, to fit in."

Mostly, Kai wanted to impress Oren, but e had shared enough already.

Abigail released her knees and looked Kai right in the eyes. "I could help."

"Oh yeah?"

"Yeah." Abigail nodded again. "I mean, I don't care about the competition. Not really. I just want to make friends with people who understand . . ." She stopped herself. "I just really need to make friends. Maybe I could try to help make sure your cabin wins any competitions both our cabins enter."

This was sounding better to Kai by the second.

"And if I do that . . ." Abigail paused to take another deep breath. "Would you help me, too? Teach me how to pretend to be confident?"

The corners of Kai's mouth twitched up. There were other Crocheter cabins to compete against, of course, but this would shift the odds. And when e got eir sling off in a few days . . .

This could work. Like, really.

"Deal." E pushed away from the wall and offered Abigail eir hand.

She took it, then brushed the dirt off her shorts. Even standing at her full height, Abigail was a head shorter than Kai.

"We should probably head back inside before anyone realizes we're missing," Kai said. As e led Abigail toward the cafeteria entrance, e glanced over at her. "My mom works at a natural products store and she gave me tons of this lavender oil to keep mosquitos away. You can have some."

Abigail positively beamed. "Okay."

While Abigail weaved her way back to her seat, Kai lingered at the buffet, which now displayed rows of desserts. There was even an ice cream machine at the end of the table. E waited in line, chose a brownie, then headed back to eir table.

Abigail caught eir eye as e sat, and Kai flashed her a grin as if to say, *We've got this.* She glanced away fast, but not before Kai saw a hint of a shy smile.

"We were wondering what was taking you so long," Oren said. "But now I see you were just waiting for them to bring out dessert."

"Smart guy." Jax hesitated. "Is that the right word?"

"Person is better." Aziza was the only kid Kai trusted to call em gendered words like a parkour *king* or *wizard*.

"Smart *person*," Jax amended. "And you picked the best one. Chef Kirstie makes the brownies and they're always *divine*."

Across the table, Kai spotted Abigail nodding along to something one of her cabinmates was saying. She still looked like a deer caught in headlights, but they could work on that.

It was only then that Kai realized e'd totally forgotten to resend Aziza's texts.

Instead of reaching for eir phone, Kai replayed the conversation with Abigail in eir head. Limbs tingling with pent-up energy, e felt more alive right now than e had in the past twelve weeks since eir injury.

ABIGAIL

(SHE/HER/HERS)

ABIGAIL HAD BEEN FEELING MUCH BETTER.

But then she made the mistake of pulling out her phone and scrolling through social media.

After dinner, they'd all gone back to their cabins. Nothing else was scheduled for their first night away at camp; it was time given (needed, in Abigail's opinion) for the campers to settle in and unpack if they hadn't and get some rest before the first full day kicked off tomorrow. It was still a little too early to sleep, but as the crickets chirped outside their cabin and the sun grew lower and lower in the sky, Abigail's eyelids were pretty heavy, anyway.

Bryn was down in his bunk with a book. He had offered Abigail one, but she had declined. Mostly because she wasn't ready for the follow-up questions, like what books do you like, and which one do you want to read, and all the other things that went into that sort of exchange. Meanwhile, below Abigail, Stick was making a ruckus as they unpacked their clothes in the most unorganized and messy way ever. Their clothes were definitely going to wrinkle, but that wasn't any of Abigail's business. Stick seemed to be having particular trouble folding their sweatshirts, which they ended up bunching into a ball and leaving at the bottom of their bunk.

Even with Stick's constant movement making Abigail's top bunk wiggle back and forth, the overall atmosphere of their cabin was relaxing. It seemed like everyone had run out of steam after dinner, and that suited Abigail fine. She wanted to curl into a ball and close her eyes and do her best to stop worrying.

She wanted to think about her pact with Kai.

Abigail could go to sleep and wake up tomorrow, and Kai would be there. E would help her. She could do this now.

Across from Abigail, Cassidy was swinging her long leg over the side of the top bunk, scrolling aimlessly through her cell phone. Abigail watched her for a bit, thinking, *Kai will help me be brave enough to ask for*

Cassidy's number so we can be friends. For now, she just pulled out her own cell phone to scroll through TikTok and Instagram.

The TikTok videos wouldn't play, and Instagram took *forever* to load. Abigail almost gave up, assuming the cell phone service in the middle of Nowhere, Minnesota, was crap. But then the page refreshed, and the picture on the screen was Stacy and the girls from school, posing in their bikinis at the beach. The caption read: *Love the ocean. Much better than any other body of water, like a lake!!!*

Abigail felt her cheeks grow warm. Stacy had never been cruel when they were friends.

That's what happens when you have crushes on people's moms.

Abigail blinked back tears, trying not to think about Leticia, especially not about Lena, or Stacy, or Stacy's mom, or Laura Dern, or anyone.

Abigail vowed she'd head over to Shakopee Lake soon and take a selfie. She'd post it so that everyone back home could see.

She'd keep the rainbows out of it.

"Hey, are you okay?"

Abigail startled at the sound of Cassidy's voice. It was a soft and quiet question, but still. Cassidy was looking at her, across the bunks, her eyebrows pinched together.

"Yeah. I'm fine," Abigail quickly responded.

Stick chimed in, "If you're homesick or something, don't worry. I was pretty upset my first night away at camp, too. It gets easier tomorrow, when everything gets going. You don't think about back home so much." Stick paused for a second, then laughed. "There's so much to do, you don't really have time to."

"I'm okay," Abigail whispered back.

Cassidy and Stick both smiled at her.

Say thanks, Abigail told herself. *Tell them you aren't homesick, but you don't want to think about home, either. Tell them you want to be their friends.*

Abigail missed her moment. Cassidy turned back over in bed, and soon the lights went out, and the crickets chirped louder, and Stick finally finished unpacking, and Abigail rolled over, too. It would all be okay. Stick was right. Tomorrow, Abigail would wake up and everything at home wouldn't matter. Tomorrow would be a good day.

She just needed to close her eyes and get a good night's sleep.

Abigail did not get a good night's sleep. At some point—between having to swat at a mosquito that had decided to live inside her sleeping bag and the sun rising and bleeding in through the window of their cabin, making the whole room super bright really early in the morning—Abigail had started to panic again.

How on earth was she supposed to keep her end of the pact with Kai? Cassidy had been so nice to her last night! Her cabinmates were so nice in general! She wanted to be their friends, and how the heck was she supposed to do that if she was planning on *cheating* so that Kai's cabin could beat them?

This was a terrible idea. What was she thinking!

"You okay?" Bryn asked her first thing.

Abigail held in a groan. *Why are all of you so nice to me! I'm the worst!* "I didn't sleep well. I kept wondering if crickets are the *Parasaurolophus* of today. They were supposedly the loudest dinosaurs ever," she added. Well, at least it was a half-truth, a mostly-truth.

"Maybe we could ask if we can get you earplugs or something?" Bryn said, too nice for someone Abigail *hadn't* made a pact with.

"It's fine," Abigail said. "Really."

"I told Jax and the rest of them that we'd sit with their cabin again!" Cassidy said, before leaping down from her bunk in one swift moment. It was pretty impressive; Abigail would be taking the ladder.

"Great!" Stick said. "Let's get going before all the cheesy bits of the scrambled eggs are gone."

"Okay. I liked the Purple cabin. They seemed really nice," Bryn added.

And then Abigail got a brilliant idea. "They were really nice. Maybe we should, um, team up with them?"

Stick looked confused. "What do you mean? For the competition? It's cabin against cabin. We can't be on the same team."

Abigail felt herself blushing. "Oh . . . well, yeah, but maybe . . ."

Maybe the idea wasn't so brilliant. Maybe she shouldn't have spoken up. Maybe she should never have made a pact with Kai. Maybe she—

"You mean like form an alliance with them?" Cassidy spoke up. She had a big smile on her face, and Abigail felt like she could breathe again. "That's a really good idea! It would at least give us an edge over the other colors. Let's get going, we can tell Juliana about your idea once we get there!"

Of course, when they got to the main cabin for breakfast, Abigail realized there was one glaring mistake in the plan: the more they interacted with the Purple cabin, the more they'd have to be around Leticia.

Who knew *full well* how Abigail felt about her mom.

After grabbing new name tags for the day, they made their way to the buffet breakfast. Stick mounded up their plate with cheesy scrambled eggs and bacon, and the smell made Abigail queasy. She took some non-cheesy scrambled eggs and a couple of pieces of dry toast.

The Purple cabin—and Leticia and MJ—were waiting for them at the table. Cassidy beelined over to Juliana to ask her about the alliance, and Abigail ducked her head and walked as quickly as possible past Leticia, her T. rex earrings swinging back and forth as she hurried. She kind of wished she hadn't put them on. At school, earrings were one of the only things they could wear with their school uniforms that made Abigail feel unique, a little more like herself. They gave her comfort. But now, she just wanted to blend in. Abigail sat down, ignoring her food. She touched one of the little silver earrings.

When she looked up, Kai was sitting across from her.

"Hey," e said. "Cool earrings."

Abigail could have kissed em. E had a plateful of scrambled eggs with some weird-looking red flakes on top, and e took a huge mouthful. Abigail stopped worrying about her earrings. She even started feeling a little hungry.

"I hear we're starting an alliance?" Kai smirked.

Abigail struggled to keep a big smile off her face. She was pleased Kai had realized she'd suggested an alliance. Kai took another giant mouthful of eggs, a bit of the flakes on top getting stuck to eir lip.

"What's on your eggs?"

"Red pepper flakes."

Oh. Ew. "Uh . . ."

"Kai! What do you think?" Someone suddenly called over to em. Abigail and Kai both turned to find the entire table looking their way. Jax continued, "It's over in the woods. Maybe we'll find Mx. Nutsford while we're out there!"

Mix what?

"That works for me," Stick said.

"Awesome," Cassidy added.

"Wait, what are we talking about?" Kai asked.

"Didn't realize you chickens couldn't hear us down there!" MJ said, standing up and leaning over, projecting his voice a little louder than necessary. "We've got a competition to start! Each day you'll have a bunch of events to choose from. They'll be posted at the back of the cafeteria every morning. See over there? A wide variety of choices. Athletic things and crafts and all sorts of good ol' fun. Jax and Cassidy, in the spirit of our new alliance, suggested we go off to an archery lesson first today. What do y'all think? You'd each earn a point for participating."

That sounded fine. Abigail didn't actually care. She probably wouldn't have to cheat at archery, at least, because she was sure to be terrible and wouldn't be helping her cabin win any extra points. And, since it was a lesson, it didn't sound like there were any extra points to earn anyway, so both cabins would finish even.

"Uh, wait. What about Kai's arm?" Oren said. He was sitting a couple seats down from Abigail. "Can e even do archery?"

Abigail watched as Kai's hand reached over to cover eir shoulder, running eir fingers over the straps of eir sling. E wasn't smiling anymore. E was actually kind of scowling, slouching a bit in eir seat.

E's embarrassed, Abigail realized. The same way she felt anytime she sat at the end of the cafeteria table at school, and someone said something about crushes or boys, and someone inevitably brought up Abigail's crush.

She had made a pact. It was her job to help em. She took a deep breath and spoke up for the first time at camp: "I'm not so great at sports. Can we do something else first? You said there were crafts?"

"Oh! Yes, please!" Juliana suddenly shrieked. "The schedule said they're making pride bracelets outside at the Benches. I want to make one to wear the whole time we're here, so I can show off my identities."

"That's a great idea!" Cassidy said. "Let's do that!"

"Anyone disagree?" Leticia asked the two cabins.

No one disagreed. Jax kind of just shrugged, but he seemed okay with the change in plans. They finished eating and picked up their trays. Kai reached for Abigail's arm before she could leave the table. "Thanks," e said.

Abigail smiled. "That's what the pact's for, right?"

Kai laughed. "Yeah. Right."

Abigail stared down a bunch of picnic tables covered with boxes of multicolored string. Someone from the Blue cabin was halfway done making a black, gray, white, and purple bracelet. The kid next to them was making a full rainbow and was on the green stripe.

"I'm going to make a nonbinary bracelet," Stick said. "Yellow, white, purple, and black."

"I might just go with a rainbow," Bryn said.

Abigail had no idea what she would make. Was there a lesbian flag? What on earth were the colors if there was? She'd never seen one before. Where would she have ever seen one? Besides, it wasn't like she could wear one of these bracelets. Could she? What if she posted a picture for the girls back home to see, and they saw the bracelet? She'd have to cut it off when she got home, because she sure couldn't go to school with it on.

This was supposed to be fun. She was actually really good at arts and crafts. Last year she helped the art teacher at school paint all the sets for the school play. (Stacy had auditioned for a part but Abigail was too afraid to.) Ms. Brophy told Abigail her trees had "wonderful dimension to them."

She and Stacy had even made friendship bracelets for each other before. They used to make a ton of them at the beach, sitting on sandy towels with Stacy's bracelet kit, so they could sell them to buy ice cream from the snack bar.

"What are you going to make?" Kai asked. Abigail wished e hadn't. E had a bunch of colors in eir own hand, blue and green and yellow and orange.

Abigail stared at them for a moment and panicked. "What identity is *that*?" she asked a little hysterically.

Kai laughed. "It's actually not. I don't think anyway. My best friend Aziza loves these colors, so I'm just making a bracelet for her."

"I don't want to do this," Abigail said, her voice hardly above a whisper. "I don't want one." *And I don't have a best friend at home I can make one for, anymore, either.*

Kai frowned at her, and Abigail felt ridiculous.

"I have an idea," Kai said. "Hey, Juliana! Did you decide which one you were going to make?"

"No!" Juliana practically howled. "I might try to make both but I am tragically slow at these and I cannot decide which one I want to prioritize!"

"Abigail doesn't think she wants to wear one. Maybe she can help you make one of yours?" Kai said.

Abigail blinked.

Kai kind of shoved her over to where Juliana, Bryn, and Cassidy were sitting. Abigail took the seat on the opposite side of Juliana. "I'm transgender and pansexual. I want bracelets to show both. Will you really help me?"

"Yeah, sure," Abigail said. She turned to look back at Kai, but e was already gone, headed toward the table where Jax, Oren, and Stick were sitting. She took a deep breath and tried not to cringe as she admitted, "But I don't know what colors to use."

"That's okay! Pansexual is pink, yellow, and light blue. You can make that one?" Juliana said. She handed Abigail the colors.

"Yes. I can do that," Abigail said. She *could* do this.

"I should have just made a rainbow, like Bryn," Cassidy said, groaning and hiding her face against Juliana's shoulder, waving her unfinished bracelet in front of her. "The lesbian flag has so much pink. I *never* wear pink."

Juliana patted Cassidy's head, and Cassidy blushed, and then leaned in to whisper something that made Juliana laugh. The whole exchange made Abigail's stomach hurt a little bit again. Cassidy and Juliana had known each other for less time than Abigail knew Cassidy, and they already, apparently, shared inside jokes.

Stop thinking and just make the bracelet, Abigail.

"Hey, Abigail?" Bryn said tentatively, leaning closer. "I just wanted to say . . . I get it. I probably won't wear my bracelet, either. I'm still a little too nervous to wear the trans flag at all."

"Really?" Abigail asked.

"Really," Bryn said. "I don't use he/him pronouns back home, at school, yet. I will soon. It's still a little scary sometimes."

Abigail breathed a sigh of relief. "Yeah. It is."

Bryn smiled, and Abigail managed a small smile in return.

They continued making bracelets. At one point, Kai turned around to look over at Abigail, and e gave her a big thumbs-up that Abigail returned.

The wind blew through the thick trees that surrounded the picnic area, blowing Abigail's hair out of her face. Her earrings swayed, and feeling the cool silver against her skin made her smile.

"How's it going over here?" MJ came over to ask. "Let me see, let me see!"

They all held up their bracelets. MJ rattled off all the identities he could see. "These both are actually mine," Juliana clarified. "Abigail helped me so I could make both, because I was having a really, really hard time deciding between the two of them. She saved me, really!"

MJ laughed. "Is that true?"

Juliana's assessment was a little dramatic, so Abigail kind of just shrugged. "I didn't mind," she said. "I wanted to help."

"Leticia! You hear this? One of my little chickens helped your little chicken out of the kindness of her heart. You know what that means?" MJ said.

Leticia, who was over by Kai and the others, sighed loudly, throwing her head back. "Oh, *fiiiiiiine*. You can do the honors."

Everyone was paying attention now.

Abigail was exceptionally curious as to what the heck was happening.

"Hear ye, hear ye!" MJ yelled. Abigail startled a little bit. "I hereby award the Yellow cabin, the *best* cabin as it is *my* cabin, an extra point toward the competition!"

Abigail's mouth dropped open.

Oh *no*.

"What? *Why*?" Jax asked. "We weren't competing!"

"Not everything is about athletic competition, or even competition in general," Leticia chimed in.

"Sometimes it's simply about being kind, and being a community," MJ finished for her. "Which Abigail here has done. Congrats on earning the first extra point of the day, chicken!"

Cassidy and Bryn were cheering, and Juliana was congratulating her, and Abigail quickly glanced over at Kai and the others. Jax and Oren were both groaning.

Kai had a deep frown on eir face.

This was *not* supposed to happen.

8

KAI
(E/EM/EIR)

KAI STAYED QUIET AS THEY LEFT THE BENCHES, ALTHOUGH e tried to silently let Abigail know e wasn't mad at her— with a small smile, a nod, whatever—whenever she glanced back at em. Which happened literally every few seconds, because Abigail didn't seem to be getting the message. By the time they made it to the cafeteria, Kai's cheeks ached from all eir fake smiles, although e figured that was better than the whiplash Abigail probably had from constantly twisting her neck over her shoulder.

A line formed at the front of the cafeteria. It snaked toward a table with brown paper lunch bags. The Yellow cabin chose their bags first, and Kai dropped eir too-cheery expression the moment Abigail stopped looking back at em. Oren stood directly in front of Kai, so Kai couldn't help studying his kippah. It was white today, with fancy gold lettering across the center. It looked just like the Hebrew in prayer books at the temple Kai's cousins attended—not that Kai could read it. E wondered if Oren would think it was rude to ask what it meant.

"Ladies first," Jax said, pulling Kai away from eir thoughts. Oren and Kai paused to let Juliana choose her lunch.

"That is an incredibly outdated gesture." Juliana picked a bag marked *Turkey*, then turned back to Jax, as though something had just occurred to her. "But I think you meant well, so thank you."

"You're welcome." Jax shot her a grin. "And got it for next time."

As Jax grabbed his own bag, Oren turned back to Kai. "It's kind of a bummer how the points worked out this morning."

"Yeah." Kai pressed eir lips together and couldn't help looking back over at Abigail. She was following Cassidy and Stick and Bryn to a table. "The competition's barely started, though. We still have plenty of time to earn extra points ourselves."

Kai couldn't tell if e was trying to reassure Oren or emself.

"Yeah, totally."

Oren smiled and Kai's chest fluttered in response. It felt like a butterfly had gotten trapped behind eir ribs.

"Were you going to grab a lunch bag, or . . ."

Oren tilted his head toward the table. Kai realized Oren had already picked a bag of his own, marked *Vegetarian*. It was just Kai who was holding up the line.

"Oh! Yes." Kai swiped at the nearest bag, then let Oren lead the way to the table where Yellow, Purple, and Blue campers were seated.

"So," Leticia called once everyone got settled. "What is everyone thinking of doing this afternoon?"

"I want to do whatever activity will earn us extra points, like Abigail got this morning," Oren said.

"For real." Jax laughed, then glanced at Kai. "I still want to try archery. But that can wait. I'm sure they'll offer it other days, after you get your sling off."

MJ aimed a thumbs-up at Kai's end of the table. "You'll definitely have a chance to do most of the things you want." He winked, and Kai felt a measure of relief that eir chest didn't flutter. At least e wasn't crushing on every single guy at camp.

E reached for eir lunch bag, then froze. It read *HAM* in big capital letters. E'd been so flustered talking to Oren, e hadn't looked before grabbing it. And while Kai didn't personally have anything against ham sandwiches, Oren might. It was one of the few foods Kai remembered that Jewish people who keep kosher don't eat.

And here e was, about to dig in, right in front of Oren.

"Crap," Kai blurted. "I didn't realize I'd grabbed a ham one."

"You don't like ham?" Oren asked, unwrapping his own sandwich. "I bet you can get a different bag. There are still some left."

"No, I just mean, I'm Jewish. Kind of. And I eat ham, but you probably don't, right? So I feel like I should've picked something else, except I wasn't paying attention." Kai sucked in a breath, cheeks burning. "I just don't want to be offensive or anything."

"You're—" Oren stopped himself, brows furrowed like he was trying to process everything Kai had just said. He shook his head a little. "I'm not offended. You can eat whatever you want."

"Oh, okay." The word came out high and squeaky.

Kai looked over at Jax, then at Juliana, then farther down the table. Anywhere but at Oren or the stupid ham sandwich that'd started this awkward conversation. If Aziza were here, she'd know what to say to break the tension. Kai's texts from last night finally showed as sent. But Aziza hadn't answered. Or if she had, they hadn't come through yet.

A few kids away, Cassidy said something Kai couldn't hear. Her gaze was aimed at the bulletin board with the day's activity list. Stick, Bryn, and Abigail were looking at it, too.

Cassidy turned back toward the Purple campers.

"How about a nature walk? That'd be exercise, and everyone would be able to do it, I think."

Kai might've scowled at Cassidy's comment if Abigail hadn't chosen that exact moment to look over at em. Her pale cheeks flushed pink as she shot em another apologetic look. As irked as Kai was about eir cabin already being behind, e knew Abigail hadn't earned that point on purpose. Plus, a pact was a pact. E sat up a little straighter.

"Sounds fun." Kai looked at eir cabinmates. "What do you guys think?"

"I'm not a guy," Juliana said, but she didn't give Kai a chance to correct emself. "Otherwise, I think that would be nice."

"Same," Jax said. "Maybe we can even find Mx. Nutsford while we're out there."

Oren nodded, while Juliana just rolled her eyes.

"Excellent." MJ rubbed his hands together like some sort of melodramatic villain. "And this isn't just any walk, for the record. Stay tuned for more after lunch."

"Hey!" a kid in a Blue cabin T-shirt called from the far end of the table. "Can we come, too?"

"The more the merrier," Leticia said, as MJ nodded agreement. "It'll be a great way to get to know some other campers, which is actually the purpose of camp, not the extra points. Now, eat up, chickens!" Leticia's voice transformed into a perfect imitation of MJ's accent, which earned her a few giggles. "Y'all've got about ten more minutes."

Everyone turned back to their food. Kai popped a potato chip into eir mouth, trying to avoid eir sandwich. E could only hope the chips and cookie would tide em over until dinner—and that eir cheeks would return to their normal color before the hike.

"Head on outside, my pretties," MJ hollered. "I'll just be a second."

The Purple, Yellow, and Blue campers all left the cafeteria together, then waited until MJ reappeared with a stack of cards. He passed one out to everyone, and offered markers to every other camper.

"Share the markers with your neighbors," MJ said. "And don't lose your card. They're laminated so we can reuse them."

They performed a quick head count, then MJ, Leticia, and the Blue cabin's counselor, Sol (they/them), led their group past the cabins, in the opposite direction of the Benches and lake. Kai looked down at eir card as e walked. It was a five-by-five grid listing things like *pine tree*, *chipmunk*, *loon*, and *Canada goose*. Instead of saying BINGO across the top, though, the card said PRIDE.

"We'll be taking you up into the hills, then looping around and back down so you'll get a chance to see the lakeshore up close," Sol called back over their shoulder. "Keep an eye out for wildlife and other nature-y things. You'll all get a point for completing the hike, plus one lucky camper will earn an extra point for being the first to call a PRIDE bingo." Sol was white and their hair was yellow. Not like Kai's natural blond but bright like a neon highlighter pen. It hung loose, just under their chin, swaying above their shoulders.

"Seems like it would've made more sense for Sol to be the Yellow cabin's counselor," Jax said.

"With that logic, Oren should've been in Blue," Juliana said, "since his last name is Blau and that's what it means in German."

Kai glanced at her. "I thought you said you take French?"

She shrugged. "I know a little bit in a lot of languages. My papa calls me a dabbler."

A pair of Blue campers slowed, then turned back to them.

"Hey, I'm Ash," a camper with olive-toned skin and spiky black hair said. The pronouns on their name tag read, *she/her/hers*.

The white kid with light brown hair beside Ash waved. "Siobhan."

Kai glanced at Siobhan's name tag, but there was nothing else to see. When e looked up, eir eyes met Siobhan's.

"No pronouns." Siobhan seemed to know exactly what Kai was thinking. "Just use my name when referring to me, please. It's pronounced 'Sha-vonne,' in case you didn't know."

Kai waited for eir cabinmates to introduce themselves, but they were all looking over at em.

"Um, hey. I'm Kai."

"Cool." Ash grinned, then wedged herself between Juliana and Jax as the group entered a more heavily wooded area. Siobhan strolled a couple of feet ahead of them, just behind Cassidy.

"It's weird how almost none of us are in the same cabin with anyone from last year," Ash said.

"Oren and Jax were both in Blue last year, with Stick," Juliana cut in.

"Right, that's why I said 'almost.' But besides them, Siobhan was Red, I was Purple, and you were Yellow." Ash nodded at Juliana.

Cassidy slowed, glancing at Juliana over one shoulder. "And you've been here three years now, right?"

"Yes," Juliana confirmed. "Siobhan and I were also in Green together two years ago."

"They probably switch it up so we can meet new people every year," Jax said.

"Or to avoid another mac-and-cheese tragedy." Oren's comment was followed by laughter. Even Juliana cracked a smile.

Kai felt like the only one who was left out, even though e knew Cassidy hadn't been there last year, either. E cleared eir throat, feeling awkward.

It felt like this shouldn't matter to someone who didn't want to make friends. Yet somehow, it did.

"Some of us snuck food back to our cabins last year," Oren explained, looking over at em. "So we'd have it for—well, that's not all that important, but one of the campers forgot where they'd stashed their mac and cheese."

"Until it started to smell." Siobhan twisted around, walking backwards. "It was in our cabin and it was *awful*."

"But hilarious now," Ash said.

Oren grinned. "Totally."

Kai's attention wandered as they continued to talk about events e hadn't been a part of. The trail wound left, then right, becoming steeper by the minute. E glanced down at eir PRIDE card, wondering if e should start looking for wildlife. But no one else in eir group seemed interested in playing.

Kai looked ahead. Just behind the counselors, Abigail was walking beside Bryn when she came to a jerky stop and slapped her hand against the side of her leg. Suddenly, Kai remembered a different promise e'd made to her last night.

"Be right back," e murmured.

Kai sped up until e was walking alongside Abigail.

"Hey."

"Hi." Abigail looked up at em with an uncertain expression.

"It looked like you were getting along pretty good with Bryn."

"Yeah, I guess." A small smile lifted the corners of Abigail's mouth.

"So hey, I forgot to give this to you earlier." Kai reached into a pocket and pulled out a small bottle of lavender bug repellent.

"Oh, thanks." Abigail's eyes immediately lit up. "I feel like I'm getting eaten alive out here."

"Not anymore. Hold out your arms."

She raised them both, zombie-style, and for the first time today Kai's smile was completely genuine. E spritzed both of her arms and her legs. Then, e shielded her ponytail with one hand while coating the back of her neck.

When e was done, Kai offered the bottle to Abigail, whose brows pinched together.

"Are you sure?"

"Yeah. Seriously, take it," e said. "This is just a sample my mom gets free at work. I have like a hundred of them."

She pocketed the bottle, then Kai and Abigail walked quickly to catch up with Bryn and the others. These campers actually seemed to be searching the woods for the animals and nature items on their PRIDE cards.

Soon Kai was engrossed in the search, too, and e wandered off to the side of the trail, hand shielding eir eyes as e squinted up at a tree. By the time Oren stepped up beside em, Kai was a few yards away from Abigail, who was inspecting a hole in a different tree trunk with Bryn.

"Hey, Kai," Oren said. "Want to see something cool?"

Kai looked over Oren's shoulder but didn't see anything other than trees and dirt. ". . . Sure?"

"You're talking about the place from last year?" Jax sprinted up to them.

"Yep." Oren's curly hair bobbed as he nodded.

"I'm down to go too, then."

Go? As in, off the trail?

"Are we allowed to?" Kai asked. "I mean, won't we get in trouble?" Internally, e cringed at how babyish eir question sounded.

"Nah. There are a bunch of us out here," Jax said. "And if this is anything like last year's hike, they won't do a head count again until we get to the lake. We've got plenty of time."

Something didn't feel right. Kai shook eir head. "I don't know if—"

Oren took Kai's hand in both of his, and Kai's words sputtered out. Suddenly, eir body temperature felt like it doubled.

"We'll totally cover for you," Ash chimed in from behind them. Siobhan nodded.

They all looked over at Juliana, whose shoulders lifted, then dropped as she sighed. "I won't say anything."

"See? We're good." Oren turned back to Kai, giving em a lopsided smile that made the fluttering in Kai's chest speed up. "What do you say? I promise it's awesome."

Kai glanced back at Abigail, but she was still with Bryn. Stick and Cassidy had joined them, too. They were all talking and nodding and smiling. Even Abigail.

And honestly, she was the reason Kai was feeling uncertain, right? Because e didn't want to leave her behind after promising to help her. No other reason. At least not any e wanted to think about. By the time she noticed e was gone, Kai told emself, e'd already be back and ready to check in on her again.

This would also give em some time with Oren. Maybe e could finally ask the questions that had been piling up since yesterday. Kai could even practice showing off some of that pretend confidence e'd promised to teach Abigail.

E pushed the last hint of discomfort aside and turned back to Oren. "Okay," e said. "Lead the way."

The farther they walked, the softer the voices of the other campers got. Oren hiked beside Kai, and they both followed Jax, who was a few feet ahead of them. It was just enough space for it to feel like Kai and Oren were alone. Kai could probably ask eir questions without Jax hearing.

Except eir tongue felt thick, like it was three sizes too big for eir mouth. Eir throat felt dry, like e'd gone an entire parkour practice without a single sip of water. Kai had never liked a boy like this before. Or anyone. This was completely new for em.

It was called "breaking a jump" in parkour whenever you tried a new skill for the first time. You'd break a jump to get past your fear and prove you could do something that'd felt impossible just moments before. What Kai had learned, first from gymnastics and then parkour, was that *thinking* about doing a skill always felt scarier than *actually* doing it.

Maybe it'd be the same with talking to Oren.

"So, you're Jewish?" Oren asked.

"Um." Kai stumbled over a dead branch. All the things e had planned to say flew straight out of eir head.

"That's what you said at lunch, right?"

"Yeah." Kai's shoulders tensed up. "Although I'm not sure it counts."

A fallen tree blocked their way. Jax climbed over it, then waited as Kai did the same. Oren decided on a different approach. He took a few sprinting steps, then hurtled over it, using his hand as a pivot. Kai couldn't help feeling that Oren would be great at parkour.

Say something to him, then!

But the words just wouldn't come.

"Why wouldn't it count?" Oren asked once they'd resumed their hike. He kept his voice low, like it was meant for Kai alone.

"My mom's Jewish but my dad's not," Kai explained. "And my parents aren't really religious at all. We sometimes go to church for Christmas and temple for stuff like Rosh Hashanah, but not every year or on any kind of real schedule."

"That totally counts," Oren said. "Technically, you're Jewish because your mom is Jewish, but I know a couple of kids back home who only have Jewish dads and still go to temple. I don't think anyone would say they don't count either, so you're fine—even if you eat ham sandwiches."

"That makes a lot of sense."

"Of course it does." Oren grinned. "It's the truth."

Oren's grin washed Kai's tension away, and the warm, fluttery feeling that was becoming so familiar returned. And that was when it hit em: Oren made Kai feel like e didn't have to put on fake smiles if e didn't feel like smiling, like e didn't have to pretend to act confident around him. Kai liked being able to let down eir guard. And e really liked Oren.

Jax disappeared around a big tree, and Oren picked up his pace. "If you ever want to be around more Jewish kids though, there are summer camps just like this one for Jewish campers who are like us."

Jewish campers who are like *us*.

"How come you're here if there are Jewish summer camps?" Kai asked.

"Because of Jax," Oren said. "We wanted to go to camp together. My mom and his dad are both college math professors. We met when we were like seven, when our parents were at the same work conference, so we've known each other practically forever."

"Almost there." Jax waved to them. Both Oren and Kai fell silent as they navigated their way around logs and over thick underbrush.

Kai heard the trickle of water before e saw it, the sound getting louder and louder until they broke through the trees and saw the bubbling creek. Sunlight peeked through the tree branches overhead, making the creek shimmer. Between the sound and the dancing sunlight, this part of the forest felt alive. It made Kai feel alive to be standing there beside Oren.

"Cool, right?"

Kai nodded.

"We found this place last summer." Jax kicked off his shoes and socks, then dipped his foot into the water. "Frigid. Just like last year."

"It probably comes from the lake," Kai offered as Oren slipped off his shoes and joined Jax on a big, flat rock where the forest floor met the shallow edge of the water.

"Makes sense." Oren dropped his feet into the creek, then kicked them up, splashing Kai a little. He shot Kai an impish grin, then patted the rock beside him.

Kai's face heated up. E ducked eir head, then settled onto the rock's edge, close to Oren, tucking eir legs underneath em, shoes still on.

All of a sudden, e realized this was the first time e had been alone with two boys since a few months ago at school. But e felt fine. Comfortable. Kai didn't have to brace emself for insults here. E didn't have to watch eir back or dodge eir classmates' attempts to hit or shove or punch, either.

E glanced over at Oren and Jax. To Kai's surprise, Oren was looking back. Flustered, Kai looked down fast. "What?" e asked.

"Nothing," Oren said. "Just wanted to make sure you're doing okay."

"I'm good. You were right. This place is really cool," Kai said, eyeing the water. "Plus, it's kind of nice to get some time away from the others." E swallowed, then looked up again. "Not that I don't like everyone. It's just—"

"—there's a lot to remember with all the changing names and pronouns," Jax said. "Right?"

"Yeah." Kai blinked, surprised that Jax had read eir thoughts so well.

"It can be intense if you're not used to it." Oren leaned over, placing his hand on Kai's good shoulder.

He gave it a gentle squeeze, which sent a pleasant spark down Kai's spine. "At least, that's how it felt for me my first year here."

"Same," Jax said. "At least you don't have to worry about that with us. Our pronouns aren't changing anytime soon, right, Or?"

Jax wrapped his arm around Oren and Oren leaned into him. Kai's breath caught in eir throat as Jax gave Oren a kiss. It was quick, and just on the cheek, but Kai still felt like eir world was crumbling.

Had e missed something? Did Jax and Oren like each other? Were they dating?

"Or with liking people. It's always been boys for me. Nice and simple." The corners of Oren's mouth turned up, just a little. "Not that there's anything wrong with people who like more than just boys or girls, or with having lots of different pronouns and switching names," he said. "Everyone's different."

Jax nodded, and any confidence Kai had been feeling around Oren vanished. Kai forced emself to smile. E pretended e was beside Abigail, demonstrating how to look confident. The conversation moved on. Kai managed a few words, but Oren and Jax did most of the talking. If either of the boys noticed something was off, they didn't say anything.

By the time they got up and started heading back toward the other campers, Kai had almost managed to convince emself that everything was fine, that eir smiles were genuine.

Almost.

9

ABIGAIL

(SHE/HER/HERS)

"THEY SHOULD HAVE PUT MX. NUTSFORD ON THE BINGO card!" Stick shouted.

And this was pretty much the last straw for Abigail. This whole bingo hike was unbelievably stressful, which seemed the opposite of how a brisk hike through the Minnesota woods should be. But Abigail was actually really good at this, apparently, and had spotted the little yellow warbler hiding in the tree before anyone else (which was an R item on her PRIDE bingo card) and was the first to identify the ostrich ferns, too (which was third down on the D column).

Basically, she was *killing* it at PRIDE bingo, and it was stressing her out, because her cabin was already ahead in points and she couldn't get anyone from the Purple cabin to focus enough to give her a chance to give them the answers first. She practically had to stamp the warbler and the ostrich fern on Juliana's bingo card *for* her, just so that they could at least be even.

Somewhere along the way, though, she *did* start having fun. She forgot about how, even though she hadn't wanted to make a bracelet, she now wanted to wear one. She forgot about how inadequate she felt every time her name tag fell off (which only seemed to happen to *her*) and someone had to ask for her pronouns, which she still stumbled over every time she said, "*She*, please." She forgot how bad she felt earlier for messing up and getting points for her cabin instead of Kai's.

At the start of the hike, she'd helped steady Bryn when he tripped over a root, and Bryn had stayed close ever since, which was extra nice since most of the kids at school wouldn't stand too close to her these days. She hadn't gotten bitten by any mosquitos since Kai gave her the lavender spray, and when she said something dumb about velociraptor footprints while Juliana and one of the Blue campers tried to look for bear prints, they actually seemed interested instead of laughing in her face.

Kai told Abigail to pretend to be confident, and she could do that, she *could*.

But then Stick brought up that stupid squirrel again, and Abigail felt clueless all over again. Maybe she *didn't* actually belong here and maybe all these kids who knew about pronouns and other sexualities and squirrels, and really *were* confident and didn't have to fake it, wouldn't want someone as hopeless as Abigail for a friend.

"I said the same thing! Mx. Nutsford should *absolutely* be in this game!" MJ shouted excitedly, which made Stick stand even taller and smile even wider.

Leticia groaned. "Don't encourage them! You and my mom are like the worst when it comes to that damn squirrel."

"Just because you don't believe in the power of Mx. Nutsford doesn't mean zie isn't real," MJ fired back. "Sol's seen zem. Tell them!"

A couple of the campers gasped. Siobhan, with wide excited eyes, said, "You did?"

The Blue cabin counselor blushed, ducking their head. "I mean. It was a long time ago. And it was only just a glimpse."

"Like for real, for real? You're not joking?" Juliana squinted at Sol.

"No joke," Sol confirmed.

"I can't believe—I mean, I just didn't think—you were chosen!" Juliana suddenly screamed. A few birds in the trees above them scattered at the outburst. A couple campers jumped. "This is my third year here." She lowered her voice. "And I honestly didn't think zie was real. I've never actually met anyone who was chosen!"

Cassidy, who had been strolling arm in arm with Juliana throughout the majority of the hike, cocked her head and asked the question Abigail was practically *bursting* to ask. "Okay. Someone needs to explain this Mx. Nutsford thing for us newbies."

"Leticia, would you like the honors?" MJ asked.

Leticia rolled her eyes. "Apparently, there's an albino squirrel that—"

"That has been around the entire time the camp has been open!" Stick excitedly interrupted.

"—as Stick said, has been around for all the years the camp has been open, which—"

"That's *eight years* this summer!" It was MJ who interrupted this time. A few of the campers, including Abigail, started giggling.

"How long do squirrels live?" Cassidy asked.

"Between six and ten years. Up to twenty-four years in captivity, though," Juliana answered. Abigail, who was known for spouting random facts about dinosaurs, was impressed by Juliana's knowledge. Juliana shrugged. "I looked it up after my first year here. But the odds of a squirrel being white are one in one hundred thousand, so I assumed it was just a myth—until now, anyway."

"*Anyway*," Leticia said, stern but with a dimpled smile that reminded Abigail so much of Lena that Abigail felt her chest squeeze. "Camp legend says that each summer, Mx. Nutsford—"

"Who I helped Lena name, by the way, as part of the inaugural camp," MJ chimed in.

"Do you want to tell the story?" Leticia said.

"But you're doing such a good job." Sol smirked.

"I'll finish! Can I finish?" Stick said, raising their hand as high as they possibly could, which was exceptionally high.

Leticia nodded, and Stick continued, "Every year, the albino squirrel Mx. Nutsford shows zemself to *one* camper, one *chosen* camper. And legend has it that *that* camper is the one who needs Mx. Nutsford the most. Mx. Nutsford brings them good luck for the rest of camp, and beyond. So, like, if someone is having a really hard time at home, with their parents or something, Mx. Nutsford shows zemself to them and when they go home things get better."

Stick's voice went soft at the end of that sentence, and the energy of the other campers kind of deflated, too.

They all got quiet, listening to the birds and the breeze around them, taking it all in, glancing at one another.

Abigail supposed she wasn't the only one who didn't have an exceptionally easy time back home.

She thought that it must be nice, to have a magic squirrel make things miraculously better when she left camp.

She knew better, though.

Which was confirmed when Sol said, "Honestly, most of the stories I heard just involved zem stealing food right out of campers' hands."

Abigail was scarred for life three years ago when a seagull on the boardwalk stole an entire slice of pizza right out of her hands just outside of Timoney's Pizzeria. As much as she'd like a magical albino squirrel to make things better with Stacy, she'd rather not encounter a food-stealing squirrel, thanks. She'd just hope she wouldn't be chosen.

Even though part of her *also* kind of hoped she'd be chosen.

"Hang on. Wait a minute," Cassidy said, her hands on her hips. "Who decided the squirrel's pronouns were *zie* and *zem*?"

The campers all looked at Sol, who shrugged. "Honestly I don't know, but until zie tells us otherwise, it just seems to fit zem. Oh! We're just about at the top.

This is my favorite view in the entire camp," Sol said, as the group began walking again.

They came to a clearing that overlooked the lake. Leticia told them all to stay away from the edge, but it wasn't that sharp of a drop. If they wanted to, they could probably roll all the way from here to the water. It was beautiful, though. As much as Abigail loved the beach back home, and as much as she would never trade the ocean for anything, she couldn't stop gazing out at the lake.

They could see bright little rainbow specks as other campers gathered around the edges of the lake down below, and Abigail could see their cluster of cabins from up here, too. She could see the tips of the trees in the distance, and the boats far out on the other side of the lake, and the reflections the sun was making on the surface of the water. She shielded her eyes with her hands as she squinted out, thinking, *Stacy and the girls would think this was beautiful, too. They'd have to.*

A Blue camper, Ash, came to stand next to Abigail. She pointed up at the sky, at a large bird that was flying across the lake. It disappeared into the trees below them. "That was an osprey," Ash said. "Did you see it?"

Abigail nodded. She had ospreys at home, too, ones that made their nests in the marshes by the bay. It felt almost weird seeing one here. As if Minnesota and New Jersey weren't all that far apart.

Ash tapped the bingo card in Abigail's hands. "We both got bingo."

Abigail looked down at her card. Sure enough, right across in a neat little row, she had filled the spots for P-R-I-D-E.

She panicked for a moment, because did the Purple cabin get bingo, too? Or was it just her and the Blue cabin? She needed to make sure that Kai got eir cabin the extra points, too, so they'd need to all get bingo together. She needed to find someone from Purple so she could tell them to fill in the osprey.

But Ash was the only other person who had seen the osprey, and she knew that only Abigail had seen it, too. Maybe it was still in the trees, and Abigail could have Juliana or Kai or someone try to find it. Maybe they could get bingo, too, before Abigail put Yellow an entire *second* point above the Purple.

Ash raised her hand. "Hey! We got bingo over here!"

Abigail frantically tried to find someone from the Purple cabin, but she quickly realized no one else was actually playing bingo anymore, even as Leticia came over to look at her and Ash's cards. Everyone was posing for photos with the lake and view behind them. Cassidy had her arm outstretched, taking a selfie with Juliana, their faces pressed close together. Bryn was snapping pictures on his phone, too—of the lake, of the other campers as they made silly faces at him. Stick and MJ were posing together, and Sol and Leticia were taking pictures together, too.

"Abigail, come get in the next picture. We can take a cabin photo!" Cassidy called over.

"I'll take it for you," Juliana offered.

Abigail looked back out at the lake. She pulled out her phone and snapped a quick picture herself. Maybe she could post it for Stacy and the other girls to see, to prove that she was at a lake like she said she would be. Shakopee Lake probably looked just like the upstate New York lakes, right? A lake was a lake, right?

Though, if she wasn't in the picture, maybe Stacy would say she got it off the internet or something, and didn't actually take the picture herself, and was definitely lying about what her plans were this summer.

She could take a selfie, but she had to make sure her camp shirt wasn't in the picture. She couldn't post a photo with *Camp QUILTBAG* written across her chest. And the other kids, they all had their bracelets, rainbows, and other flag colors on proud display. She couldn't ask them to hide those things. She'd never be able to post these pictures.

Maybe Kai could help! Abigail trusted em, she could tell em the truth about the picture, and maybe Kai could use eir longer arms to get a picture of just their heads and the lake in the background. No shirts shouting *Camp QUILTBAG*, and neither one of them were wearing bracelets. She could tell Stacy and the girls that Kai was a family friend spending vacation at the lake house with them.

"Come on, Abigail, get in the picture!" Cassidy said, waving her over.

Abigail turned around, looking for Kai. The Yellow cabin, except for her, was all clumped together for a photo, and all the Blue campers and the counselors were scattered around, still taking pictures, too. But Juliana was the only purple shirt Abigail could find.

"Hey, Juliana, do you know where Kai went?" she asked.

Juliana just kind of shrugged in response.

Abigail looked over at the counselors and the others. "Hey, does anyone know where Kai went?"

She made eye contact with Ash, whose eyes went wide as she slowly shook her head. Abigail's eyebrows creased together. Behind Ash, Siobhan was holding a finger against Siobhan's lips. "What—"

Before Abigail could figure out what Siobhan was trying to say, Leticia pushed through the group. "Hey, wait a second. Juliana, where are the other three? Everyone, seriously, where's the rest of my group?"

"Oh crap," Sol said.

"Don't freak out, they probably just wandered off for better pictures," MJ said, reaching out a hand to gently grasp Leticia's forearm. "We'll find them."

"My mom's going to kill me," Leticia said. "Okay, seriously, does anyone here know where they went?"

Abigail and a few others shook their heads, but she noticed Ash and Siobhan exchange glances. Juliana looked down at her toes.

Leticia noticed, too. "Seriously. If any of you know, you need to tell me where they are."

"It's okay, little sweets," MJ added, his voice a lot gentler but also stronger than Leticia's. "You're not in trouble, but we really need to know where everyone is."

"There's a spot Oren and Jax found last year," Ash finally said. Juliana looked at her, practically shooting daggers with her eyes. Ash looked away, but she didn't stop talking. "They wanted to go see it, with Kai. They only left the path a little bit."

"Where's the spot?" Leticia asked.

Juliana looked over at the Blue campers again, eyes narrowed.

Ash caved first, again, with a deep sigh. "Down a bit, there's a second path that leads to a creek. You know the part with the big flat rocks?"

"Show me," Leticia said, holding out a hand for Ash to take. "MJ, Sol, stay with the rest. I'll be right back with my kids, and then we're heading back to the main camp."

Leticia and Ash walked back down the path, Ash looking a bit like she was an *Albertadromeus*, the smallest plant-eating dinosaur, being led by the hand to the jaws of a *Tyrannosaurus rex*.

Siobhan came to stand next to Abigail. "Oof. Looks like you just got those kids in *big*, big trouble."

"I didn't mean to," Abigail said, her voice high and squeaky.

Not that it mattered. Everyone grew quiet as they waited for Leticia and Ash to bring the others back. No one took any more photos, no one tried to find anything more on the bingo card. They just waited.

Abigail could only think, *You got bingo and Blue got bingo and Purple still has no extra points,* and *you got Kai in big trouble, too.*

She was officially the *worst* person to make a pact with, ever.

She was also officially the worst cabinmate ever, too.

After a very, very quiet dinner—where Siobhan and Ash met up with the rest of their cabinmates, and neither the Yellow campers nor the Purple campers seemed up for much talking after the tense trek back to camp—Abigail lay in her bunk, trying to get anything on her phone to load. Kai hadn't so much as looked at her during dinner, and Oren and Jax didn't seem particularly interested in making small talk, either.

Abigail got enough service for a picture to finally load, another one of Stacy at the beach. Abigail sighed and shoved her phone under her pillow without reading the caption this time. She had nothing to show for her trip to the lake, nothing to post to make the girls back home think she was telling the truth about her summer plans.

Not that she *was* telling the truth about her summer plans.

"Hey, Abigail?" Cassidy called over from the adjacent bunk.

"Yeah?"

"Don't feel bad. Everyone knows it wasn't your fault. They shouldn't have wandered off, and Juliana said they actually got in trouble for it last year, too," Cassidy said.

It didn't really make Abigail feel any better, because it wasn't as if Cassidy knew about her pact with Kai, but it was nice to hear, anyway. "Thanks."

Cassidy glanced down at the two below them. Bryn had his headphones on while he read, the music loud enough that Abigail could faintly hear it. Stick was already sleeping. Cassidy leaned over, bridging the gap as much as she could without falling. She lowered her voice and said, "Can I tell you something?"

Abigail nodded.

"I was thinking about the competition. And we're doing really well so far, right, and that's mostly because of you," Cassidy said, and Abigail felt the back of her neck grow warm. She didn't need the reminder. "I was hoping, well . . . the thing is, I think maybe . . ."

Seeing Cassidy struggle to say what she wanted to say loosened something in Abigail's chest. She was used to being the one stumbling over her words. Cassidy had seemed so sure of herself. "Whatever it is, you can tell me," Abigail said, trying to tamp down the hope that maybe things were going her way. Maybe she actually *was* making friends, even if she was messing a bunch of other things up, too. Only friends confided in each other like this, whispering in a dark room during a sleepover.

"I like Juliana," Cassidy said, in one quick exhale. "Like, I *like* her. A lot. And she told me how badly she wanted the camp's name to change, how hard she worked to get the camp to agree, so all of this is super important to her, you know?"

Abigail slowly nodded. She did know. It was important to Juliana, and the Purple cabin, and Kai. That was why she was supposed to help Kai's cabin win in the first place.

"And I know that since we have an alliance, no matter if Purple or Yellow wins, Juliana can help pick the name, which is what's important, but . . . Well, I still want to do really well, you know? To stand out a little, maybe? And I was thinking, you know, since you've been so good at getting extra points, maybe you can help me get some extra points, too? To impress Juliana," Cassidy said, and then paused for a moment. "Do you think that's silly?"

Abigail wanted to say, *Yes, that is absolutely silly,* even though that definitely wasn't true. *That's really sweet, and you're so nice, but I have a pact with Kai and I need to help* em *get extra points, not you.*

She couldn't exactly tell Cassidy that, though. Not when Cassidy was trusting Abigail with the honest truth of her crush on Juliana. The last time Abigail had trusted anyone with a crush of her own, all the girls in her grade had made her feel small and silly and gross.

She would not make Cassidy feel even a little bit like they had made her feel.

"I think that's really nice, Cassidy. But we have an alliance with Purple, so we all kind of have to help each other get extra points, right? And, anyway, I've really just gotten lucky. I'm not actually any good at this, I promise."

Cassidy shrugged, and gave Abigail a small little

laugh. "I just thought, well . . . I just really want her to notice me. I was just hoping you could maybe help."

Abigail sighed. *Shoot.*

"Okay," she said.

Cassidy smiled big, so big, and Abigail had those pterodactyls in her stomach all over again. She was going to end up hurting Cassidy. She was going to ruin this friendship before it had really even begun.

But her pact with Kai, her friendship with Kai, that came first, right? That meant something, right?

"Thanks, Abigail," Cassidy said. "Good night."

"Good night." Abigail sure as heck wasn't going to sleep any better tonight. She kept making more and more and more mistakes, and camp had barely even started.

One day down, Abigail thought as she rolled over and closed her eyes. *Twelve to go.*

END
OF DAY
1

CROCHETERS COMPETITION
STANDINGS!

RED: 11

YELLOW: 10

BLUE: 9

PURPLE: 8

ORANGE: 8

GREEN: 8

10

KAI

(E/EM/EIR)

KAI USUALLY SLEPT ON EIR BACK. BUT SINCE EIR INJURY, e'd had to lie on one side and get creative with pillows if e wanted to have any real chance to rest. Over the past couple of months, e'd gotten used to it.

Until Camp QUILTBAG.

Now e tossed and turned, unable to get comfortable. Kai couldn't even blame eir shoulder since it was pretty close to healed. A twinge here, an ache there, but nothing major anymore.

The Incident was history, eir sling the only lingering reminder. And Kai was supposed to get it off in a few hours—if the camp nurse gave em the okay. Then it'd be *ancient* history.

Across the room, someone rolled over in bed, then sighed—a long release of breath that'd come from either Oren or Jax. Kai studied that side of the cabin closely, but no one moved again. Part of em felt disappointed that Oren hadn't woken up or sensed anything was off. Since Leticia and Ash had found them on their return from the creek, Kai hadn't had a chance to talk to Oren, at least not in the way e wanted. Kai supposed e should be thankful Leticia had only lectured them about wandering off without permission, rather than giving them a worse punishment, like losing points or calling their parents.

Because it'd been so nice, so perfect, to spend time alone with Oren. Kai thought back to their conversation, remembering the way Oren's smile was just a little crooked, and the shock of cold creek water he'd splashed at Kai before patting the rock and inviting em to sit beside him. E also remembered how wonderful it felt to finally let eir guard down around someone here besides Abigail. To be completely emself.

But there'd also been Jax, with his arm around Oren's shoulder. And the kiss: Did it mean what Kai suspected it did? Was Oren just being nice to Kai because Oren was a boy who was nice to everyone, whether he liked them or not?

All these questions reminded Kai that e barely knew either of these boys. E knew eir classmates at school a whole lot better and even then e couldn't have guessed how mean some of them would be after e changed eir name and pronouns.

Oren hadn't technically answered Jax's question yesterday, about the two of them not planning to switch their pronouns. But he *had* said he only liked boys. Kai's hair was short and e usually preferred boyish clothes, but e wasn't a boy. E hated being misgendered as *he* just as much as when people called em *she*. Plus, Kai didn't feel comfortable taking off eir shirt in front of other people. Maybe all of this would be a problem for Oren.

All Kai knew for sure was that e wished e had someone to talk this through with. Now, more than ever, Kai missed Aziza.

Kai pulled the sleeping bag up over eir head, then reached for eir phone. The screen flickered on. E blinked away the stars in eir eyes, then glared at the upper right corner, which indicated e only had a single bar of service.

There were no new notifications. Either Aziza's response hadn't come through or she hadn't sent anything yet. It was also five a.m., so the chances of her being awake were about as high as Kai's current chances of successfully pulling a bow to play archery. E typed out a message anyway.

Kai:
Hey, if someone says they
only like boys (or girls, or
whatever), do you think that
means no exceptions like at
all ever?

Asking for a friend who might
like a camper here (no jokes
or else teaching you a full-
twisting layout when I get
home is 10000% off the table)

E sent both messages, then watched the little green progress bar move across the top of eir screen. Processing . . . almost sent . . . *still* processing—

A scratching sound made Kai poke eir head out of the sleeping bag. E waited for eir eyes to adjust to the dark, but when they did, there was no movement within the cabin.

The sound came again, and Kai twisted toward the window beside eir bunk. It sounded like a tree branch scraping against the cabin.

Except there were no trees close enough to do that. Kai reached for the curtain and pulled it back, just enough to see outside.

Abigail stared up at em with wide eyes. She held a long stick, a piece of paper speared through the far end.

"What the—" Kai cut emself off before e woke up eir cabinmates.

Abigail dropped the stick and gave em a small wave, then moved her hands: up, down, close to her body, then arms apart with fingers spread out. Kai couldn't begin to guess what she was trying to tell em.

One second, e mouthed, then held up eir index finger to make sure she understood. Carefully, Kai climbed out of bed, slipped into eir shoes, and tiptoed across the room. E paused near the other bunk. From this angle, e couldn't see Jax in the top bed, but Jax wasn't eir main concern. On the lower bunk, Oren slept peacefully, his hair partially obscuring his face and curling around his ears. Kai watched Oren's sleeping bag rise and fall in a slow, steady rhythm. E resisted the urge to brush Oren's hair away from his face.

Barely.

Outside, Kai glanced around. Abigail was nowhere in sight. Then she poked her head around the side of the cabin, and Kai headed over to her.

"Did I wake you up?" she asked, then barreled on without giving em a chance to answer. "I didn't mean to. I was just trying to slip a note through your window. The curtain was open before lights out and I saw you have a top bunk, so . . ."

She trailed off, maybe because she wasn't sure how to finish or maybe because she needed to take a breath after that flood of words.

"I'm here now," Kai whispered back. "What's up?"

Abigail stayed silent, one hand tucking a strand of loose hair behind an ear, the other using the tip of the note-delivery stick to doodle in the dirt.

"Is everything okay?" Kai asked.

She bit her lip but kept quiet.

"If you tell me what's wrong, maybe I can help."

Abigail's eyes darted from Kai to the cabins. First Purple, then Yellow.

"How about we go to the bathrooms so we don't have to whisper. Sound good?"

This time, Abigail nodded. She set the stick down and let Kai guide her around the cabins to the communal bathrooms. The lights flickered on with their movement, and Kai caught a glimpse of Abigail's pajama shorts. An army of little blue dinosaurs stared back at em.

The moment they came to a stop by a row of sinks, Abigail started talking. "Cassidy wants me to help *her* get extra points, and I felt like I pretty much had to say I would so I wouldn't look suspicious, but then how am I supposed to help *you* get extra points?"

Kai stared at her. "Wait, what? Why does Cassidy want to earn extra points? Our cabins have an alliance."

Abigail pressed her lips together.

"I mean, I get it," Kai said. "I want to win, too. That's why we made our pact. Part of the reason, anyway. But I still don't see why she has to—"

"I'm sorry," Abigail burst out, shoulders inching toward her ears. "About the extra points I've been earning for my cabin. They were all accidents though, not because of Cassidy. She only talked to me last night, I promise. I told you as soon as I could."

Kai lifted eir hands. "Hey, hey, hey. Breathe."

Abigail did as e said, her breath catching a little as she inhaled. She breathed out and Kai saw her shoulders relax.

"And then I got you in trouble earlier, because I'm the worst. I just don't want you to be mad at me . . ."

"Do I look mad?"

Abigail shrugged and kept her eyes down.

Kai leaned against the closest sink. "I know we don't know each other all that well yet, so let me tell you a story. When I was eleven, all the way back in sixth grade, my mom and I had a disagreement about letting me cut my hair short."

Abigail looked up. "She didn't want you to cut it?"

"Yeah. Well, actually, I think I said I wanted to shave it all off and she was worried I'd regret it." Kai ran the fingers of one hand through the tuft of hair at the top of eir head. "She was probably right. I like it longer, like this.

"Anyway, my younger sister, Lexi—she was eight at the time—heard us arguing and decided she would help me out . . . by literally cutting my hair when I was asleep that night."

Abigail's eyes widened. "Oh my God, she didn't."

"She did." Kai nodded grimly. "And it looked like someone had run a lawn mower over my head. I was *pissed*. I actually screamed at her."

Abigail's mouth opened, forming a small *o*.

"So," Kai continued, "the point is, you didn't make my hair look like a crappily mowed yard, and I'm not screaming, so I can't be that mad at you, can I?"

"I guess not." Abigail ducked her head, but not before Kai spotted the hint of a smile. "My mom would've freaked out if that happened to my hair."

"Oh yeah, Mom flipped. But Lexi did me a favor, actually. Mom had to take me to get my hair fixed and I got them to do it just like this." E flipped eir tuft a little. "Lexi solved my problem for me, in her own way. And maybe you're doing just fine with our pact. Maybe things'll even out soon and then your extra points won't matter."

"Maybe." But Abigail seemed to deflate a little. "It doesn't feel like I'm doing fine. It's not even just about the competition. Also, I"—she shuffled her feet, voice dropping enough that Kai had to lean forward to hear her—"have a crush on someone."

"Yeah?"

"Yeah." Abigail spoke to the floor.

"That's okay, though. It's normal."

Kai's comment didn't seem to make Abigail feel better. She flinched away at the last word, like it might bite her.

"It really is fine." Kai tried a different approach. "You don't have to tell me who it is."

"It's Lena. I'malesbianandIlikeLena."

Abigail spoke so fast, the sentence sounded like a single long word. It took Kai a moment to untangle it and another to realize who she was talking about. E'd just assumed she had a crush on one of her cabinmates.

"You mean, like the founder of the camp? That Lena?"

"Yes." Abigail looked up at em, face pinched. "I know, it's so weird."

"I mean . . ." Kai didn't know what to say. E'd never had a crush before Oren so e didn't know if it was bad to like someone eir parents' age. Or weird. Was it weird?

Not any weirder than crushing on a kid who said he only liked boys, Kai figured.

And Abigail looked so miserable, so embarrassed. Kai couldn't just let her stand there thinking she was the only one who felt like the odd one out here.

"I like someone, too."

She blinked. "You do?"

Kai nodded. And shrugged. E glanced at eir reflection in the mirror, then back down. "Oren."

"Oh."

Kai had the good sense not to frown at Abigail's obvious disappointment, but she still seemed to pick up on eir mild annoyance.

"I just thought you meant you liked someone a lot older than you, too," she explained. "But Oren's the same age as you."

"He's a year older, actually," Kai said. "And also? He's gay."

Confusion clouded Abigail's face, like she wasn't quite following. Suddenly, all Kai could see was Jax and Oren together. Jax, who didn't think twice about wrapping his arm around Oren's shoulder, or calling Oren a nickname no one else at camp used, or even kissing him. Jax, who was definitely a boy and used *he*, *him*, and *his* pronouns. Kai's muscles tensed.

"As in, Oren likes other boys," e forced out. "And I'm not one."

"*Oh.*"

Same word, different tone. Abigail understood now.

"So I guess we're both a little hopeless?" She stole a glance up at em.

"Yeah, probably." Kai allowed emself a small smile. "We should probably also get back to our cabins before anyone notices we're missing."

"Right."

Kai led her toward the exit, then paused to look back. "And you're good?" e asked.

"I'm good."

"Awesome." Kai held the door open for her. "Now, let's see if we can both get a little more sleep before breakfast."

Kai did not get a little more sleep before breakfast.

E tossed and turned some more, until eir shoulder started to feel sore, thoughts racing. They started out hopeful—Oren hadn't technically answered Jax's question about pronouns so maybe it was a sign that Oren's identity wasn't as set as Jax believed—and then shifted to doubts. Every insecurity weighed Kai down.

As the cabin filled with the soft light of morning, Kai's focus narrowed to name tags—specifically, how Oren would list his pronouns today. He and his cabinmates took turns changing behind the privacy curtain, then filled out their name tags for the day. To Kai's disappointment, Oren's pronouns hadn't changed. Still the same *he, him, his* it had always been.

Leticia came to collect the four of them for breakfast. As they rounded the corner of their cabin, Jax crouched down, studying something on the ground. Kai saw this out of the corner of one eye, but eir attention was mostly on Oren.

At least that's where it stayed until Jax wedged his way between Kai and Oren.

He turned to Kai with a grin that made Kai's stomach twist a little. "Since you're the only one in our cabin whose name starts with a K, I'm guessing this is for you."

He passed Kai a sheet of paper. Kai unfolded it, noting the hole where a stick had once speared it.

> K.,
> I need to talk to you.
> Can we meet outside the
> cafeteria during breakfast?
> —A.

Abigail must have dropped it earlier.

Jax cleared his throat, and Kai wasn't the only one to look over at him. Oren was looking too. A few steps ahead, even Juliana and Leticia glanced back at them.

"Is this from Ash or Abigail, do you know?"

"Abigail." No point in hiding it, Kai figured. Abigail was smart enough to keep her note vague, so their pact was still safe.

Jax's grin widened. He nudged Oren.

Kai slowed, then studied them both. "What?"

"Someone likes you." Jax's voice turned singsong.

Kai blinked, thoughts immediately back on Oren, who was smiling a little now too. Eir cheeks warmed up.

But how had Jax figured it out? Had Kai given something away?

"That's adorable," Juliana said, and even though Kai couldn't tell what she thought from the monotone way she'd said it, e really didn't mind. Not if Oren felt the same way. And he was smiling so that had to be a good sign.

"Isn't she younger, though?" Oren asked. "Like barely twelve?"

The realization hit Kai fast.

"But you're younger too, aren't you?" Jax looked over at Kai, whose face was hot for an entirely different reason now.

"I'm thirteen," e managed. "But that's not—"

"So it could work," Jax spoke over em. He really seemed to be getting into this now. Oren didn't seem quite as excited, but he was smiling at what Jax was saying, like it made more sense for a lesbian to have a crush on Kai than him.

When Jax next spoke, he lowered his voice. "Maybe you two can get to know each other even more at the bonfire on Saturday."

"What bonfire?" Kai asked.

Jax and Oren immediately shushed em.

"It's a secret, just for the older campers," Jax whispered.

"Not part of the official activities," Oren supplemented. "But the counselors know about it and just look the other way. It's basically a yearly tradition."

They reached the cafeteria and the boys went quiet. Leticia held the door open for them.

Kai entered last.

"Hey," Leticia said to em. "My mom told me you've got an appointment with the camp nurse coming up. I can get you to the front of the line for breakfast, so you have time to eat. It's possible you'll miss the first part of the presentation, but I'll make sure you get your attendance point since you won't be missing the whole thing."

Kai nodded.

"You'll need to go with someone, according to the rules of our glorious buddy system," Leticia said. "I'll see if MJ will keep an eye on my campers so I can take you."

"Okay."

"I know where the nurse's office is too." Oren turned back to them. "I could take Kai if that'd make things easier."

Leticia looked from Kai to Oren, then nodded. "Sounds like a plan, as long as you promise not to run off into the woods again. Straight to the nurse's office. No detours."

"Promise," Oren said.

"Okay, then." Leticia waved them toward the front of the breakfast line. "Follow me."

The visiting activist for the presentation was named Mel Solomon, and she was all Kai's table wanted to talk about. Mel was going to be a twelfth grader next fall, only a few years older than the oldest Crocheters, but she'd already gone to court to fight her school district's rules that forced her to use the boys' bathroom and kept her off the girls' swim team. She was going to discuss advocacy with them, about how kids could work for change within their communities.

Juliana and Cassidy seemed especially excited. Kai half listened as Juliana told their table about the organization she volunteered for in Oakland, which helped LGBTQ+ people who were experiencing homelessness. E nodded along as the Purple, Yellow, and Blue cabins decided on a morning activity to do after Mel's presentation: something about learning how to write letters to state representatives.

As Kai finished eating, eir thoughts kept shifting to why Oren had volunteered to take em to the nurse, especially after the misunderstanding about Abigail's note.

Actually, maybe that was the reason. Oren might want to talk to Kai about it, which was pretty much the *last* thing Kai wanted.

By the time Oren hopped up from his seat, Kai was an anxious mess.

"We should get going," Oren whispered. "You ready?"

"Sure," Kai said, even though e felt the exact opposite. E stood tall and put on a brave face anyway.

"The admin buildings aren't too far from the parking lot," Oren told em as they exited the cafeteria. "But they aren't totally visible through the trees either. Good thing you've got me."

Oren's smile still had the power to send a nervous flutter into Kai's stomach.

"Yeah," e managed. "Good thing."

Oren glanced at Kai as though he expected em to say something else, but Kai's mind was blank. Eventually, Oren looked away, gaze shifting to the path.

The silence dragged on, becoming awkward. It felt like an eternity until the parking lot came into view. By then Kai had thought of a million different ways to tell Oren e didn't like Abigail the way Jax thought, but e still had no idea how to get emself to say a single one of them.

It was Oren who broke the silence.

"How do you feel about the competition?"

"Um." Kai immediately thought of Jax and how disappointed he was that their cabin decided not to try archery because of Kai's injury. "You mean the activities we've been doing? Or . . ."

"Like about how far behind we are with the points, since we haven't earned any extra yet."

"Oh." Kai breathed a little easier. "Well, that part sucks. I know it's not the point to beat other cabins but I'm an athlete so I kinda can't help wanting to anyway."

"I'm competitive too," Oren said. "I'm not an athlete, but I have two older sisters and they both get straight As so I kind of have to, as well."

"Oh, wow." Kai did okay in school, but e definitely didn't get straight As.

"What kind of sports do you play?" Oren asked.

"I do parkour. Do you know what it is?"

"Yep!" Oren's brows rose, disappearing under his curls. "So, you can do like flips and twists off buildings and stuff?"

"Yeah. Or I could before . . ." Kai glanced down at eir shoulder, then changed the subject. "But when I get my sling off, we'll be able to do more stuff and catch up in the standings."

Kai expected Oren to shoot em one of his adorable, crooked smiles, but Oren looked down.

"Except I won't be able to help earn points for most of Saturday."

"Why not?"

"It's Shabbat," Oren said. "I mean, I guess I can technically do sports. There's no rule that says you can't play them on Shabbat."

Kai wasn't sure what to say to that, just knew e didn't want to say the wrong thing. E kept quiet as they headed down a wooded path at the far side of the parking lot.

"But if I were at home, my family and I would spend Friday night and most of Saturday at shul. We pray and reflect and spend time together. That's what I'm used to," Oren continued. "These two weeks I'm here at camp, I'll attend virtual services. That was fine last summer, but I'm afraid I'm going to get us further behind in the standings this year, since I won't be at any of Saturday's events to get a point for participating."

A cluster of buildings appeared through the trees. Oren came to a stop in front of one, then turned to Kai.

"Anyway, it's whatever. I'm sure we'll figure something out." He nodded toward the building. "This is the nurse's office. I'll wait for you."

"You don't have to," Kai said. "I can probably ask the nurse to take me back when we're done."

"But I'm gonna." Oren offered em a small smile.

Kai entered the nurse's office. A white man with dark brown hair, a thick lumberjack beard, and a name tag that read, *Micah Peterson: he/him/his*, looked up and waved at em. "Kai Lindquist! Welcome to my office."

Kai sat down in a tall chair. While Nurse Micah inspected Kai's shoulder, he asked questions that Kai dutifully answered. Through it all, Kai's mind wandered, trying to work through everything Oren had just shared with em. While it was a relief to know e wasn't the only one worried about their cabin falling behind, this was also the first time Kai had seen Oren act anything other than confident.

The obvious solution would be to try to cram in an extra activity one day without letting the Yellow cabin know.

Except then Yellow would probably think they were trying to break their alliance.

Plus, Kai didn't know what other activities were open to the Crocheters today. E'd been so distracted at breakfast, e'd read the Weavers' list instead.

"This is looking good," Nurse Micah said, but Kai barely heard him.

An idea was starting to take shape in eir mind.

"Seems to be healing nicely," Nurse Micah continued. "I'd say you can probably bid adieu to your sling."

That got Kai's attention.

"Right now?"

"Right now." Nurse Micah nodded. He leaned over and unfastened the first clip on Kai's sling. Kai quickly reached for the second. E glanced at the room's wall clock. The presentation wasn't even done yet.

What if . . .

"Take it easy the rest of camp though, kiddo. And don't be surprised if that arm feels weaker than your other for a while still. It'll take time for you to regain strength in those muscles."

Kai nodded, but e was barely listening, thoughts going a mile a minute.

"Thanks!" e said, then practically flew out the door, down the steps, and back to Oren, who was sitting up against a nearby tree.

"That was fast." Oren pushed himself up to standing. "And you got your sling off!"

"Yeah." Kai nodded. "I'm still supposed to be careful doing sports and stuff, but hey, guess what? You don't have to worry about losing points on Saturday."

Oren tilted his head.

"You know how Abigail got a point for helping Juliana make a second bracelet yesterday?" Oren's nod encouraged em to go on. "The Weavers are down by the

Benches today, according to the activity list. They're going to act out the story in a queer picture book. What if we volunteered to help them?"

"We're supposed to head back to the cafeteria, though," Oren said slowly. "We promised Leticia."

"Yeah, but you said it yourself: My appointment finished fast. There's no reason to expect us back yet. We can help the Weavers and get you the point you'll miss on Saturday. I bet we won't even miss much of Mel's presentation so there would be no reason for Leticia not to give us our points for it."

Oren's face lit up. "That's *such* a great idea, Kai. Seriously."

Kai couldn't control eir wide grin. E turned away from Oren fast to hide it, ready to head toward the Benches, but Oren caught eir hand.

"Hey, remember I said I attend virtual Shabbat services?"

Kai nodded.

"Lena lets me use her office for that. Would you maybe want to come with me for the Friday service?"

Oren rushed on before Kai could utter a word.

"I know you're not super religious, and that's totally okay. I just thought it might be nice to hang out together. But if not, that's totally cool too, obviously."

Oren let go of Kai's hand and brushed his hair from his eyes. To Kai, in this moment, Oren couldn't be any cuter if he actively tried.

"That'd be awesome," Kai said. "As long as you don't mind me not really having a clue what's going on."

They started walking in the direction of the Benches.

"Don't worry," Oren said. "I can explain it to you. But only if you want. If not . . ."

"That's totally cool, too?" Kai finished.

Oren grinned. "Yep, exactly."

END
OF DAY
2

CROCHETERS COMPETITION STANDINGS!

RED: 19

PURPLE: 18

YELLOW: 18

BLUE: 17

GREEN: 16

ORANGE: 16

11

ABIGAIL
(SHE/HER/HERS)

"DANG. THE RED CABIN IS STILL AHEAD," STICK OBSERVED as they all gathered around the next morning to see the current standings.

Abigail was just relieved to see that both Yellow and Purple were still holding their own. Yes, Red was still doing really well, but so were they. In fact, the Purple cabin was tied with Yellow now, somehow.

Cassidy noticed, too. "How did the Purple cabin get enough points yesterday to tie with us?"

Abigail shrugged. Yesterday was a surprisingly okay day for her. There wasn't much competition involved, thankfully. They'd all gotten points for attending the lecture with Mel Solomon, and the activist had captured the heck out of Abigail's attention. Mel was younger than Leticia and MJ—only a handful of years older than Abigail—and she had done *so* much. When things got unfair for her at school, Mel had *done something* about it. Abigail couldn't imagine doing that. She could imagine what Stacy and the other girls would think if she had so much as *tried* to make their school more LGBTQ+ friendly. Not to mention the uphill battle of doing so at a Catholic school.

After Mel's speech, Cassidy and Juliana had practically dragged their cabinmates over to talk to her. When it was Abigail's turn to say something, she wanted to say, *You're so cool, I wish I could be just like you, I'm sorry I'm such a chicken,* but all she could do was smile.

Mel smiled back, and Abigail had to duck her head and look away before she fell in love with *her,* too.

It wasn't until after Mel's presentation, when all the cabins were practicing writing letters to their state representatives, that Abigail realized this was something she could actually *do.* She was one of the best writers in her class—her teachers, who barely ever took the time to praise the quiet little lesbian who sat in the back row in all her classes, always complimented her when they gave back her writing assignments, the tops of her papers always displaying giant As and smiley faces.

She was good at this, and fast, and before Juliana even finished her first, Abigail had finished writing two letters. With help from MJ, she had googled her state's representatives and the important LGBTQ+ bills that may or may not be passed, and she was so proud of what she wrote that she was determined to find stamps while she was here, at camp, so she could mail them.

Abigail felt good. She liked knowing she could do something without having to speak up, which she was never any good at anyway.

Maybe she didn't have to be as brave as Mel, or as determined and loud as Juliana, or as confident as everyone else.

Afterward, the Yellow, Purple, and Blue cabins, even a few of the Greens, decided they'd earned enough points for one day, so they'd gone down to the lake to go swimming.

Abigail, who grew up by the beach, was the best out of everyone at holding her breath under water. It was the most fun she'd had so far at camp. That night in her bunk, though, she was disappointed that she hadn't taken any pictures. She'd been having too much fun to even think about Stacy. She'd try to remember to take a picture today.

Cassidy was right, though. The points didn't seem to make sense. Purple had gotten more somehow. "Maybe they got the extra points for something like I did when I helped Juliana? Or something?" Abigail guessed. "We weren't with them *all* day. Maybe we just missed it."

"Yeah. Maybe," Cassidy said, still frowning.

"Does it matter? We're still in the top three, and we want Purple to do really well, too, don't we?" Abigail said.

"Yeah, we do," Cassidy said, then shook her head. "It's fine. I was just confused. I guess you're right."

The first real snag of the day came a little bit later, as they all gathered around the Daily Activities board, deciding what to do that morning. "Well, since Kai finally has eir sling off, can't we do the roller derby demo?" Jax asked, tapping against it twice on the board. It was the one super athletic thing on the list for the day, besides kayaking.

Kai fell quiet, but Oren spoke up for em. "Kai still isn't supposed to do too much with eir shoulder. It's still healing, and weak." He turned to Kai. "Right?"

"That's what the nurse said, yeah." Kai didn't look like e was happy to be referred to as weak.

Abigail quickly scanned the board for an alternative to suggest. "Why don't we—"

"We could split up," Cassidy said, watching the Purple cabin carefully, her eyes moving from Jax, to Oren, to Kai, before settling on Juliana. "Maybe some of us can do the roller derby demo, and some of you can do something else. As long as they give us *an even amount of points*." She emphasized the last part hard.

"Yeah, we got it," Jax said.

Oren still looked uncertain. He turned to Kai. "Are you okay with us splitting up like this?"

"Whoever wants to do roller derby can do roller derby," e said. "I don't mind; it's fine."

Abigail tried to smile at Kai, maybe wink at em conspiratorially, but she sort of just blinked weirdly. Kai gave her a confused look, but Oren smiled at her, at least.

Of course, her attempt at having a moment with Kai made her completely miss what Cassidy was saying, until she caught her name. "Okay, so we'll meet up with you all at lunch. Abigail, you coming?"

And, because she didn't want Cassidy to know she wasn't paying attention, she said, "Yep, yeah, I'm coming," only realizing what she'd agreed to when Cassidy chattered excitedly about roller derby.

The basketball court was bordered by the woods on one side, the lake on the other, and the camp buildings right behind it. Abigail could see almost everything from on the bleachers. She could see the little Weavers in their rainbow shirts gathered at the Benches for Drag Queen

Story Hour, she could see other campers scattered in kayaks in the lake. She could see the main cabin where Kai, Oren, Bryn, and Stick were inside with the Blues, tie-dyeing shirts.

Abigail was a little disappointed that Bryn hadn't joined their group. She felt like she could breathe around Bryn. Cassidy still made her a little nervous, and she still didn't know the Purple cabinmates (other than Kai) as much as she'd like to. Splitting up the cabins made her feel a little unsteady before she even got roller skates on her feet.

Jax, Cassidy, and Juliana (who didn't actually seem very interested in roller derby) sat next to Abigail, the heat from the sun making Abigail's sweaty thighs stick to the aluminum bench. Leticia sat next to her, leaning forward expertly so only her shorts were touching the hot seat.

Abigail shifted a bit, putting her hands under her legs, to get herself unstuck, and knocked right into the girl on her other side in the process. "Oh, sorry," she said, turning to find the Red cabin had joined them.

The girl she knocked into was big, double the size of Abigail in both height and weight, and she looked at Abigail with big green eyes that lit up her entire face. "It's okay," she said, and Abigail read her name tag. *Hannah:*

she/her/hers. She looked Hawaiian and had black hair so short it might as well have been shaved, and an attractive mole next to her left eye.

Abigail glanced over at the rest of the Red cabin, realizing that all four of them were very tall. No wonder they were ahead in the points. Abigail felt hopelessly small. She especially felt small when the Minnesota Roller Werewolves skated onto the court.

There were five of them. Three had thighs that Abigail figured could squeeze a watermelon right down the middle. One of them was shorter, closer to Abigail's height, but much, much wider. Four of the five of them had visible tattoos, and three of the five had brightly dyed hair.

One of them, with tattoos snaking up her arm and a bright pink braid going down her back, took center. "Hey, all, I'm Pushy Much, she/her, and these here with me are some of my very best and most hard-core teammates. So, who here knows anything about roller derby?"

Hannah's hand went up so fast, she nearly knocked Abigail over. "I've seen *Whip It* a bunch of times," she said.

Abigail had never seen *Whip It*. She'd never even heard of *Whip It*.

Cassidy's hand also went up. "It's a sport played on roller skates. I'm not sure exactly how to play, but you skate around the rink in a group and one of the skaters has to get the points for the team, right?"

"Yep! All right! So we've got some of you with some knowledge, and others with none. That's fine! We're going to do a brief intro to roller derby, and then we'll see if we can get some of you on skates," Pushy Much explained. "We won't have you do any roller derby today, because despite the fact that bruises and bumps are common, we don't actually want any of you getting hurt. Our goal for today is to teach you how to skate and build some confidence on the rink."

She motioned toward another one of her teammates, who had dark hair pretty much the same style as Kai's. "I'm Elliot Rage, they/them, and I, too, have seen *Whip It* more times than I can count." They winked at Hannah. "I'm one of our team's jammers. What that means is I'm the one who scores the points. I get a point for every person on the other team that I pass, so speed is important to be a jammer! Everyone else is called a blocker. They don't score any points, but their job is super important. They block the other team's jammer from passing and they *also* have to help me get through the pack to earn as many points as possible."

"But that's a lot of talk and not a lot of play, so why don't we just show you what we mean?" Pushy Much chimed back in.

The Minnesota Roller Werewolves got into their pack formation, gliding on their skates as if it were as easy as walking. Elliot Rage was at the back with another one of the Werewolves, and Pushy Much, who was at the front of the pack, blew a whistle, and off they went. They skated in that pack, that werewolf pack, around the basketball court, seamlessly, like they were one body. And then Elliot Rage and the other jammer started pushing their way through.

Cassidy and Jax started whooping and hollering, and Hannah and the rest of the Red team started cheering, too. Abigail flinched a little when it looked like Elliot Rage took an especially hard hit from one of the blockers who tried to keep them from getting through. "I want to be a blocker so bad," Hannah said, and then added, "I bet you'd make a good jammer."

Abigail couldn't imagine trying to push her way through Hannah or Pushy Much.

But Elliot Rage did make their way through, passing all the blockers and skating faster than everyone and looping back around to the back of the group. Abigail found herself cheering along with everyone else, and Elliot Rage pushed through the pack again, and then Pushy Much blew her whistle, and all of them skated to a stop.

Everyone on the bleachers applauded.

Pushy Much skated back to the center. "Now, before you come check out the loaner equipment we brought for everyone to try, I want to make something perfectly clear. Roller derby is for everybody, and I want to emphasize that it is for every *body*. Take a look at all of us. There is no right body to play roller derby. You just have to get out here and skate with us. Roller derby is about community and inclusivity, and it doesn't matter if you've skated every day since you were eight or if you've never tried until today. You can be the worst player in the world, and I'll still be proud of you for getting out here and trying. So, on that note, let's get going!"

There was a big pile of equipment on the side of the court: helmets, kneepads, elbow pads, wrist pads (Abigail hadn't realized there were so many kinds of pads), and, of course, the skates.

Abigail hung back. She figured if she walked slowly and was the last to the pile, they might run out of her size and she could just sit and watch everyone else skate. "Abs, what size are you? I'll help you find a pair," Leticia said, ruining her plan.

Abigail had the smallest feet, of course, so she didn't have any competition for her skates. Leticia helped her into her pads and helmet. Cassidy and Juliana helped each other, and Jax was on the court skating laps with Hannah before Abigail was even finished getting ready.

"Once you have your skates on, get comfortable with them," Pushy Much called out. "Anyone who needs help, we'll pair them up with one of us. Don't be shy!"

Oh, Abigail was not going to be good at this. She knew that the moment she tried to stand, and the wheels under her feet started rolling, and she immediately fell back down. "Here," Pushy Much said, holding a hand down for Abigail to take. "Lemme help you up, friend."

Pushy Much stayed close to Abigail as she attempted to skate around the court. She felt super unsteady, but when Pushy told her to bend her knees a bit, she started to move a lot easier. "That's it! You've got it!" Pushy said, and Abigail thought that was a bit of an exaggeration, but she blushed under the praise, anyway.

After everyone was able to skate at least a little bit, Pushy Much said, "Okay! Here's your first lesson in skating *and* roller derby: know how to fall!"

Oh, wonderful, Abigail thought. She was already quite good at that.

"Falling is inevitable in roller derby," Pushy Much continued. "The key is knowing how to *safely* fall to avoid injury. To do that you fall small, and fall forward. Use those kneepads! You'll notice how scratched up all your loaner kneepads are—that's because we fall on them. A lot. I want you all to try it, too. Look at me," she said, and then demonstrated.

Abigail had never fallen as gracefully as Pushy Much did. She skidded right down to her knees and got up without touching the ground with her hands. "It's important *not* to put your hands down. And I'll be completely honest with you, it's so you don't get any fingers crunched by your fellow skaters."

Oh good grief. As if Abigail needed anything else to worry about.

"Now fall!" Pushy said, and the Werewolves immediately dropped down to their knees. Some of the kids did, too. "And get back up!" Pushy said, and everyone did their best to do just that. The second time she yelled, "Now fall!" Abigail did, too. It wasn't exactly graceful, and she definitely put her hands down (and quickly pulled them up out of fear of losing her fingers), but she fell, and she managed to get back up, and she didn't get hurt at all.

They all laughed each time they went down and got back up again, and when Hannah fell right in front of Abigail and Abigail fell nearly on top of her because of it, Hannah only laughed and helped Abigail get back up again.

Abigail wouldn't say she was a great skater by the end of practice—her only goal was to be steady and balanced on her feet. Some of the other campers learned to skate backwards, which seemed impossible to Abigail.

But Pushy Much was right—it didn't really matter. Some of the campers were good, some of them were bad, but Pushy and the rest of the Werewolves only seemed to notice the kids who were laughing and the ones who needed an extra push. Pushy Much even noticed Abigail.

"You're looking good," Pushy said. "Thinking about getting a pair when you get home?"

"Oh God no," Abigail replied, and then immediately felt her face flush. "I mean! It's great! You guys are so cool! But I don't know that it's for me."

Pushy Much laughed. "Well, I'm proud of you for giving it a try, anyway."

"Hey! Abigail!" Cassidy called from where everyone else was gathering. "Come here. Leticia's gonna take a group picture of us in our gear!"

Abigail went over to the group, and on the count of three they all held up peace signs and made funny faces and had big smiles. Leticia sent the group picture to everyone who asked for it, and as Abigail sat on the ground untying her skates, she looked at the photo on her phone, at Cassidy's arm wrapped around her shoulders, at Hannah's big toothy smile, at the way Jax's shirt was completely damp with sweat, at the Werewolves smiling right alongside them.

She *loved* that picture. She loved how cool she looked with her friends beside her and Pushy Much right behind her. Even Stacy and the girls back home would have to notice that.

Without hesitating, Abigail posted the picture online with the caption: *Roller derby is so much fun!!!!!*

Jax, Juliana, Cassidy, and Abigail all decided they definitely needed showers before heading to lunch, so they went to the bathrooms to clean up. The rest of both their cabins showed up a little bit afterwards, wanting to clean the tie-dye off their hands, too.

The Yellows and Purples all exchanged stories from their morning until Jax's stomach growled loudly enough for them all to hear it. "Oh, man, I'm starving."

"Are we all ready to go eat?" Juliana said, looking around the group to make sure everyone was accounted for.

"Bryn's not here," Stick said. "He must still be in the bathroom."

Abigail knew that if she were the one still in the bathroom while everyone was waiting, she would die of embarrassment. "I'll wait for him," she offered for Bryn's sake. "We'll meet you all there."

They all agreed, and Abigail watched as the group headed toward the main cabin. It was quiet at the bathrooms with all the other campers at lunch. Abigail could hear the caw of a hawk, or some other large bird, as it flew off in the distance. She strained her ears, wondering if she could hear the lapping water of the lake like she could hear the ocean at home, but she couldn't.

She couldn't hear any movement from the bathroom, either, and Abigail had a hot moment of panic that maybe they were all playing a joke on her and Bryn was with the others at lunch, waiting to see how long she would wait here alone. But they wouldn't do that, would they? Besides, Abigail had volunteered to stay behind, and she hadn't seen Bryn come out of the bathroom, either.

"Bryn?" Abigail said as she poked her head into the bathroom. She breathed a sigh of relief when she saw Bryn's sneakers underneath the doors to one of the stalls. "Hey, you okay? Everyone else headed to lunch."

"Just leave, Abigail. You can go to lunch, too," Bryn said. His voice sounded a little stuffy.

"Um. I don't think that's a good idea?" Abigail said. "You aren't supposed to be alone, because of the buddy system, and also I think if we don't get to the main cabin soon we'll be in trouble."

Bryn didn't say anything.

"Bryn? Is something wrong?" Abigail asked.

There was another pause, where Bryn said nothing, and Abigail was about to ask again—or maybe go find someone to help—when Bryn finally said softly, "I . . . got my period."

"Oh," Abigail said. Okay, this she could do. Stacy had gotten her period before all the girls in school last year and she'd been more than happy to explain everything to Abigail. She'd even been the one to show Abigail how to use a pad, though Abigail let her mom show her, too, so her mom didn't feel bad that she already knew how. "Do you need a pad or tampon or something? The nurse might have some. I can go ask?"

Again, Bryn was silent.

Abigail tried to remember the things Stacy had told her. "It's okay, Bryn. I know it's weird, but it's totally normal. I think I'm due for mine next week. It's okay."

"It's *not*," Bryn said, and Abigail realized he sounded stuffy because he was crying. "It's not okay for me. It shouldn't . . . I'm not . . . I *hate* this."

Well, yes, Abigail hated getting her period, too. She was about to say so. She was about to open her mouth and say, *All girls hate getting their periods, Bryn.* But she closed her mouth tight, because that was when she understood.

Bryn was not a girl.

Bryn hated getting his period in ways that Abigail could never understand. She felt wholly useless. She had no idea what Bryn needed right now. "I'm sorry, Bryn. I don't really know what to say," she admitted. "But . . . I'm here for you though, okay? Let me go get you stuff from the nurse. Okay?"

Abigail waited, holding her breath and unsure of what more she could do, until Bryn finally said, "Okay."

The nurse was a big burly bearded man named Micah, which was the opposite of what Abigail was expecting when she burst into his office to ask for menstrual supplies. She almost couldn't get herself to ask this lumberjack-looking dude for pads and tampons out of sheer embarrassment, but then she realized she was being ridiculous. He was a nurse, and people with uteruses got their periods. It was just something that happened, and Abigail shouldn't be embarrassed, especially when Bryn was counting on her.

She was practically sprinting back to the bathrooms, arms full of different-sized pads and tampons, not knowing what Bryn wanted or would be comfortable with. Abigail figured the more options, the better. She was hurrying so quickly, so determined to help Bryn, even if she felt totally inadequate to handle this situation, that she didn't realize anyone was standing in her way until she collided with the body in front of her.

The pads and tampons scattered all over the ground, and Abigail bent down to start gathering them back up. "I'm sorry!" she said, and then she looked up.

She had run into Lena. She stood above Abigail with a sun-reflected halo around her head like the absolute goddess she was.

Oh my God.

"Should I even ask?" Lena asked, as she bent down to help Abigail pick up all the sanitary supplies. No matter how much Abigail kept telling herself there was nothing embarrassing about menstruation, her entire face flushed anyway. "You should be at lunch with everyone else."

Great, now she was also getting in trouble. "My friend. He's . . ." Was it okay to tell Bryn's business to Lena? Would Bryn be mad? "My friend needed help. So I went to the nurse and got all these, and I was just headed back to the bathroom. And then we were going to lunch. We *will* go right to lunch! I'm sorry."

Lena didn't scold her, though. She just held out her hand to help Abigail stand back up again. "Let me help you carry these, and then you can help your friend, and then I'll walk you *both* to lunch. Sound good?"

It sounded both amazing and terrible all at once, really.

Lena waited outside the bathroom while Abigail told Bryn how to use the pads, and when Bryn finally came out of the stall, his face was still a little wet. "I'm sorry," Abigail said again, because she didn't know how to make this better for him.

"Don't tell the others, okay?" Bryn asked.

"I won't," Abigail responded. "But, there's probably other kids at the camp who feel like you do? I'm sorry I'm not any help."

Bryn shrugged. "That's okay. Thanks for just . . . being here. And for, well, all of this." He waved his arms indicating the giant pile of sanitary supplies on the floor. "It was a lot scarier when I was in here alone."

"I should warn you, though, Lena is waiting right outside. I didn't tell her your business. I mean, I dropped all these pads and stuff by her feet so she probably knows. I'm sorry. She's going to walk us to lunch, so we don't get in trouble for being late," Abigail said.

Bryn stared at Abigail for a moment, and Abigail thought maybe he might still be mad she told Lena anything, but then Bryn just opened his arms and pulled Abigail into a hug. "Seriously," he said. "Thanks for being here."

Abigail hugged him back.

They left the bathroom hand in hand, and Lena smiled at them. "You two ready? I bet you're hungry."

"Oh, yes," Bryn said, and Abigail was happy to hear he didn't sound so stuffy anymore.

As they walked to the main cabin, Lena asked them about their day, and Bryn told her all about tie-dyeing, and Abigail found herself excitedly talking about roller derby. Lena listened, and laughed in the right places, and kept looking over at Abigail as they walked, and it felt good, and Abigail let herself enjoy it. She tried not to walk too fast so that they could keep talking to Lena as long as possible before getting to the lunchroom.

When they got to the main cabin, Abigail and Bryn took their seats with the rest of the Purples and Yellows, and Bryn stayed close, and Kai waved hi, and Cassidy said, "Abigail! We were just talking about how awesome Pushy Much was! Juliana was trying to come up with roller derby names for everyone! Stick could be *Stick It to 'Em*! Leticia can be *Gore-Ticia* Addams!"

"*Jammin' Jax*!" Jax shouted.

"Abigail could be *Bruisasaurus*," Kai said.

"Only because I'd be the one getting the bruises," Abigail replied.

"Hey, speaking of Abigail, you guys want to go swimming again after lunch?" Stick asked. "I wanna try and beat her record for holding her breath under water!"

"Yeah, me too!" Jax said.

"I don't know that anyone's going to beat Abigail! She's basically a fish," Cassidy said.

Abigail felt good. She felt like maybe, just maybe, she really had found her people, and was fitting in, and could finally relax and have fun, like she was supposed to. She finally felt like these were her friends, like maybe camp was giving her exactly what she needed.

Across the room, Lena caught Abigail's eyes and winked.

END
OF DAY
3

CROCHETERS COMPETITION
STANDINGS!

RED: 23

PURPLE: 22

YELLOW: 22

BLUE: 21

ORANGE: 21

GREEN: 20

12

KAI
(E/EM/EIR)

FRIDAY WAS KAI'S FAVORITE DAY OF THE WEEK. WHEN E was younger, eir gymnastics meets usually took place on Fridays, right after school let out. Last year, after e'd quit gymnastics, Fridays meant getting two whole days away from eir classmates, especially the ones who hadn't accepted Kai's new name and pronouns. Fridays had become a relief from the mean comments and sharp elbow jabs from two boys in particular.

Fridays were also times to hang out with Aziza and the rest of eir parkour friends.

At camp, Friday was all about Oren and Shabbat.

But while Kai was no stranger to looking forward to Friday nights, the nervous birds flapping in eir chest were new. They started the moment e woke up and stayed with em for breakfast. This was different than the kind of anxiety e got before gymnastics meets. That had been manageable. All Kai had to do was remind emself how hard e'd trained to be ready to compete. Competition nerves were expected.

Kai didn't know what to expect tonight with Oren. E carefully dissected eir hash brown patty as eir cabinmates chattered around em. What if e said something wrong? What if e said something accidentally offensive and Oren no longer wanted to hang out with em?

Crappity crap. Accepting Oren's Shabbat invitation had been *such* a bad idea.

While Kai was silently freaking out, they'd apparently watched an entire episode of a docuseries about the history of the queer rights movement in the US. But Kai couldn't have answered a single question about it. E also couldn't remember what activity the Purple and Yellow cabins had decided on at breakfast.

So Kai followed eir cabinmates' lead, hanging back with the Yellow cabin, plus the Red kids, once everyone got dismissed. E glanced at Abigail first, but she was deep in conversation with Bryn at the far end of the table. Maybe Abigail was finally starting to feel comfortable with other kids at camp, or at least with Bryn. Kai turned eir attention to Oren next, who had just enough time to smile at Kai before an adult with a shaved head and a name tag that said, *Chef Kirstie: any pronouns*, approached them.

Chef Kirstie gestured to them, and all the campers plus their counselors got up and followed her. (*Him? Them?* Kai was having a hard time wrapping eir head around the idea that someone truly might not care what pronouns people used for them when e'd fought so hard to claim eir own set.) They veered right, to a set of doors behind the buffet tables, and into a large kitchen. It was all silver appliances and rows of tables for preparing food, plus a few stools.

"Grab a station," Chef Kirstie called, and Kai followed the others. Kai was behind Oren, who got the last station at a table that also included a Red camper, Juliana, and Jax. Bryn stepped up to the station beside Kai. Abigail and Cassidy took the other two spots. Abigail and Bryn traded a look, then switched places so Abigail was next to Kai.

Kai studied the ingredients in front of em: yeast, water, flour, oil. There was also a saltshaker and small boxes of sugar and cornmeal. E wasn't a huge fan of cooking so e couldn't guess what they'd be making.

Chef Kirstie didn't make them wait long.

"Welcome to Pride pizza-making, taught by me, Chef Kirstie. Wash your hands at the sink behind me first. Then, there are recipes for each table, as well as a set of measuring spoons and cups. Share with your neighbors. Help them out if they need it. More on the Pride part once you've all got your dough made."

They washed up, then returned to their tables. Cassidy eyed the recipe sheet as Bryn and Abigail hopped up onto stools. "Okay! The easiest way to do this is probably for one of us to read out the measurements, then the instructions. Unless anyone has a better idea."

When everyone stayed quiet, Cassidy snatched up the sheet. "First up: two and one-fourth teaspoons of yeast!" She grabbed the measuring spoons and carefully measured each scoop before putting it in her mixing bowl. She passed the spoons to Bryn who passed them to Abigail when he was done, who then passed them to Kai.

"One and a third cups of water," Cassidy said the moment Kai was finished portioning eir yeast.

They continued the process until all the ingredients were in their mixing bowls.

"Now it says to hand-mix until your ingredients are all consistent!" Cassidy set the recipe back on the table, then thrust her hands into her mixing bowl with a *squelch*. Bryn, Abigail, and Kai copied her.

Abigail glanced over at Kai. "How are you doing?"

"Fine." Kai looked at Oren's table. Oren and Jax were making their own *squelch* sounds with the Red camper, probably on purpose based on their laughter. Kai couldn't see Juliana's face from this angle, but e bet she was rolling her eyes. "Oren invited me to attend a virtual Shabbat service after dinner tonight. Just the two of us."

"That sounds nice." Abigail's hands slowed. "That's nice of him, right? A good sign?"

"Maybe." Kai nodded, gaze drifting back to Oren. Whenever e had attended temple in the past, there'd been ushers handing out kippot and prayer shawls—Kai couldn't remember the Hebrew name for them—to people who hadn't brought their own. Plus, everyone dressed nicely. There'd be no ushers at camp to give em a kippah or prayer shawl, and e definitely hadn't packed dressy clothes. Kai picked up the pace, kneading eir dough harder. "Or it could just be him being polite, because I'm probably the only other sort-of Jewish kid at camp."

Oren had said e counted as Jewish, but Kai wasn't quite convinced.

"Oh." Abigail went quiet and Kai mentally kicked emself for being so negative.

"Anyway, it's fine." Kai changed the subject. "How are *you* doing? Did you have fun yesterday?"

"Yeah." Abigail's expression immediately brightened. Kai listened as she talked em through her first roller derby lesson.

"That sounds awesome," Kai said, and e actually meant it. "Plus, we've got the bonfire tomorrow, so this should be a fun weekend. Are you going?"

"Stick told me about it." Abigail nodded. "It sounds fun. And so does that gala on the final weekend. Or—" Abigail hesitated, and then kind of whispered, "*gay-la*? I guess that's what everyone is calling it?"

Kai vaguely remembered hearing some talk about the end-of-camp get-together. Chef Kirstie was making the rounds, giving kids pointers on how to mix their ingredients. Before Kai could respond to Abigail, Chef stopped in front of Kai's table, nodded, then turned to address the rest of the campers.

"Looks great, everyone! My assistants will now pass out a greased mixing bowl to each of you. Place your dough into the bowl, flip it over, cover it with plastic wrap, and write your name on the label so you'll know which one is yours. After lunch, once the dough has had time to rise, we'll have you return and prep them for the oven."

While Chef Kirstie spoke, MJ, Leticia and the Red cabin counselor passed out new bowls.

"As promised," Chef Kirstie continued, "time to explain why I call this activity Pride pizzas. Before you all head out for lunch, you'll get to pick the ingredients to put on your pizza. You're free to choose whatever toppings you want, *but* if you're feeling particularly festive, you can choose rainbow-colored ingredients. We have peppers in lots of different colors, plus corn, broccoli, cherry tomatoes, mushrooms, and even food coloring. If you can think it up, we probably have it. Be as creative as you like!"

Chef Kirstie waved them toward a pantry on one side of the room. "Now, go wild."

As they all made their way to the pantry, Oren fell back to walk beside Kai. "Having fun?"

"Not as much as you and Jax," Kai said, remembering the sounds coming from their station.

Oren laughed, then paused along with the other campers to grab a plate. He passed one to Kai, then headed for the pantry.

"I usually just put mushrooms and olives on my pizza, which is like the opposite of rainbow colors," Oren said. He studied a shelf with precut red and yellow onions. "What do you like on your pizza?"

Kai swallowed, suddenly nervous. Oren had the same effect on em as trying a new parkour move. Talking to him made Kai feel giddy but also anxious. "My favorite toppings are pineapple and jalapeño."

"Wow." Oren looked at em. "I know people who like

pineapple and Canadian bacon together, but I don't think I've ever heard of anyone choosing *that* combination."

Kai's cheeks flushed. "I just like how the sweet and spicy blend together. My friends think it's weird, too, though."

"Not weird," Oren said. "I actually think it'd be cool to try."

Kai stole a glance at him. "Yeah?"

"Totally." Oren grabbed a jar of olives, then squinted. "I'm not seeing either of those ingredients here, though."

"There's definitely pineapple!" a voice called.

Both Kai and Oren turned toward Abigail, who was crouched down and reaching across the bottommost shelf. She straightened and held a tin out to Kai, who tried not to make a face.

"Thanks, but I think I'm going to try other ingredients today," e said. "My favorite pizza place uses fresh ingredients, not canned, and I don't want the pizza to get soggy from the extra pineapple juice."

"Oh, okay." Abigail put the canned pineapples away. "Timoney's always uses fresh ingredients, too. That's my favorite pizzeria back in New Jersey. It's right on the boardwalk."

Out of the corner of eir eye, Kai saw Oren looking between em and Abigail. Studying them.

"Cool." Eir throat got tight.

Thankfully, Bryn pulled Abigail away before she could notice anything was off. Kai grabbed some yellow peppers and a handful of asparagus stalks, then moved on. Oren followed as e moved to the next shelf.

"Are you excited about tonight?"

"Yeah," Kai said, but the word came out high. E shook eir head and eir tuft of hair fluttered. "A little nervous, actually."

"Don't be." Oren put his free hand on Kai's shoulder and gave it a quick squeeze. "I'll walk you through anything you don't understand. It'll be a chill night, I promise."

Kai couldn't be sure if it was Oren's touch or his words, but suddenly e was able to breathe a bit easier.

After a dinner of rainbow-colored Pride pizzas but before dessert, Kai and Oren headed back to the Purple cabin. They had special permission to skip the Knitters' skit performances tonight. As Oren rummaged around for clothes to take with him to the shower, Kai perched at the edge of Juliana's bed and noticed e had a pair of new texts, both from Aziza.

Queen Aziza:
Idk, I think some people make exceptions for people they click with and others don't? It probably depends on the person

> And the pass will be easier to explain over the
> phone! When can we talk??

The first one related to eir question about people who only like boys or girls. The second text took em a beat longer to figure out. Kai skimmed the message chain, scrolling up to eir first day at camp before e remembered. Aziza had told em she had an idea for a sick new tumbling pass. And yeah, it would definitely be easier to talk through a pass than explain it in writing.

But one glance told Kai e was out of luck again. Eir phone was barely holding on to a single bar in this cabin.

Kai made a frustrated sound, and Oren looked over.

"Something wrong?"

"Not really." Kai shrugged. "I've just been trying to chat with my best friend, Aziza, all week but my phone isn't cooperating."

"The signal here is really terrible, yeah." Oren folded a set of clean clothes, then gathered them up in his arms. To Kai's relief, he'd chosen a T-shirt and a pair of shorts. Nothing super dressy. "I usually only get two bars, tops."

"That's more than I have." Kai scowled at eir phone as the smallest bar flickered out. "I'm at zero bars right now."

"That sucks. Do you want to use mine?"

A spark of hope. Kai looked up. "Really?"

"Yeah." Oren unlocked his phone, then passed it to Kai. "I don't need it while I'm showering, plus I don't use technology once Shabbat starts at sunset. Someone might as well get some use out of it."

As soon as Oren left the cabin, Kai tapped in Aziza's number. It took her so long to pick up, Kai worried it would go to voice mail. Finally, it connected.

"...yeah?"

"It's Kai," e said. "My phone barely works here so another camper let me use theirs."

"Oh! Heyyyy." Aziza's tone immediately brightened. "I'm glad I decided to answer then. How's it going?"

"Good," Kai said, and e realized this was the truth. E may not have wanted to come to camp, but e also wasn't hating it as much as e'd imagined. "The kids here are cool—but not as awesome as you and the rest of the crew, obviously."

"Obviously." Kai could hear the grin in Aziza's voice. "So, this pass—you ready for me to break it down for you?"

"One hundred percent ready."

Kai listened as Aziza explained her idea, which involved an aerial cartwheel into a one-handed back handspring into a full-twisting layout.

"I was thinking that you doing an aerial and then the handspring with just one hand would up the difficulty but also keep you off your bad shoulder—"

"—which would be great, since the camp nurse told me it'd take a while to get my strength back," Kai finished for her.

"Exactly. You think you can do it?"

Kai could do an aerial and a layout, no problem. E could do a back handspring too, but e had never tried a handspring with only one hand before. "I think so. I'd just need to practice a bit."

"Well, get started. You don't have to do it at the next event or anything, but it'd be cool to start running it." Aziza paused. "Assuming you can come next week, I mean."

"I should be able to," Kai said. "I just need to talk to my parents at the end of the weekend. But they said they'd get me early if I 'made an effort' to try out the camp and still wanted to come home. They promised."

"Cool, cool. So that just leaves your crush on that other camper. Time to spill."

"Oh. Um." Kai felt eir cheeks flush, even though Oren wasn't around. "There's this boy at camp. Oren. He's really nice—"

"And cute?"

"Definitely cute. But he's also gay. As in, likes other boys. And I don't know if he'd ever be into me because of that."

"Have you asked?"

Kai blinked. "No?"

"You should ask."

Aziza made it sound so simple.

"Like . . . just go up to him and say, 'Hey, Oren, I know you said you only like boys but would you make an exception for me?'" Kai felt a little queasy just thinking about it. "That would be seriously awkward."

"Well, yeah, if you say it like *that* it's awkward as heck." Aziza laughed. "But what if you find a way to ask when you're already talking about a similar topic? You're at a queer camp so it wouldn't be that weird to talk about stuff like that anyway and then hint at it, right?"

"Maybe."

The cabin doorknob twisted, and Kai startled, almost dropping the phone. E ducked eir head as Oren entered, trying to hide eir flushed face.

"Hey, Zeez? I've got to go."

"All good. Keep me posted?"

"Yeah." Kai took a breath to center emself, then held out Oren's phone to him.

"Can you put it on my dresser, actually?" Oren asked.

"Oh, right." Kai glanced out the window, where the daylight was quickly dimming. E pushed off the bunk. "No technology on Shabbat."

"Yep." Kai felt Oren's eyes on em as e made eir way to the dresser. "Also, I had an idea while I was in the shower."

If Kai's cheeks were hot before when e was just talking to Aziza about Oren, they were positively on fire now at the thought of Oren showering.

"I was wondering if you wanted to borrow one of my kippot. You don't have to, obviously," Oren rushed on, "but I just thought, you know, if you wanted one but didn't have one with you, you could . . . yeah."

All the teenage boys and men at the services Kai sometimes attended would wear a kippah in the temple, and a small handful of the girls and women would wear headscarves. Oren's offer made em both nervous and excited.

Kai stole a quick glance at Oren's head, then ran a hand through eir hair. "Sure. That'd be cool. I'm not sure it'd stay on, though?"

"It totally will." Oren pulled open his top dresser drawer, eyes narrowing as he studied its contents. "Hmm . . . I think a dark blue one would look really good on you."

He pulled out a solid navy kippah and showed it to Kai.

Kai nodded. It did look nice.

"If you lean forward a little, I can clip it in."

E did as Oren instructed, breath catching the moment Oren's hands came in contact with eir temple.

"Your hair is so cool," Oren said, his voice soft. "Sometimes I think about changing my hair but I honestly don't know what I'd do."

Kai liked Oren's curls, but eir mouth was too dry to let him know.

"Done!" The clips snapped into place, and Oren stepped back. "I unfortunately don't have an extra tallit for you."

"That's okay," Kai managed, hands reaching up to carefully pat eir head. The kippah stayed in place.

"But you can share my siddur." Oren retrieved a shawl—*tallit*, Kai silently recited—and a prayer book from his dresser. He placed the tallit over his shoulders, then Kai followed him out of the cabin.

Lena's office was among the administrative buildings on the other side of camp, not far from Nurse Micah's office.

"How was your friend?" Oren asked.

"She's good. I definitely miss her, though," Kai said. It'd only been a week, but it felt like e hadn't seen Aziza in forever.

"That's tough." Oren brushed his hair out of his eyes. "I'm really lucky Jax is here with me—in the same cabin again, too!"

"Yeah." Kai swallowed, trying to push away a surge of jealousy.

Aziza had said to start a conversation about a queer topic and then work eir way toward what Oren thought about making exceptions. As Oren led the way to Lena's office building, Kai tried to think of how e could manage that without being super obvious.

"It must be nice to be around someone who really gets you and likes the same . . ."

The same what? Gender of people? Awkward.

"It totally is." With just three little words, Oren saved Kai from further embarrassment. He held open the door to Lena's office and let Kai enter first.

Lena was waiting for them inside. "Hi, you two."

"Hey," they both said.

Lena treated them to a big smile and Kai could kind of see what drew Abigail to her. Lena felt safe and strong and accepting all at once.

"Come pull up a pair of seats." She gestured to a stack of folding chairs against one wall, not far from a card table.

As Oren and Kai chose their chairs, Lena placed a laptop on the card table and opened a browser. She clicked into a live feed that had an opening slide with the date and a countdown ticker on it. Less than five minutes until the service at Oren's temple started.

"Okay, you're all set," she said. "No need to touch anything. Just leave the laptop as-is when you're done and

I'll deal with it later." Another dimpled smile. "Shabbat shalom."

"Shabbat shalom." Oren smiled back.

The moment Lena left, his expression grew serious. He turned to Kai. "So, I had a question . . ."

Kai's heart fluttered. Maybe Oren had picked up on what e'd been planning to ask on the walk over.

". . . are you and Abigail, um . . . ?"

Kai stared at him. "Are me and Abigail what?"

E realized where this was going at the same time Oren spoke again. "The note that Jax found. The way she's always looking at you at meals. And getting you canned pineapples and stuff. I was just wondering if you two were . . . you know."

"No." It came out louder than Kai intended. Oren raised his eyebrows. "Sorry. I just mean, I don't think of her that way. She's more like a little sister to me." E could explain that Abigail also wasn't into em, but considering how embarrassed Abigail had seemed when she'd admitted her crush on Lena, Kai figured e shouldn't bring her into the conversation any more than necessary.

"Oh, okay." Oren's smile was back.

Finally, they were getting somewhere.

But then the laptop screen changed and the live feed flickered on. Oren's attention shifted.

"So, every temple's service is a little different, but here's how mine does it . . ."

For the next hour, Oren walked Kai through the service, letting em know when to sit or stand, sharing his prayer book, and explaining the meaning of each song as they went. Kai's worries faded as e soaked it all in. Every detail, however small. With Oren here to walk em through it, Kai felt like e really was a part of the service. E didn't have to pretend e knew something e didn't or worry about acting confident.

Oren stood as the service came to an end, and Kai followed suit, then folded eir chair and placed it against the office wall.

"So usually, everyone meets in my temple's community room after services and we all eat and chat," Oren said. "It's called an oneg."

Kai nodded to show e was following along.

"That obviously can't happen here, but I asked Chef Kirstie to save some dessert for us since we had to leave before dinner ended. So . . . did you maybe want to have an oneg with me?"

Kai's chest filled with warmth.

"What kind of dessert?" e asked with a serious look, as if e was carefully considering Oren's offer.

Oren placed his folded chair against Kai's, then

headed for the door. "Two brownies. One for me, and one for you. Sound good?"

As Kai opened the door and let Oren exit first, e couldn't conceal eir smile any longer.

"Sounds perfect."

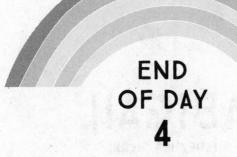

END
OF DAY
4

CROCHETERS COMPETITION
STANDINGS!

RED: 31

PURPLE: 30

YELLOW: 30

BLUE: 29

ORANGE: 29

GREEN: 28

13

ABIGAIL
(SHE/HER/HERS)

ABIGAIL WAS WHAT HER DAD ALWAYS REFERRED TO AS A "water baby." She was born in the spring, lived by the beach, and had spent many long days in the sun by the ocean. She took her first steps in the sand. She'd become intimately familiar with the taste of salt water, as it splashed into her mouth and nose, by age two.

Stacy preferred the pool. "For someone who freaks out about almost everything, it's weird to me you don't freak out about the ocean," Stacy had said more than once. That was because Stacy didn't like that she couldn't see through the murky water when they swam in the ocean.

But Abigail actually liked that. She liked that she could swim in the ocean and no one could see below her neck if she didn't want them to. At Stacy's pool, even when they were all swimming in the deep end, the girls would comment on each other's bathing suits. "Are you sure you don't want to borrow one of my bikinis?" Stacy would say. Or, "You're going to get a weird tan line if you leave your board shorts on."

Abigail liked her board shorts, and her one-piece with the thick straps that didn't make her feel too self-conscious. Back home, these things made her the odd one out at pool parties.

Not here, though.

Abigail was absolutely not the only one wearing board shorts at their morning swim at the lake—Cassidy wore a bikini top with her board shorts. Abigail wasn't the only one wearing a one-piece, either—Juliana had a really pretty mermaid-scale one that changed colors when the sun hit it just right. Kai had on long navy blue swim trunks and a white swim shirt, Stick had on much shorter green swim trunks and a black tank top, and Jax was the only one who took his shirt off to jump into the cool lake water. No one said anything when Bryn jumped in wearing what looked like just his regular clothes.

"It's nice not to worry about what to wear when we swim here," Juliana had quietly admitted, and Juliana never really did anything quietly. Kai had eagerly agreed with her. So did Stick and Bryn. And even though Abigail didn't know how they felt about their bodies or how *other people* made them feel about their bodies, she understood.

Because Juliana was right. It *was* nice not to have to worry. To let herself feel comfortable and wear what made her feel like *Abigail*, without Stacy's opinions in her ear.

Thinking about Stacy and home reminded Abigail she was supposed to take a picture of the lake, this beautiful Shakopee Lake—which wasn't as great as the Atlantic Ocean, but was still pretty wonderful—and post it to show all the girls back home that Abigail was doing just fine this summer without them. And this moment was perfect, because they were all in their swimsuits and not in their camp shirts.

She climbed up the ladder at the dock, waving at the lifeguard at his post when he smiled down at her as she headed toward the belongings that they'd all flung into a pile before jumping into the water.

"Abigail!" Jax called as she was digging through the pile for her bag. "What's the name of that really freaking big shark-looking dinosaur dude that was in the newer *Jurassic Park* movies? You know, the one that swam around and jumped out like a giant whale to eat people?"

"Mosasaurus," Abigail called over her shoulder.

"See?" Cassidy called out. "I told you she'd know it. She knows *everything* about dinosaurs and the *Jurassic Park* movies!"

Abigail didn't correct Cassidy that she was only an expert of the movies Laura Dern was in, which didn't include two out of three of the newer trilogy.

"Could you imagine if there was something like a Mosa-whatever in this lake?" Jax said, before using his hands to make a shark fin as he swam straight at Juliana, who screamed. Kai splashed at him.

"Jax, stop! There's no dinosaurs in this lake!" Cassidy said.

"The Mosasaurus lived in salt water, anyway," Abigail said, finally finding her phone. "Though they might have found a new type of mosasaur that lived in freshwater."

"That's it, I'm getting out," Juliana said.

"Wait!" Abigail said, scrolling through her phone apps. "I want to take a picture, let me just . . ."

Oh no.

Oh *no*!

Between all the camp activities and the spotty service and the fact that no one really texted Abigail anyway, she hadn't checked her phone since she posted the picture after the roller derby demo.

The picture where she stood happily with all her fellow campers in their roller gear.

The picture where they all wore their camp shirts with the rainbows and *CAMP QUILTBAG* written across the front of them.

The picture she had posted that now had a bunch of comments:

> *Lindsay Pinto: looks awesome! wish I could try!*
> *Stacy Mackenzie: uh whats camp quiltbag??*
> *Stacy Mackenzie: why does it say your in*
> *minnesota???*
> *Maya Higgins: I found a link!*
> *Stacy Mackenzie: OMG!!!*

This was bad. This was really bad. Everyone knew she lied. Everyone knew she was at *gay camp*! Her fingers hovered over her phone to text Stacy and say . . . what? What was Abigail supposed to do? Say, *Sorry I lied but I didn't want you to know I was coming here*? That was the truth, sure, but admitting it . . . Abigail couldn't do that.

How was she supposed to go home now? It didn't matter how much fun she'd been having this morning, or how much fun she'd had at roller derby, or how much she liked her new friends. At the end of next week, she would be going home.

Abigail deleted the post. She deleted the photo off her phone, too.

Even though she had loved that photo.

God, she had been so *stupid*!

What was she going to do?

"Abigail? Are you okay?" It was Bryn who asked, as he swam to the ladder and pulled himself up and out of the lake.

Abigail turned to find everyone else was looking at her, too.

"It's fine. It's just—it doesn't matter," she said, tossing her phone back in her bag.

"I thought you wanted to take a picture?" Kai asked, pulling emself up the ladder, too.

Don't cry, Abigail. Pull yourself together. "No. I mean, yeah. I mean, my phone died," she lied. "It's fine."

Cassidy swam over to the ladder next. "You can use mine," she said, digging through the pile to find her bag and phone. Juliana got out right after her, probably because of the mosasaurs, and then one by one everyone else started getting out, too, and the dock was a little too crowded and the sun was a little too hot, and Abigail was finding it a little too hard to breathe.

She jumped when Bryn's hand reached for her shoulder. His palm was cool on her skin. "Are you sure you're okay? You look a little funny."

Abigail looked at Bryn. She should just tell him. She'd helped Bryn the other day, and Bryn had been nice ever since Abigail got to camp. He'd smiled at her and stayed close when none of her friends back home did either of those things anymore. Or Kai. She could tell Kai what was happening. Kai had been her friend since day one, since e found her having her *first* meltdown, and e'd been nothing but nice to her ever since. Maybe e would know what to do to help her through this disaster, too.

She opened her mouth to tell Kai *and* Bryn everything.

But before she could, a group of younger kids in bright orange shirts came running onto the dock. One of the smallest of them, a Weaver with teeny blond pigtails and a name tag that said, *Jayme: she/her/hers*, flung her arms around Kai's middle, nearly knocking em and her both into the lake. "Kai!" she exclaimed.

"Hey! Come back here, by the shoreline! I'll get the kayaks ready!" The camp counselor was calling to their group of tiny orange missiles. "MJ, mind helping me with these?"

MJ, who had been sunbathing with Leticia while the older group swam, popped up to give the Weavers' counselor a hand.

Meanwhile, Jayme had yet to let go of Kai. "Are you kayaking too?" she asked.

"We're just swimming," Juliana answered.

"Make a new friend when we weren't around, Kai?" Jax joked.

"Um." Kai hugged Jayme back and then wiggled out of her grasp. "Yeah."

"Kai and Oren helped us put on our play! Kai helped me with my lines. I got to be one of the princesses!" Jayme said.

Cassidy's eyebrows flew up her forehead. "When did you do that?"

"Jayme! Let's go, kid, I've got a kayak with your name on it!" Jayme's counselor called. She leaned in to give Kai another squeeze before jogging off to join her cabinmates.

"When did you and Oren go off and do something without the rest of us?" Stick asked, looking equally as baffled as Cassidy. They looked at Jax, who shrugged.

"Is that how you got so many extra points the other day? I knew those points weren't adding up right," Cassidy said. She turned to face Juliana and asked, "Did you know about this?"

"No!" Juliana said, her eyes wide.

"Did you both sneak off to get extra points?" Stick asked. "Did you do that on *purpose*?"

Kai looked extra small as e stood on the end of the dock, rubbing at eir newly freed elbow, eir eyes flickering from one person to the next until e settled on Abigail.

E needed her to stick up for em. E needed her to say, *Hey, maybe e didn't do it on purpose*, or, *It's fine, we're still ahead in the points, and we have an alliance to both try to win*, or, *Let's let Kai explain emself, I'm sure e didn't mean to upset anyone.*

But what if everyone else got mad at her, too?

Abigail didn't have any friends at home. All she had was *one week* left here.

She didn't know what to do. "M-maybe . . . ," she started to say, and everyone turned to look at her, which made her close her mouth right up again.

"We have an alliance," Cassidy said, turning back to Kai. "We're supposed to keep each other in the loop. That's the *point*."

"Wait, look," Kai interrupted her. "It's not like that. Oren and I got a couple extra points for helping the Weavers and didn't tell anyone, yeah. But it's not like Abigail hasn't been getting a bunch of extra points for doing that stuff all the time! We were just trying to even the playing field. Oren couldn't compete today because he wanted to observe Shabbat and so we just thought we'd do something extra then, instead. So that we wouldn't fall farther behind. That's all."

"You should have just told us that in the first place, Kai," Juliana said.

"Maybe we should just go back and change. It's almost lunchtime," Bryn said. He pointed over to where MJ had finished helping the Orange Weavers with their kayaks, and he and Leticia were starting to gather their own things.

"Yeah," Juliana was quick to agree. She reached for Cassidy's hand and said, "Let's go refresh."

Cassidy stared at Juliana's hand in her own for a moment before saying, "Fine."

"Fine," Kai echoed.

Everyone got quiet as they started gathering their things, but it wasn't the nice kind of quiet. It was the kind of quiet that came after someone like Stacy said something about Abigail being gay. The kind of quiet that came after Dylan Donnell mumbled something rude under his breath in class but Sister Patricia heard anyway and yelled at him for it.

The kind of quiet that maybe could have been avoided if Abigail had stuck up for Kai and helped smooth things over before they got weird.

Kai was the last to grab eir stuff, and Abigail waited for em. She stood in front of em, blocking eir way off the dock as e put on eir shoes. She wanted to say something to em. Apologize, maybe, even. But she still was finding it a little too hard to breathe, and even harder to speak.

Kai sighed. "Just move out of the way, Abigail. I'm hungry."

She stepped aside.

She walked slowly. Leticia stayed back with her but didn't try to make small talk, which Abigail appreciated. Her head was full of stomping triceratops feet, and she kind of wished a freshwater mosasaur had swallowed her whole while she was swimming. Then she wouldn't have let Kai down. Then she wouldn't have to go home to face Stacy.

Don't cry, Abigail. Especially not in front of *Lena's daughter* of all people. Abigail blinked quickly and glanced away from Leticia toward the woods. She couldn't even enjoy the view.

A dash of white suddenly caught her eyes, the leaves of the brush along the edge of the woods rustling. Abigail stopped short, holding her breath as she leaned in, squinting her eyes. *It couldn't be . . .*

"Did you see something?" Leticia asked, as she came to a stop beside her.

"I thought I saw . . ." A flock of birds suddenly flew out of the trees, and Abigail ducked as their shadows moved over her and Leticia, little warblers that Abigail recognized from their bingo nature walk.

Birds. It was just birds. Even if Abigail believed in magical albino squirrels, she was absolutely not the type of kid who'd get to see Mx. Nutsford. "Nothing," she said. "I thought maybe I saw . . . but it was nothing."

"My mom talks about that squirrel every summer," Leticia said, immediately understanding. "And every summer, I always keep my eyes out, even though I don't actually believe a word of it. It'd be nice, though, wouldn't it? To get a little bit of camp magic and luck?"

Yes. Abigail would love a little bit of camp magic and luck. That was why she wanted to come to Camp QUILTBAG in the first place. That was why she was here.

But she was starting to think maybe there was no such thing as magic albino squirrels, or good luck, or even a place she could be comfortable and happy and understood. Even if she had thought for a moment—for one really, really good moment—that maybe she had finally found a place she belonged.

14

KAI
(E/EM/EIR)

IN KAI'S EXPERIENCE, GOOD MOMENTS BUILT ON TOP OF other good moments. Like, if e was having a good week of parkour practice, where e nailed all eir tricks, e was also likely to perform well at an event that took place the following weekend. Same for when e was training as a gymnast.

So, after what felt like a perfect end to Friday and a fun start to the weekend swimming in the lake, Kai felt unfairly blindsided when Cassidy called em out about the extra points e and Oren had earned for their cabin.

E felt worse that no one—including Abigail—had defended em.

Maybe e should've expected it. Abigail was the girl who needed to learn how to pretend to be confident, after all. But Kai had really needed her support. They were supposed to be friends, and friends stood up for one another.

Kai's foul mood stayed with em through lunch. The Yellow and Purple cabins were still seated at the same table, but the mood felt different. There had been less talk, no laughter. Oren was still observing Shabbat in Lena's office, so Kai felt alone. When e did talk, it was to the Green campers at their table. Their cabin was in last place, but none of them seemed to mind. In fact, when Jax asked them about their score, a kid named Lin (they/ them/their) just laughed and explained that none of them cared about winning; they just wanted to have fun.

That made zero sense to Kai. Eir entire life, e'd been focused on winning.

At one point, Kai's gaze traveled to Abigail's side of the table. But unlike earlier this week, Kai never caught Abigail looking eir way. She sat between Stick and Bryn, with Cassidy nearby, directly across from Juliana. When she wasn't talking with her cabinmates, her eyes were down, checking her phone in her lap.

Just hours earlier, Kai had been looking forward to seeing Oren. E'd been excited about the bonfire. But now that e was back in eir cabin waiting for dinner with

Jax and Juliana, arms sore from an afternoon of racing kayaks, Kai was worried things would be just as awkward after Oren returned.

So when Jax asked Kai if e wanted to come with him to get Oren from Lena's office, Kai shook eir head. "I think I'll stay here if that's okay. Maybe ask Leticia to go with you?"

"Yeah, no problem," Jax said. "Be back soon."

And then there were two.

Kai held eir breath, waiting for Juliana to say something about the lake argument. But the silence dragged on. At first, e was grateful for it, but then eir thoughts turned to how Jax would be walking with Oren back to the cabin. And that got Kai thinking back to the moment at the creek, when Jax had kissed Oren.

Suddenly it was all e could think about.

E glanced down at Juliana on the bed under em. She was reading a book, something called *The Best Liars in Riverview*. Its dust jacket was torn and folded at some of the corners, like it'd been read multiple times. The cover was all river blues and forest greens, which just reminded Kai of Jax and Oren all over again.

"Are you mad at me?" Kai finally asked. E figured it was better to distract emself, even if e probably wouldn't like Juliana's answer.

But the book stayed up, concealing Juliana's face. "No, I'm reading."

"I mean about earlier," Kai tried again. "About Oren and me getting extra points for our cabin."

"I'm not sure what I feel," Juliana said. "I think it would've been nice to know what you were up to. I didn't like feeling confused, and I don't think Cassidy did, either."

Before Kai could respond, the cabin door opened. Oren appeared first. He nodded at Juliana, then looked up at Kai. Their eyes met.

"Hi," Oren said.

"Hey," Kai said back. For a moment, it felt like they were the only kids in the room. Kai and Oren. Just the two of them.

Then Jax barreled in, severing the connection.

"Jax told me what happened, about Cassidy getting upset about our extra points," Oren said. "We probably should've let everyone know after we got back from helping the Weavers, huh?"

Kai shrugged. Oren was most likely right, but e couldn't speak over the lump in eir throat.

"You probably should've," Jax jumped in, "but it's not like they're super behind now or anything. The only cabin that's ahead of them still is Red. So . . . dinner?"

"Yes." Juliana bookmarked her page, then hopped up. "Dinner."

Kai kept eir eyes on the ground as they made their way to the cafeteria. Oren walked beside em.

"You okay?" Oren asked.

"Yeah. Fine." But Kai kept eir eyes down. "I guess my great idea wasn't so great."

"It was fine. You were just trying to help the cabin because of my situation. Technically, it was more my fault than yours."

"Lena should have just given you a point for Saturday up front," Juliana said. "It would've been the inclusive thing to do."

Kai glanced at Oren right as he looked down. His hair fell into his eyes, and Kai desperately wanted to brush it away as easily as Oren sometimes put his hand on Kai's shoulder. Because there was no reason for Oren to feel bad about observing Shabbat. It was an important part of who he was, and if other kids didn't get it, that was their problem.

Before Kai could figure out how to express eir thoughts, Oren spoke up again. "It's whatever. We can try to smooth things out more with the Yellow cabin, though. Maybe at dinner."

"Or at the bonfire," Jax chimed in. "Don't sweat it.

Things will be fine by then. Pretty much no one can be annoyed during that."

"That's true," Juliana said. "It's one of the best parts of camp."

Oren's hand brushed against Kai's as they walked. It was probably just an accident, but Kai suddenly felt a little better.

"Okay," Kai said. They'd figure things out at dinner, or at the bonfire later tonight. Jax and Juliana both seemed certain that everything would be back to normal very soon.

～

Things felt more comfortable at dinner. The conversation between the Purple and Yellow campers seemed to come more easily, but Kai still couldn't help feeling like e had royally messed up. All through the meal, e tried to act confident by sitting up straight and joining in the conversation. Yet e was still quieter than usual.

Even after lights out, after the Crocheters crept out of their cabins and headed toward the bonfire site, Kai felt off-balance, like e was walking the hallways of eir school, braced for an elbow jab or a mean comment.

The Yellow campers sat in a row on one of the logs arranged in front of a firepit that was currently crackling with a small flame. Purple was on their own log next to them. An Orange camper stoked the fire with a stick, occasionally raking wayward embers back toward the center.

The other campers seemed excited, laughing and chattering and passing around paper cups filled with water they had poured from a spouted jug, as well as s'mores ingredients. But Kai could still feel the tension knotting up eir shoulders. Juliana stared into the flames, while Jax and Oren spoke in low voices. Abigail and Bryn were sitting next to one another and talking quietly. Same for Cassidy and Stick.

Kai let eir eyes wander toward another campfire that was just visible as a soft glow through the trees.

"That's the counselors."

Kai glanced at Oren, who pointed toward the glow in the distance.

"Even though we're not technically supposed to be outside our cabins after lights out, this is like an unofficial tradition for the Crocheters, so the counselors look the other way," he explained. "But they also have their own bonfire on the same night, probably so they can keep tabs on us. Or help if we need anything."

"Which we never do," Juliana said, without looking away from the flames.

"Yep." Jax grinned. "Eight years of not burning the forest down and counting. Go, Camp QUILTBAG!"

Juliana made a face, reminding Kai that more was at stake than just winning this competition. As bags of marshmallows, trays of chocolate bars, and boxes of graham crackers made their way around the firepit, Kai wondered if Juliana already had a new camp name picked out.

"Storytime!" A Green camper stepped up to the fire. "Tonight, it's Mx. Nutsford, *horror edition*."

The camper described how, on a full moon, Mx. Nutsford's claws grew into razors, zir teeth transforming into fangs. Kai figured this might be a story that'd scare the Weavers. The Crocheters? Not so much.

"It sounds like a squirrel on steroids," Cassidy called out once they were done.

"Or a were-squirrel," Jax chimed in.

Laughter erupted around the campfire. Cassidy grinned at Jax.

Then Cassidy's gaze shifted to Kai and her smile changed, dimming a little. It wasn't a lot. She didn't scowl or anything, but it still made Kai's insides twist. Beside her, Abigail finally glanced at em, only to look away fast, back at Bryn.

Kai felt a queasy lurch in eir stomach. Why hadn't Abigail stood up for em?

"Be back in a bit," Juliana said, oblivious to Kai's turmoil. She pushed up from the log and headed over to Cassidy.

Oren glanced at Jax, then Kai. "Want to go hang out with some of the other campers?"

"Nah." Jax popped a whole marshmallow into his mouth. "Ahll sday ober here, sanks."

Oren and Kai stared at him.

Jax swallowed. "I said, I'll stay over here." He held up the marshmallow bag. "Want to make s'mores?"

"Sure," Kai said, but Oren shook his head.

"Not kosher." He pointed at the nearest box of graham crackers. "I'll just have some of these. You two go ahead, though."

Kai studied Oren carefully out of the corner of one eye. Was Oren slouching more than usual? Did he feel bad? Kai couldn't tell for sure, and e wasn't brave enough to outright ask, either.

"I'm good with just this, actually." Kai reached for one of the chocolate bars.

"Suit yourselves." Jax headed over to a pile of sticks other campers had collected for roasting marshmallows. He had just speared his first one and was reaching for a second when music blasted through the clearing. Half of the campers jumped. All eyes turned to Ash, who lowered the volume a second later.

"Sorry," she said. She placed a portable speaker on a tree stump, then waved her cell phone over her head. "I've got a playlist that'll go for like an hour, but feel free to add any songs you want."

While other kids moved closer to the fire to roast their marshmallows, Stick jumped up and made their way over to Ash's cell phone.

"This should be good." Oren sat up straighter as he reached for the graham cracker box.

Kai followed his gaze to the other side of the campfire just as the music changed to a pop song. Stick danced over to the Yellow cabin's log and beckoned to Abigail, who blushed and shook her head. Bryn shook his head, too. Even Cassidy seemed hesitant to dance with Stick, her eyes darting to Juliana, then to the ground.

Oren's eyes never seemed to leave Stick. Even though Kai had never been interested in dancing, e found emself wishing e knew some fancy choreography that would make Oren turn and watch em instead.

It was Juliana who ultimately stood and accepted Stick's outstretched hand. Stick beamed as they helped her up. Juliana moved to the music, her long hair loose and fluttering as she spun around, but Stick was in a league of their own. Their movements matched the song perfectly, sharp on the beats, softer on the in-between melody.

"Stick can seriously dance," Kai said, begrudgingly impressed.

Oren nodded and kept his eyes on Stick and Juliana. "Last year, Stick told me they did ballroom competitions with a partner and everything. Not sure if they still do them, but I bet they're going to be the best dancer in class next week."

Kai froze, a square of chocolate halfway to eir mouth. "There's a dance class?"

"Yeah. Maybe it'll be different this year with the competition and all, but last year's teacher said they wanted us to learn traditional dance holds for men and women, so we can modify them if they don't feel right for us." Oren shrugged. "It was also good practice. It's not required or anything, but lots of kids danced together at the gala last summer."

"Ah."

As Siobhan joined Stick and Juliana on their make-shift dance floor, Kai tried to imagine dancing with Oren in front of the rest of the camp. Eir whole body got hot. E popped the square of chocolate into eir mouth, then hunched forward, elbows resting on the tops of eir legs.

"So, I've been thinking . . ." Oren turned to Kai, whose stomach flipped. They'd just been talking about the gala. Was Oren about to ask em to go with him? Did kids even ask other kids out as their dates here?

"Yeah?" Kai tried to look cool and unconcerned.

"Yeah. This camp is kind of like one big parkour course."

"Oh. I guess."

"Like, the dock, the Benches, and even the forest, with all its rocks and trees and stuff."

Kai nodded absently. Just a moment ago, e'd been nervous about the thought of Oren asking em to the gala, but now that he hadn't, disappointment settled like a rock in eir stomach.

"There are even things that could be obstacles here." Oren glanced around the campfire, then back at Kai. "Right? I don't know a ton about parkour, but couldn't you use the logs somehow? Or, um . . . the campfire?"

There was an eagerness in Oren's voice that Kai couldn't help responding to.

"Probably not the fire. My coach says parkour's about taking calculated risks, but not actually risking your life trying something life-threatening." Kai smiled a little, remembering eir coach's lecture when one of eir friends had attempted a trick he hadn't been ready to do without help. "But the logs? Sure. They'd make great obstacles."

"That sounds so cool." Oren's brows rose. "Can you do something on this log?"

"Uh . . ." Kai's smile wavered.

"Only if you want," Oren was quick to say. "Or if you can, I mean. Forget I said anything if your shoulder's still hurting."

"It's fine." The last thing Kai wanted was for Oren to feel sorry for em. "I can show you some stuff."

E stood up on the log, testing it out. The balance beam had always been Kai's favorite gymnastics apparatus. This log was wider than a balance beam, and nowhere near as high off the ground. E took a breath, bent eir knees, then jumped. Kai tucked eir knees and twisted a full revolution, landing in the same spot e'd started in, arms over eir head.

"Awesome." Oren's face lit up.

"It's nothing," Kai said, but excitement tingled through eir limbs. "Usually, you want to do multiple tricks in a row, connecting them together and using more than one obstacle. My friend Aziza just thought up this tumbling pass that's so cool because it's mostly no-handed. Lots of flipping. I'm not sure what I'd flip off of yet, but figuring that stuff out is part of the fun."

"You can seriously do flips?" Oren seemed in awe just thinking about it.

Kai nodded. Eir coach always said e had some of the

best technique of their crew because e'd spent years training in gymnastics before switching to parkour.

"What's this about flips now?"

Oren and Kai turned to Jax, who'd just returned from the firepit.

"Kai said e can do flips," Oren said.

"Show us!" Jax said.

Suddenly both Jax and Oren were looking at em.

Kai swallowed hard. "I mean, I haven't tried this pass before, and definitely not on a log." But e was already thinking through how it would work, calculating how much space e would need. E would need to simplify it a little since e wasn't confident e could do an aerial on the log's bumpy surface. Plus e'd never tried a one-handed handspring before.

But Kai bet e could do a one-handed back walk-over into a simple back tuck off the end of the log. E'd graduated from walkovers to handsprings on the beam years ago.

E glanced around the campfire. The music continued to play. More people had joined Stick and Juliana and Siobhan, dancing around the fire with various levels of coordination. No one was looking their way.

"Okay, I'll try something."

Jax and Oren took a step back as Kai hopped onto the log.

With the heat and music and the chattering of other kids, it almost felt like a parkour event. Kai had learned how to block out distractions long ago. E did that now, focusing only on emself and the feel of the log under eir shoes.

Kai lifted eir good arm over eir head, pointing eir left foot out in front of em. E arched eir back and leaned backward. The moment eir hand touched the log, e kicked one leg over, then the other.

This had always been a simple move when e'd had two arms equally holding eir weight. But the log wasn't smooth like a balance beam or even a sidewalk curb. Walking over on one hand was very different than using two. Kai found emself slightly off-balance as eir feet connected with the log. Then muscle memory took over and Kai punched into eir backflip automatically.

Coach had called Kai a cat more than once because e was usually able to straighten emself out in the air if e ended up tilted. But it'd been months since Kai had last tumbled.

E landed on eir heels instead of the balls of eir feet. Over-rotated.

Kai stayed on eir feet just long enough to hear Jax's *Whoop!* before eir momentum threw em backwards. E shot eir hands out behind em without thinking and landed on straightened elbows.

White light sparked behind eir eyes. Kai rolled onto eir back as pain shot into eir shoulder.

"Are you all right?" Oren crouched beside em.

Kai blinked. Bit the inside of eir cheek. Nodded.

"You sure?" Jax offered em a hand.

Kai let Jax pull em up, then rolled eir shoulder a little, testing it out. It still stung, but the pain felt more like a dull ache now. What stung more was the embarrassment of having missed an easy landing. Kai's cheeks burned as e glanced around the campfire.

E met Abigail's gaze from across the firepit. She looked away fast once again. No way to tell if she'd seen what had just happened. No one else was looking at the three of them. Everyone was watching Stick, who was doing a complicated-looking set of dance moves.

Kai nodded slowly. Yes, e was fine.

Neither boy looked convinced. Jax crossed his arms. Oren's brows pinched toward the bridge of his nose.

Kai rolled eir shoulder experimentally again. Same dull ache. E reached up with eir good hand and brushed the leaves out of eir hair.

"The ground was uneven, so I just lost my balance there at the end," e said. Kai was positive e'd only tweaked eir shoulder. Nothing serious. There was no need to make either of them worry. "I'm honestly fine."

"Oh, okay," Jax said, lowering his arms. Oren's face

relaxed. "Well, that was an incredible trick before you fell."

"It totally was." Oren's curls bounced as he nodded. "Maybe we can watch some parkour videos online later. I totally want to see more."

"Same!" Jax grinned.

"Sure." Relief washed over Kai. "If we can get them to load out here, anyway."

"Right." Oren laughed, then glanced over at the other campers. "Should we go dance or something?"

Kai was just about to say that dancing was the last thing e wanted to do, but Jax beat em to it.

"I'll wait until dance class for Stick to show me up, thanks." He spotted the marshmallow bag and grabbed it. "More s'mores for me."

Oren reached for his packet of graham crackers, then held out a Hershey bar to Kai. "More chocolate for you?"

As Jax headed back toward the firepit with the marshmallows and his stick, Kai settled in on the log beside Oren again.

"Sounds good."

E reached for the chocolate with eir good arm, even though the other one was closer.

END
OF WEEK
ONE

CROCHETERS COMPETITION
STANDINGS!

RED: 35

YELLOW: 34

PURPLE: 33

BLUE: 33

ORANGE: 33

GREEN: 32

15

ABIGAIL

(SHE/HER/HERS)

THEY ALL STILL SMELLED LIKE STALE CAMPFIRE SMOKE,
even though they'd changed into their pajamas. Abigail
could smell it in her hair as she pulled it away from her
face and into a high ponytail. She laid her head onto her
pillow, hoping the odor wouldn't rub off on the fabric,
wishing she'd been able to take a shower to wash it all
away.

Stick, who shone with sweat, their hair sticking up
in odd directions from running their hands through the
damp strands, was still wired from the campfire. They
couldn't stop telling bad jokes, trying to make the rest of

them laugh. Abigail really just wanted to sleep the day off, not think about how she and Kai were avoiding one another, how e was probably still upset with her, how Stacy and everyone knew she'd lied about her summer plans.

She felt like she'd lost her best friend here like she had long ago lost her best friend at home.

"What's the difference between Black Eyed Peas and chickpeas?" Stick said. Their voice was loud in the dark and quiet cabin.

"What?" Bryn asked. He was the only one playing along.

"Black Eyed Peas can sing us songs, but chickpeas can only hummus them!"

Cassidy groaned. Abigail stifled a giggle. She'd always had a soft spot for bad jokes. She wished she were in the mood to enjoy them.

"Abigail, this one is for you," Stick said, and Abigail rolled over, leaning her head over her bunk to look at them. "What do you call a dinosaur fart?"

"Oh my God," Cassidy grumbled, though Abigail could see, now that her eyes had adjusted to the dark, Cassidy had a smile on her face.

"What?" Abigail asked, smiling too.

"A *blast* from the *past!*"

"That was terrible," Abigail said, even though she was laughing. She could hear giggles coming from Bryn and Cassidy, too.

"That's why it's so good," Stick replied.

Something shook loose in Abigail's chest as their little giggles died down. She settled more comfortably under her blankets. The smoke smell wasn't so bad anymore. "Hey, Stick! Did you know that the dinosaurs in *Jurassic Park*, they could change their gender? The scientists used frog DNA with the recovered dinosaur DNA, and even though they made all the dinosaurs girls, the dinosaurs were able to change so they could make babies."

Stick was quiet, and Abigail for a second wondered if maybe it was the wrong thing to say.

But then Stick shouted, "*They're Nonbinarysauruses!*" And then they started roaring.

"Sex and gender aren't the same things," Cassidy said, rolling over to face Abigail. "Juliana can explain it better, but basically the dinosaurs technically changed their sex, not their gender. But I see where you were going with that! And, anyway, who am I to decide how the dinosaurs identified."

"Oh," Abigail said, though she didn't feel silly for once for not knowing. It felt good to learn, and not to feel judged. "Okay."

"Like Mx. Nutsford," Bryn chimed in. "So, they definitely could be nonbinarysauruses."

They all fell quiet again, but Abigail could tell Cassidy wasn't sleeping. She was staring up at the ceiling above her bunk, her arms behind her head, seemingly lost in thought.

Abigail's mind drifted back to Kai. She'd thought about sitting with Kai at the bonfire to apologize. But e was busy with Oren and Jax, and then e fell, and Abigail was worried she would just make things worse for em all over again.

Kai kept making camp better for Abigail. Abigail was pretty sure she was doing the opposite for em.

"Cassidy?" she said, taking a deep breath and gathering up every ounce of courage she could find. "I think . . . I mean, I know you were upset that Oren and Kai got extra points, but I really don't think they meant to be sneaky. Kai just wanted to help Oren, I think."

When Cassidy didn't reply, Abigail slowly shifted to look at her. She had a deep frown on her face. "I don't think I'm really mad at Kai and Oren. I mean, I get it. And, well, I want to get a lot of points and get ahead, too, so . . ."

Stick and Bryn had both gone quiet in their bunks below.

Cassidy's voice lowered to a whisper that Abigail had to lean over in her bunk to hear. "I just . . . you know how important this is to me. I just don't want to look bad, so I guess maybe I was jealous? I just don't want them to pull too far ahead of us."

"It'll be okay, Cassidy," Abigail said. "No matter what, okay?"

"Will you please help me earn extra points? Like we talked about?"

Abigail swallowed. It went hard down her throat. "Yes."

Cassidy grew quiet again. But then she looked over at Abigail with a soft smile and said, "Thanks, Abigail."

Abigail was relieved for about half a second before she realized that she shouldn't have made the promise. Not when Abigail and Kai had their own alliance they would put above everyone else. Above *Cassidy*.

The first week of camp was officially over. Abigail had to figure out what to do. She had time to fix this. She had time to get back to the feeling she had a few days ago, when things were going right. Maybe she could help Cassidy impress Juliana and find another way to make Kai happy with her again. Then they would *both* be her friends, and maybe the mess back home wouldn't matter as much.

She had an entire week to fix this.

She just had to figure out how.

Abigail was getting used to not sleeping, to staring at the wooden ceiling and listening to the cicadas chirping throughout the night, watching the flutter of the moths as they chased the sparse light that bled through the window from the lamps lining the paths outside.

She spent a lot of time that night swatting at a mosquito that had made its way into the cabin and danced along the wall next to her bunk. She was nearing sleep, her eyes heavy, as she thought, *I'll have to ask Kai for more lavender spray.* But then her stomach clenched when she remembered Kai probably would rather she got eaten all up by mosquitos right now, and that knocked the sleep right out of her.

Luckily, Sunday was Relaxation and Recovery Day. There were no scheduled activities, no chances to earn participation *or* extra points. It was an entirely points-free day. The goal was for any campers who needed to rest to do exactly that before they kicked off the second and last week of Camp QUILTBAG.

It suited Abigail just fine. Cassidy had plans to meet up with Juliana, Stick was still snoring, and Bryn had asked MJ to walk with him to the main cabins so he could call his dad since his phone wasn't getting service. Abigail thought about going with him and calling her mom, too, but decided to text instead. Her mom's last text, when it was finally delivered, had said, *How's my girl doing? Having fun? Making friends?*

Abigail had quickly shot one back that just said, *It's really nice here!* Which didn't really answer any of her mom's questions but was true enough. Abigail was about to put her phone away when a text suddenly came in.

Stacy:
Are you really at gay camp what is that like omg

Abigail turned her phone off.

Truth was, Abigail always knew that her crush on Stacy's mom was going to cause a problem. And not just because it was Stacy's mom—Abigail knew that if she admitted about Laura Dern or Teri Polo or any of the women she liked, her friendship with Stacy would be in trouble. Stacy said things like, "Don't be gay" when someone put their sleeping bag too close to hers during sleepovers. She didn't like seeing gay people kissing on TV shows; she'd commented more than once to Abigail that she "just didn't want to see that."

Stacy said she didn't care that people were gay, but Abigail had a list of other things Stacy had said to prove otherwise.

That hurt—and it also made Abigail wonder if Stacy's mom said those things, too, when Abigail wasn't around.

Stick let out a really big snore below her. Abigail surrendered and climbed out of bed. She wasn't supposed to go anywhere without a buddy, but she didn't want to wake up Stick and she kind of wanted to be alone, so she gathered her clothes to head to the bathroom by herself.

She felt better after she showered and dressed, like a new week promised a fresh start. It felt like forever ago that she'd arrived at Camp QUILTBAG, and it was only halfway over. She wasn't sure if that was a good thing or a bad thing. An entire week left of this. It felt impossibly short and impossibly long all at once.

Abigail stepped out of the bathroom and took in a deep breath of fresh Minnesota air. She closed her eyes and tried to enjoy the shade of the trees in the heat of the summer. She couldn't smell the lake like she could always smell the ocean at home, but she could see the Pride flags that lined the paths, rainbow colors fluttering with the leaves.

Why do I have to be gay?

It wasn't the first time Abigail thought it. It wasn't even the tenth.

Why, out of all the people in the world, and the members of her family, and the students in her school and the patrons of her church, did *she* have to be gay? Why did she have to be the one to get made fun of for having a crush on a friend's mom, and why did she have to be the one who slunk in her seat, blushing, during religion class anytime something even remotely close to homosexuality came up during their readings?

She wished she didn't need to come to this stupid camp in the first place.

Then she wouldn't have lied. She would be at home, on the beach, with all her friends. Maybe she'd have a crush on Hudson or Elijah or one of the other boys in her class. Maybe she'd get dressed up with the rest of her friends before the seventh-grade dance next year, borrowing Stacy's favorite lip gloss, and she would hope that one of those boys would ask her to dance.

Maybe they would. And then Abigail would have a boyfriend and she would rip all the Laura Dern posters off her walls because they wouldn't matter to her anymore.

Abigail's nose started to burn, and she had to blink back tears at the thought of ripping up her posters, and that made her eyes fill with even more tears. She loved Laura Dern *so much.*

She loved Laura Dern because she was gay, and she wanted to feel like the other kids did at this camp *so much.* She wanted to be proud of who she was *so much.*

But she couldn't. She couldn't even hang her Laura

Dern poster on the walls of her bunk here, where it should be safe.

She just . . . *couldn't*.

There was a rustle from the bushes and brambles in front of her and Abigail paused, holding her breath. Was that a flash of white? Was that a squirrel's tail? Abigail wasn't even super sure she believed in magical squirrels, and especially nonbinary albino ones, but she wanted to so badly. She wanted it to be zem so badly. *Please*, she thought. *Mx. Nutsford. Please. I need good luck. I need you to choose me. Help me.*

"Hey."

Abigail screamed at the sound of the voice behind her, and the voice behind her let out a shout, too. She quickly looked back into the bushes, but she didn't see anything. If something had been there, all that shouting probably scared it away.

She turned to scowl at whoever frightened her and came face to face with Oren. He had his hands up in surrender. The sun made the little blue Jewish hat on his head shine brightly. "I didn't mean to scare you," Oren said. "You were just . . . standing here by yourself. I thought it'd be weird if I didn't say anything."

Abigail sighed. "It's okay. Are you here by yourself?" She looked around. "Is Kai with you?"

Oren shook his head. "No. E went to get breakfast with the others, and I didn't wake up early enough to go with them. I think Kai hurt emself last night, but e's being kind of stubborn about it and I didn't want to push. I'm here by myself. I guess I'm breaking the rules again."

"I'm by myself, too."

"Well, at least we can pretend we're here together if we get caught?" He smiled at her, but Abigail couldn't bring herself to smile back. His shoulders slouched a little. "You're not mad at us for getting extra points or anything, right?"

She quickly shook her head. "No. I know why Kai did it. I mean! I understand why you needed extra points."

Oren stuck his hands in his pockets, rocking on his feet a bit. "Yeah. I couldn't get any points because of Shabbat, and I was feeling kind of bad about it, so Kai thought it'd help me feel better, is all."

"Shabbat?" Abigail asked. It was a Jewish thing, but that was all she knew. "Is that like . . . going to church?"

Oren smiled softly. "You're Catholic?" Abigail nodded, and he continued. "So, you'd go to church on Sunday, right, if your family is religious and it's what you observe each week. We observe Shabbat from sundown on Friday until sundown on Saturday. That's why I wasn't around all day yesterday until dinner. Which means I couldn't do any of the competition activities during the day."

Abigail slowly nodded her head. "Kai helped you get extra points because you were going to miss out yesterday. That . . . definitely sounds like something Kai would do."

"E came with me to virtual Shabbat service on Friday night, too. It was nice having someone to share it with," Oren said.

And before Abigail could stop herself, she asked, "You went to your Shabbat service *voluntarily*? Even though you're here?" She couldn't imagine voluntarily going to church. Not while she was at gay camp, of all things. She realized what she had said a second after she said it and quickly added, "I mean! I just . . . hate going to church. It makes me feel bad. Doesn't it ever . . . make *you* feel bad? Or is Jewish church nicer to gay people?"

Abigail felt her face completely flush. Here she was, standing in the middle of the woods in front of the camp bathrooms, asking Oren personal questions about a religion she hadn't any clue about. She opened her mouth to apologize, but Oren started answering her question anyway. "My family is Modern Orthodox. I was really afraid to come out to them for a while."

Abigail nodded. She didn't know anything about being Modern Orthodox, but she knew about being Catholic, and how that made her scared to come out to her parents, too.

"My parents were great about it, but our religious community kind of . . . wasn't. We switched temples, which is what our version of a church is called. It was hard, especially for my parents." Oren paused, kicking at a rock embedded in the dirt. He took a deep breath and looked back up at Abigail. "My mom told me that it's important to honor our faith, but it's impossible to fully do that unless you honor yourself and your identity first. The whole thing's a little messy, but it's all part of me, you know? Being Jewish and being gay both make me, well . . . *me*."

Oh, Abigail thought. That sounded nice.

Oren's eyes suddenly grew really wide. "Oh. I'm sorry! I didn't mean to make you cry!"

Abigail didn't even realize she *was* crying. "No! I'm sorry! It's okay. I'm okay. I'm just having a bad . . ." *Week? Year? Life?* ". . . morning."

"I hear you. At least it's Sunday. I needed a chill day," Oren said.

Abigail wiped her cheeks, pulling herself together. She would have to tell Kai later that she fell apart in front of Oren. They could laugh about it, maybe, if e wasn't still upset with her. Maybe e would even be a little mortified on her behalf since e liked Oren so much.

Wait a minute.

That was it! That was how Abigail could get Kai to be her friend again! The only reason Kai wanted to do well in the competition was to impress Oren. Same as Cassidy with Juliana. But Kai was worried that Oren couldn't like em back, because Oren was gay and Kai wasn't a boy. But maybe Oren *could* like em back! Maybe all she had to do was ask, and Oren would say, "Yes, I like boys and I like nonbinary kids, too," and she could tell Kai and e'd be happy and everything would be okay again!

"Can I ask you another question?" Abigail asked.

"About Judaism?"

"No, about, well . . ." She stopped to think for a second. "About being gay. Like, do you only like boys or . . . ?"

Oren blinked. He cringed a little as he looked her up and down.

"Oh God! Not for me! I'm not asking about me!" she practically shouted when she realized what he was thinking. He seemed visibly relieved. "I just mean, like, if another kid, like, a nonbinary kid? If a nonbinary kid had a crush on you? Is that something you would . . . like?"

Oren's eyebrows pinched together. "A nonbinary kid has a crush on me?"

"What? No! I mean! Maybe! I mean . . ."

And then Oren's eyebrows shot up. "Abigail, are you saying *Kai* has a crush on *me*?"

Oh God! Abort! The dinosaurs are out of their cage! Abort!

"I'm just asking! You know, just wondering! No specific reason!"

But Oren was smiling as if he was in on a secret that Abigail told him. But she didn't tell him, did she? She didn't mean to, anyway! This was bad. This was really, really bad. "Please don't say anything!" she pterodactyl screeched at him.

"It's totally cool, Abigail," Oren said, still smiling a little too big for Abigail's nerves. "Like, seriously. No worries. I gotta get back to my cabin. But I'll see you later, okay?"

"Okay," Abigail said, a little dazed.

She watched Oren walk away, praying to God (it *was* Sunday, after all) that she hadn't completely ruined any chance at reconciling with Kai.

16

KAI
(E/EM/EIR)

OREN WAS AWAKE WHEN KAI, JAX, AND JULIANA RETURNED from breakfast. He was in clean clothes, his hair still damp from the shower, but something seemed off. His smile seemed forced when he looked at Kai, his jaw tense.

"Hey," Jax greeted him. "Cassidy seemed a little less pissed when we saw her in the cafeteria. At least, she wasn't side-eyeing Kai and even said a few words to em. I'd say that's progress. Also, we brought you some breakfast."

Jax nodded at Kai, who was holding a paper plate filled with toast and scrambled eggs.

"Cool, thanks."

As Oren stepped closer, Kai tried to meet his gaze. Oren's eyes darted away, making Kai's heart sink. E thrust the plate toward Oren, elbows locking, and pain shot through eir shoulder. E grimaced as the plate wobbled.

Oren gently took the plate from em, then set it on his dresser.

"Are you okay?" he asked.

"Yeah, fine." The words came out sharp and fast. Kai held eir breath as Oren studied em.

Inwardly, Kai was cringing. How quickly yesterday's fun at the bonfire had turned into awkwardness. Kai could still smell a hint of smoke and burnt wood in the air, scents that had always comforted em. It reminded em of the fires eir parents would make during long Minnesota winters, of watching snow through eir family room window as it fell and blanketed their front yard, and Super Bowl parties surrounded by all eir relatives.

After last night, the same smells reminded Kai of Oren.

Oren and his perfectly curly hair. His laughter. The way his smile made his eyes crinkle at the corners.

Oren, who had also suggested multiple times last night that e have the nurse check out eir shoulder after eir fall. Kai had told him e was fine so many times, e had started to believe it emself.

Now, Kai was telling Oren e was fine again, despite the stinging pain that still coursed through eir shoulder. Oren didn't look convinced, but eventually he turned and started eating his breakfast.

"So, they posted Monday's activity schedule early," Jax said. He followed Oren over to his bed and flopped down beside him while Oren ate his breakfast. "Juliana has one she really wants to do."

Oren's gaze traveled across the room, past Kai, to Juliana.

"Blackout poetry," she said. "It's when you take a piece of text—like from a magazine or a book or newspaper—and use a Sharpie to mark out all the words except the ones you're going to use for your poem. So, on top of creating poetry, you're also making a piece of art."

"That sounds cool." Jax looked from Oren to Kai. "What do you guys—sorry, what do you *two* think?" He corrected himself on his own, earning a small nod from Juliana.

"Sure," Kai said, at the same time that Oren said, "Okay."

Kai glanced over at Oren, expecting him to smile, but Oren still wasn't looking at em. Something felt off. Had e said something wrong last night? Kai was pretty sure e hadn't. Oren had seemed fine through the end of the bonfire, and Kai hadn't noticed anything wrong after they'd returned to their cabin, either.

"Hey, I'm going to ask Leticia to take me to the admin buildings so I can call my parents," Jax said. "Anyone else want to come?"

Kai shook eir head at the same time Oren pushed up from his bed.

"Yeah, I'll give mine a call, too."

As Jax turned to Juliana, Kai felt a twinge of discomfort that had nothing to do with eir shoulder. Oren's phone worked fine in the cabin, Kai knew, since e'd called Aziza on it a couple of days ago. Was Oren trying to avoid em now? Or was e overthinking this?

"I'll call my family later." Juliana reached for her book. "I'm getting to the good part."

Jax and Oren headed out. As Juliana settled down on her bed to read, Kai carefully climbed back up the bunk bed ladder using only eir good hand. E took a deep breath to calm emself, but all it accomplished was the realization that the smoky bonfire smell was fading away—and taking all of Kai's happy feelings along with it.

Kai was no closer to figuring out what was wrong when they headed to the cafeteria to grab lunch. Oren wasn't exactly ignoring em, but he seemed to be avoiding Kai's gaze, and when Kai asked how the call with his parents went, e only got "it was fine" as a response.

Lunch bags lined the cafeteria table. Today, it was wraps instead of sandwiches. Once they'd all chosen their bags, they headed outside to the Benches and sat at a picnic table close to the edge of the woods, where overhanging tree branches offered some shade from the midday sun. Two Blue campers joined them: Ash and a kid named Priyanka (she/her).

Kai stayed quiet as e opened eir lunch bag. E winced a little trying to lift eir injured arm up to table level, then resigned emself to opening eir wrap one-handed.

Which was super awkward, since it was hard to tell where the plastic wrap started. E scowled at eir food.

Once e'd made some progress, Kai glanced up. The only reason everyone else wasn't done eating by now was because they were talking (Priyanka) and laughing (Ash) and goofing off (Jax). Also, reading (Juliana).

Except Oren, Kai realized. Oren wasn't doing any of those things, because he was staring right at Kai. Their eyes met for a pulse-fluttering second. Then Oren's gaze dropped to Kai's arm before he looked away, eyes skittering from Kai out toward the shores of Shakopee Lake.

And that's when the thought came to Kai: maybe Oren was acting all weird because he was mad at em for not going to the nurse. Kai was pretty sure Oren had seen how e was favoring one arm over the other.

Could that be it? Was this why Oren was acting distant?

It *had* to be. And that meant there was a simple way to get things back to normal. Kai hopped up fast.

The conversation died as everyone turned to look at Kai, including Oren.

"I'm gonna . . ." Kai's throat felt tight. It should've been simple to say e was going to the nurse to get eir shoulder looked at, but e couldn't form the words. ". . . go check and see if they made any more brownies."

That should work. E'd sneak off to the nurse and if everything was fine, Kai could tell Oren where e'd gone. Problem solved. And if everything *wasn't* fine . . . well, Kai didn't want to think about that just yet. One thing at a time. Nurse first.

But then Jax hopped up from the table. "I'll go with you. I freaking love those brownies."

"Me too!" Ash called.

Kai's heart sank as she scampered around the table to join them.

Short of saying never mind, sitting back down, and looking like a weirdo, Kai was out of options. E followed Jax and Ash back to the cafeteria, where one of the two big brownie pans had indeed been refilled.

"Let's grab some for the others too," Jax said, reaching for a fresh paper plate. "I know for sure Oren will want some."

As Jax and Ash stacked brownies onto their plates, Kai silently ran through excuses for not heading back to the Benches with them.

"I actually need to go to the bathroom first," Kai said.

"We'll wait," Ash said, but Kai waved her off.

"It's fine. I know we're supposed to be doing the buddy system or whatever, but it's not like I'm going to get lost."

"Right?" Jax took a bite out of one of his brownies. "I get why they make us go places together, but it's literally a two-minute walk. We'll just see you when you get back."

The two of them headed out, leaving Kai on eir own, but eir relief quickly faded. Even though e'd gotten away from Jax and Ash, Kai realized it'd been dumb to think e could make it all the way to the nurse's office without getting caught by a counselor along the way.

E dropped into a chair at the table closest to the front of the room, watching as campers wandered in, grabbed food, then headed back outside. Everyone had at least one other camper with them.

Frustrated, Kai slouched in eir seat. At the far end of the cafeteria, the adult who'd taught Kai's cabin how to make Pride pizzas appeared, holding another fresh brownie pan. Chef Kirstie headed over toward em, apron ties swinging, then set the pan down on the table.

Kai got up. Might as well grab another brownie while figuring out eir next move.

Chef Kirstie waved at em as e approached the table. "Well, hey! Did you ever pick a great time to get dessert. These just came out of the oven."

"Yeah, they look good." Kai reached for a brownie.

Chef Kirstie glanced around the empty cafeteria, then arched an eyebrow. "Did you come here alone?"

Kai shook eir head. "Me and my cabinmates were at the Benches having lunch, but I had to go to the bathroom, so . . ." E shrugged, not wanting to get anyone in trouble.

"So you need a buddy to get back to the Benches, is what you're saying?"

An idea sparked to life as Kai nodded. "Or, is it possible—I mean, could you take me to the nurse's office first, maybe?"

Chef Kirstie studied Kai. "Something wrong?"

"No. Not really," Kai said. "I just hurt my arm before camp started and it feels a little weird so I wanted the nurse to check it out."

"That I can help with. Just give me a sec." Chef Kirstie untied the apron, revealing a name tag, with *any pronouns* written on it in big block letters, just like the day they'd all made Pride pizzas. Chef Kirstie folded the apron under one arm, then waved Kai toward the exit. "Onward!"

Much to Kai's relief, Chef Kirstie guided em away from the Benches, toward the offices, which connected to the parking lot. It was the same route Oren had led Kai down.

Chef Kirstie talked as they went, asking Kai how camp was going and whether e liked the cafeteria food. Kai answered automatically, but eir thoughts skipped around, first to Oren, then to eir shoulder.

The woods were quiet except for the rustling of leaves underfoot and a few chirping birds. Kai looked up, almost wishing e could spot Mx. Nutsford as a sign that things would be all right—not that Kai believed in mythical albino squirrels or anything. Eir gaze shifted, moving to Chef Kirstie's name tag.

Something still really bothered em about it saying *any pronouns*, maybe because Kai had spent so much time online searching for the right words to describe how e felt when e was younger. And Kai had fought *so* hard to get eir family to use the pronouns that felt right for em once e'd finally found them, along with eir classmates and teachers. People at school still didn't use the right pronouns a lot of the time, and that stung. Kai had even had to quit gymnastics because e hadn't seen any way around having to wear a leotard and compete on apparatuses people had decided were only for girls.

But here was Chef Kirstie, walking beside em with a name tag that proudly announced people could choose any pronouns they wanted. Like those words didn't matter.

Kai thought about this as they made their way through the parking lot. Eir confusion continued to build until e couldn't hold it in any longer.

"What does that mean about your pronouns?" E pointed to Chef Kirstie's name tag. "If it's okay to ask."

"It sure is." Chef Kirstie grinned. "I'm genderfluid, so my pronouns change depending on how I'm feeling. And it can really fluctuate! Sometimes I feel like a woman for a long time, like a whole month maybe, and then I'll feel like a different gender. Then sometimes it changes daily, or even by the hour."

"That sounds complicated," Kai said, and Chef Kirstie laughed.

"It can be sometimes. It absolutely was when I was still figuring things out. Now, I just live from moment to moment and don't worry about it too much. I'm not the same person I was last year or even last week. I am who I am and that constantly changes. So do my pronouns."

The administrative buildings came into view as Chef Kirstie continued. "But that would've been *way* too much to put on this tiny little name tag, so I just let people choose whatever pronouns they think fit me best on any given day. Or I just tell them my pronouns if it feels important to me at that specific moment."

Kai didn't say anything to this. It made sense to em but it also didn't. E wasn't the same kid doing parkour as e was when e trained in gymnastics, because e was definitely a lot happier now than before. But that didn't mean e wanted people to use different pronouns every time something about em changed, either.

As they climbed the steps to the nurse's office, Kai decided that this must just mean that everyone was unique. If some people's pronouns never changed for their whole lives, it made sense that others' might change a lot, like Chef Kirstie's. And right now, to Kai, *xie* felt like it fit Kirstie best, so that's how Kai decided e'd think of xem, unless xie told em otherwise.

In a way, Kai realized as Chef Kirstie held the door open for em, Chef Kirstie was fighting for xir pronouns just as much as Kai. Xie just had a different approach, one that worked for xir identity.

"That makes sense," e finally said.

Chef Kirstie let Kai enter first, but xie didn't follow em. "I'm going to see if Lena's around and catch up with her while you're getting checked out. You know where her office is?" xie asked.

Kai nodded.

"Cool beans. Come get me when you're done."

Nurse Micah was at his desk when Kai entered.

He looked up. "Nice to see you again, Kai."

Kai's stomach clenched. E could think of a ton of things nicer than seeing Nurse Micah again, but e kept them to emself. Nurse Micah wasn't the real reason e felt anxious.

"Hi. Sorry to bug you."

"No bugs here." Nurse Micah gave em a quick smile. "To what do I owe the pleasure?"

"My shoulder's kind of hurting," Kai said. "Like, not all the time, but when I try to lift it too high and stuff."

"I see. Let's take a look." Nurse Micah gestured to the chair Kai had sat in a few days earlier.

Nurse Micah was gentle as he checked Kai's range of motion. Just like at lunch, the pain returned the moment Nurse Micah lifted Kai's arm more than a few inches. Kai winced, then chewed on eir lip.

Nurse Micah's brows pinched together. "Can you pinpoint exactly when you started feeling pain in your shoulder again, Kai?"

"No," Kai said, then thought better of it. "Actually, yeah. I stumbled yesterday and put my hand down to catch myself."

"Ah. That would do it."

Nurse Micah had Kai try a few other movements. Some of them hurt while others didn't. Eventually, he stepped back, and Kai held eir breath.

"The good news: it doesn't appear to be dislocated again."

Kai exhaled.

"Now, the not-as-good: you do seem to have over-extended it." Nurse Micah headed over to a cabinet and retrieved the familiar blue sling. "So just to be on the safe side, I want you to wear this again."

Kai looked down, but e didn't argue. As much as e had wanted to be free of the sling forever, eir shoulder had felt better when e was wearing it. And at least now Oren would know Kai had gone to the nurse and would hopefully stop being mad at em.

"Okay," Kai mumbled.

"I'm also going to call your parents."

"What?" Kai's head shot up. "You don't need to do that."

"I'm afraid I do." Nurse Micah gave em a half smile. "Parents need to be informed whenever a camper gets injured. In your case, I already let them know you were out of your sling last week. They'd certainly wonder why you were wearing it again when they picked you up, don't you think?"

Kai really couldn't argue with that one.

E kept quiet as Nurse Micah called home and explained the situation. Although Kai couldn't make out any words, it sounded like he was speaking to Kai's mom based on the high pitch of the voice on the other end of the phone.

Beyond that, Nurse Micah didn't give Kai any clues as to how the conversation was going. A few yeses, one no, a not-at-all, and then he passed the phone to Kai.

Kai lifted it to eir ear. "Hi?"

"Hi, sweetie," eir mom said at the same moment eir dad said, "Hey there, pal." They were on speakerphone.

"How are you feeling?" Eir mom's voice sounded wobbly and Kai swallowed down the irritation that had started to form. E'd just tripped, not fallen off a cliff.

"I'm fine." The words sounded clipped, even to Kai, so e tacked on a gentler, "Sorry the nurse had to call you."

"Nothing to apologize for." Dad took over. "We're just sorry to hear you had a fall."

Mom sniffled a little, and Kai bit eir lip. It felt like they were making a big deal out of something really small.

"This wasn't because of another kid, sweetie, was it?" Mom asked, and suddenly Kai realized what might be upsetting her. The first time Kai had injured eir shoulder, e'd been shoved. Eir parents had received a call from the school. Two of Kai's classmates got suspended, and e'd had to go to the hospital.

"No," e said. "I just tripped. It was stupid."

There was a pause on the other end, then some whispered words Kai couldn't make out.

"Do you want to come home, pal?" eir dad asked.

At first, Kai thought Dad had switched topics. E almost said yes, of course e wanted to come home early. E'd told Aziza e would be at her event next Saturday.

But something about the way eir dad had asked made Kai hesitate.

"What do you mean?" e said slowly.

"Do you want us to come get you?" Kai's mom spoke this time, her voice less wobbly now.

Kai blinked. "Like, now? *Today?*"

"Yes," Dad said. "We could be there by early evening if we leave soon."

Kai's eyes darted around the room, landing on Nurse Micah. He hadn't said anything about Kai having to go home now.

What about figuring out what was up with Oren? Or helping eir cabinmates win the competition? Things were also awkward with Abigail right now. If Kai left tonight, that might never change.

"No, I'm good."

"Are you sure, honey?" eir mom asked.

Kai nodded, even though eir parents couldn't see em. "You don't need to come get me. I want to stay. For the rest of camp, actually."

"Well, okay." Eir dad sounded surprised but also pleased. "I'm glad it sounds like you're having a good time, pal. Your mom and I were really hoping you would."

Kai suddenly realized that e *was* having a good time. Camp wasn't perfect, but e still wanted to be here.

E said good-bye to eir parents, then let Nurse Micah help em get eir shoulder into the sling.

"Promise me you'll come back if the pain starts getting worse?" Nurse Micah held the door open for em.

"Yeah, I promise," Kai said, and e meant it.

Kai met Chef Kirstie at Lena's office, and the two of them walked back toward the lake. Xie talked the entire way again, but Kai's thoughts were elsewhere, back at the Benches with Oren and the rest of eir cabinmates. Kai walked with a new sense of confidence. Because, if e was going to stay at camp all the way until the final day, e realized e had to make every moment count. E'd start by making sure things were back to normal with Oren, then check in on Abigail.

ABIGAIL

(SHE/HER/HERS)

THE ONE THING—OKAY, *ONE* OF THE *THINGS*—THAT *Jurassic Park* got wrong was that velociraptors didn't actually hunt in packs. That, to Abigail, was actually more terrifying. At least when Stacy and the girls at school were together as a group, Abigail knew how to avoid them. One giggling girl set off the rest of the girls, and if Abigail sat at a different table, she could avoid being laughed at altogether.

It was like that at camp, too. She had her pack of Yellows, and she could blend in and hide and keep to herself if she needed to.

But velociraptors hunted alone, and as she sat at the Benches with everyone else working on some craft project she really didn't care about, Abigail was worried that Kai was going to strike at any moment. E was going to be so mad that she opened her big mouth and told Oren about eir crush. That was apocalyptic, worst-friend-ever betrayal. That was worse than anything Stacy had ever done to her. Kai would be so mad, and e would definitely stalk her like prey to tell her off in front of everyone so they would know not to trust her, too.

So when Kai appeared out of nowhere and asked Bryn if he could slide down a bit so that e could sit next to Abigail, her back tensed up.

Bryn didn't move for a moment, looking over at Abigail, but when Abigail nodded (even though she kind of wanted Bryn to refuse), Bryn made room between them for Kai.

Abigail should say sorry to Kai before e could say anything. She should beat em to it, make sure that e knew, at least, that she didn't mean to be a bad friend, that she was just doomed to always betray people by having crushes on their moms or accidentally telling their crushes they liked them.

Kai spoke first, though, and all e said was, "Can we do one of these together? I'm not that good at poetry."

"Oh," Abigail said, blinking at em. "Yeah, sure." She caught sight of eir sling. "Um. Are you okay?" she asked.

"I'm okay," Kai said.

Abigail decided to believe em.

They sat side by side, quietly working on the blackout poetry together. They didn't talk about much. Kai would point out a piece e thought would make a good word choice for their project, and e would smile at Abigail when she made a good contribution, too. Abigail, when Kai was focused on their work, glanced across to where Oren was sitting. Oren caught her eye and gave her a brief wave. Maybe he didn't say anything after all. Maybe he wouldn't. Maybe Abigail would be okay.

"'We ride along the gray roof singing softly,'" Kai read as e continued working, their poem slowly revealing itself. "Told you I was bad at this. At least it's more fun to be doing this together."

Abigail sighed in relief. "Yeah. It's much better doing this together."

Abigail shook the weirdness away. Her mom sometimes said that maybe things weren't as awkward at school as Abigail made them out to be. Maybe she just needed to get out of her shell and break the ice herself, instead of waiting for Stacy and her friends to do it. Maybe they thought that she was icing *them* out.

Her mom didn't know about her crush on Stacy's mom, of course—so her mom didn't know much of anything—but maybe she wasn't wrong, exactly, either.

Kai was fine. Crisis averted. No harm, no foul. Abigail just needed to keep out of her shell and smile big and be extra friendly and not let the weirdness back in.

It worked, too. They all laughed at one another's bad poetry—except for Juliana's, which was actually really pretty—and made plans to do trivia in the main hall after dinner with all the Crocheter cabins. Abigail *loved* trivia. She was good at it, so she wouldn't have to worry about letting her cabin down.

That night, the counselors moved the tables around so that every cabin had its own section, far enough away from each other so they wouldn't overhear their conversations.

"Guess we can't exactly keep up an alliance for this," Cassidy said. She didn't sound too beat up about it.

"MJ said the winner gets *three* points, and the runner-up gets an extra point. So if we win, if we beat Red and Purple at this, we're officially ahead," Stick pointed out. "Like, we'd be in first place out of all the cabins. *Finally.*"

It was true. For the poetry, each camper had earned exactly one participation point, so nothing had changed in the rankings. But with the trivia game, only one cabin would really win.

"But," Abigail said, trying to be positive and brave, "we're all in an alliance, right? So, it's okay if Purple does well, too?"

Cassidy paused to think about it. "Well, I guess. But one of us needs to win. It may as well be us, right?" She smiled. "Are you all good at trivia?"

"Depends on the topics," Bryn said.

"Not really, no," Stick added.

Cassidy looked a little dejected as she turned to Abigail.

"I'm actually really, really good."

"Oh, thank God," Cassidy said, as the sound system in the main hall squawked to life.

Leticia and the Green cabin's counselor rolled in a big dry-erase board. Leticia used a black marker to separate the board into categories. On the far end of the board, the Green counselor used color markers to write each cabin's name so that they could keep score. The categories were: *movies, music, science & math, geography,* and *famous slogans.*

Abigail wasn't so great at geography—she barely knew where she was right this second in Minnesota, let alone the entire US map—but the rest she could definitely do.

Sol passed each table a clicker that connected to the tablet that MJ had in his hands. They explained that MJ would ask a question and if anyone on the team knew the answer they should click the button as fast as possible. The table that clicked the fastest would get to try to answer the question first. If they got the answer wrong, they would lose a point, and someone else would get a chance to answer instead. MJ would pick the first category, and then whoever got each question right would get to choose the category that came after it.

"Are all you chickens ready?" MJ asked. He wore a headset with a microphone so that everyone could hear his questions loud and clear.

Everyone cheered.

"Then let's begin!" MJ cleared his throat dramatically. "And the category is . . . music!"

The room grew really quiet. Abigail's cabinmates all inched closer to the clicker placed at the center of their table.

"Who was the very first winner of *American Idol*?"

Clamor and chaos erupted as everyone dove for their clickers. Stick, with their long arms, snagged theirs and clicked it as fast as they could. All the tables looked up at MJ as his tablet dinged.

"Red team, you're up first! Do you have the answer?"

Hannah from the Red cabin said, timidly, "Kelly Clarkson?"

"*Ding, ding, ding!* Correct! Leticia, give the Red team their point!"

Cassidy and Stick both groaned as Leticia drew a big tally mark in the Red team's column.

"It's just one," Abigail said, trying to keep everyone's spirits up. "We can do this."

And they could. As the questions went on, all the cabins seemed to be doing pretty well. Abigail knew the answer to the second question (she knew that it was a clock that the crocodile swallowed in *Peter Pan*), but then the Blue cabin got two easy movie questions right in a row (the nickname for the Academy Awards was *the Oscars*, and Rapunzel's chameleon's name was Pascal in the movie *Tangled*). The Orange cabin got a math question right that Abigail didn't even pretend to understand, let alone know the answer to, and Kai knew the names of the five Great Lakes.

Abigail gave em a big thumbs-up as Oren wrapped an arm carefully around Kai's shoulders in celebration, and Kai looked happier than Abigail had ever seen em.

Actually, Kai was really, really good at trivia, too, Abigail realized as the game went on. E was particularly good at geography and movies, and e answered for the Purples almost every time their buzzer dinged in first.

As the game went on, it was clear that the competition, as it had been all along, was between Red, Purple, and Yellow—until the Purple and Yellow cabins, thanks to Abigail and Kai, slowly but surely helped their teams pull ahead. The rest of the cabins—the Greens, the Blues, the Oranges—started cheering loudly any time either of them got a question right.

Abigail felt like she was running a race, adrenaline making her fingers move faster every time she reached for her team's clicker. Kai's sweaty hair stuck up in odd directions.

It was exhilarating to be doing so well. To have an entire room of people cheer every time she got something right.

"What plant was actress Uma Thurman named after in the film *Batman and Robin*?"

"Ivy!" Abigail called out loudly when MJ confirmed her clicker was first. *And Uma looked gorgeous playing her.* Abigail kept that thought to herself.

"Movie category again, please!"

"Who directed the movie *Schindler's List*?"

Abigail clicked as fast as she could, knowing the answer—because he also directed *Jurassic Park*—but MJ said, "Purple, you're it!"

"Steven Spielberg!" Kai shouted.

"Correct!" MJ said, and Kai's cabinmates went wild.

"Movie!" Kai said.

"Okay, okay," MJ said, laughing. Everyone was on the edge of their seats. "Seeing as Leticia keeps aggressively pointing at the clock on her phone and staring at me, I'm going to assume we're running out of time. So how about we end all this excitement on a tiebreaker. One more question to rule them all!"

A few campers went *oooooh!* Abigail gripped the edge of the table tightly, her knuckles turning white. She was doing well and having fun, but she wasn't used to being so heavily in the spotlight. Especially when MJ said, "Purple and Yellow cabins, choose a representative from your team, and have that person come stand up here with me!"

Abigail's entire cabin turned to look at her. "Bring it all home, Abigail!" Cassidy said, grinning ear to ear.

The Purple cabin, of course, chose Kai.

Abigail and Kai stood on either side of MJ, their team's clickers in their hands. Kai smiled at her, but eir jaw was set and eir shoulders squared.

"You've got this, Kai!" Oren called, and Kai turned to look at him, eir smile growing even wider.

"May the best cabin win," MJ said, and then winked at Abigail. "No pressure, my chickadee, even though we both know Yellow cabin is the best."

"Oh, heck no," Leticia called. "You've got this, Kai! Help me show MJ who's boss!"

Kai widened eir feet a bit, getting into a stance as if e were about to play a sport, not answer a trivia question. Abigail glanced around the room. All around them, the other campers started to pound their fists on the tables. At her own table, Stick and Bryn were excitedly watching her—Stick was standing up bouncing on their feet. Cassidy's hands were in tight fists at her side.

If Abigail got this right, they would win. If they won, they would officially be in the lead.

They could win the whole competition, and her cabin would be thrilled—especially Cassidy.

She glanced over at the Purple table. They were all cheering for Kai, who was standing in front of Abigail, looking ready to fight as e held out a hand. "May the best kid win?" e said.

Abigail shook eir hand.

And she realized that as much as she wanted to win—for her cabin, for Cassidy—she owed Kai.

Especially when she had made so many mistakes this week, and Kai was still treating her like a friend.

Her pact was with *Kai*.

"And the question is . . . On what fictional island is *Jurassic Park* located?"

The room went silent.

Isla Nublar, Abigail thought.

Everyone looked at Abigail.

Everyone *knew* Abigail would know the answer.

Abigail *did* know the answer.

But she didn't click her clicker. A second later, Kai clicked eirs.

MJ blinked as his tablet dinged. "Oh. Uh, Kai. It's all you, fast fingers! Do you know the answer?"

"Islan . . . *ISLA*," Kai shouted, correcting emself before e got it wrong, and then e paused to think.

Abigail said nothing. She wouldn't give anything away. But she knew she had mentioned it to em just last week. *Minnesota might as well be Isla Nublar, it's so foreign to me.*

It took Kai a second. "Nublar?" E remembered it.

"That is correct!" MJ shouted into his microphone, way louder than he needed to. "The Purple cabin wins!"

Everyone cheered loudly, though there were some groans, and Leticia and the rest of the Purple cabin were all jumping up and down. They ran over to Kai, barreling into em, and e had to cradle eir shoulder to make sure no one bumped into it in all the excitement.

Abigail, standing alone, smiled at the commotion. She'd made the right choice.

Right?

She glanced over at her table.

Cassidy was looking right at her, eyes narrowed, like she knew exactly what Abigail had done.

END
OF DAY
7

CROCHETERS COMPETITION
STANDINGS!

PURPLE: 44

RED: 43

YELLOW: 43

BLUE: 41

ORANGE: 41

GREEN: 40

18

KAI
(E/EM/EIR)

A FEW DAYS AGO, IT HAD SEEMED IMPOSSIBLE TO BREAK their tie with the Yellow cabin, let alone get ahead of Red.

But now Purple was in the lead. All because of Kai.

And possibly also Abigail.

Kai couldn't be sure if Abigail had thrown the final question or if e'd just been super quick to hit the buzzer. Only a day later, that memory had become fuzzy. What Kai remembered best was eir cabinmates' reactions: the sound of Jax's excited shout when MJ had declared the Purple cabin the winners, the look of Juliana's wide smile as she hopped up out of her seat, her red-to-pink ombre skirt swaying as she moved.

The feel of Oren's arms around em when e returned to eir table. The pressure of Oren's hug and the pleasant warmth it caused in Kai's stomach.

Kai didn't exactly know if Abigail had been trying to help em, at least not with one hundred percent certainty. But the more e thought about it, and the longer e savored the memories formed in that moment of victory, the more Kai felt that Abigail had probably thrown the trivia game. It had been part of their pact to help Kai and the Purple cabin win, after all. Better still, things felt balanced between the two of them again.

Not so much for the rest of eir cabinmates and the Yellow cabin, though. Cassidy seemed especially annoyed. She definitely shot Kai a few side-eyes that morning.

That was fine, as far as Kai was concerned, because Oren stepped in to help instead. Everything felt like it was back to normal between Kai and Oren now. Almost. There were still moments when Oren looked away from Kai when their eyes met, but there was usually a good reason for it.

Like at breakfast when Oren looked away because Stick was practically vibrating across the table. Their legs bounced along with the rest of their body as Stick talked about the Crocheters' dance lesson this morning.

Since their legs were just as long as the rest of them, Stick's knees kept bumping the underside of the table. Oren's juice sloshed in its cup, and Kai's red pepper flakes danced on eir plate.

Kai might've felt jealous, except it wasn't just Oren looking at Stick; almost every camper at their table was focused on them.

"Sorry, sorry!" Stick went still for half a second before they started bouncing again. "I just really love this class. Finn is an amazing dancer, plus they're nonbinary, like me. They used to be a famous ballroom dancer and they won lots of events with their partner."

"How did that work?" Kai couldn't help asking. "Like, doesn't ballroom usually require a man dancer and a woman dancer?"

"Oh, yeah, absolutely. It's very traditional." Stick nodded. "I think Finn came out after they were done competing."

Kai didn't respond, thoughts turning to gymnastics. There had been no place for em in that sport either, even though e'd loved it. There was a boys' division and a girls' division and apparatuses that corresponded to each of them. Beam for girls, rings for boys, and nothing for kids like Kai. Parkour, at least, didn't have apparatuses based on gender. The important part was just performing impressive tricks.

"But it's not like that here, promise," Stick chattered on. "You get to dance with a partner and we're obviously not all boys and girls. It's great. You'll see!"

"It was actually really fun last year," Jax said. "And I say that as someone who completely sucks at dancing."

Oren nudged Kai's good shoulder. "Literally two left feet, this guy."

"That is highly improbable," Juliana said.

"Yeah, you got me there." Oren's comment was met with laughter. Even Cassidy cracked a small smile.

The conversation moved on, but Kai tuned it out. Eir shoulder was still tingling from where Oren had nudged em. Kai's thoughts were stuck on one specific thing Stick had said.

Partners.

Kai could ask Oren to dance with em, if e didn't chicken out.

For the rest of breakfast, Kai worked out how e'd ask Oren to be eir partner. Just like training for a parkour event, Kai figured the more times e practiced the question silently to emself, the more comfortable e'd feel about actually asking it.

Kai left the cafeteria with the rest of the Crocheters and their counselors, heading to the designated dance area: the basketball court. Kai could see a hint of sunlight shimmering off the lake's surface in the distance.

Jax turned to Kai and Oren. "This is where we did roller derby last week."

As other campers chattered about unfamiliar things like jammers, blockers, and Pushy Much, Kai pulled out eir phone. Three bars of service: the most e'd seen since arriving at camp. It figured the one time e wasn't eager to message Aziza would be when e had the best chance of eir texts going through. E took a breath, then sent a string of texts.

> **Kai:**
> Hey, this is too long to explain in a text
>
> but I won't be home in time for your event this weekend
>
> I'll make it up to you tho, I'm really sorry!

"Hey, everyone! Welcome to Camp QUILTBAG's annual dance class!"

Kai looked up from eir phone. It took em a beat to locate the counselor sporting a name tag that said, *Finn: they/them.* Finn was short for an adult, about as tall as Kai, who was average height for a soon-to-be eighth grader. Finn's hair was completely shaved but they still had plenty of hair on their face. Their beard was as thick as Nurse Micah's, and a little longer.

"I'm Finn, and as some of you might already know, I used to compete in ballroom dance, which is very gendered. Back then, I looked a little different. My hair was longer in some places and nonexistent in others." They tapped their head, then their beard, making some campers giggle. "But at its simplest form, dance is movement, a way to express your feelings without saying a word. Dance has no gender."

Kai stole a glance at Oren. E imagined taking his hand and the breathless feeling of spinning around together in front of all the other campers.

"That said, for hundreds of years, society has limited who can dance," Finn continued. "For example, in eighteenth-century France, ballet was initially intended only for noblemen, by decree of the king. By the nineteenth century, it was mostly performed by girls and women because it became viewed as embarrassing for men to dance. Now, of course, you see men and women onstage. The same goes for ballroom dancing, which has specific roles and steps based on whether you're a woman or a man."

This, Kai understood well. The same was true for gymnastics.

"But what if you're neither?" Finn tilted their head. "Unfortunately, there's no easy answer. The dance world still has a lot of work to do to create a welcoming and inclusive place for *all* genders." They smiled. "Here at Camp QUILTBAG, we make our own rules. Instead of men's and ladies' steps and holds, we'll call them leads and follows. And you can choose which ones you want to do with your partner no matter your gender."

Finn signaled to Leticia, who headed their way holding an upturned baseball cap by its rim.

"So now, the moment you've all been waiting for." Finn fluttered their fingers, then lowered one hand into the hat. "Partner selections! Randomly picked by yours truly, of course."

Wait, what?

Kai stared as Finn pulled out a folded slip of paper, then called the name of an Orange camper. They repeated the process, matching that camper with a kid from the Green cabin. By the time they'd gone through all the names, Kai was partnered with Siobhan, Juliana with Ash, Abigail with a tall camper with short dark hair from the Red cabin, and . . .

Oren was with Jax.

As Siobhan stepped toward em, jealousy sparked in Kai's chest. E vaguely heard Finn appoint Stick as their assistant, then introduce various ballroom dance hold positions. But e was mostly focused on Oren and Jax. They came together, holding one set of hands while Jax placed his other on Oren's shoulder. By the time Oren slipped his hand around Jax's waist, Kai couldn't hold back eir frown.

"Did you want to try waltz position first, too?"

Kai jerked eir head toward Siobhan.

"Sorry, what?"

Siobhan lifted both hands, copying Oren's hold with Jax. "What they're doing. I can be the lead if you can't lift your arm that high."

A prickle of irritation ran up Kai's spine as Siobhan studied eir sling.

"Yeah. Sure."

Except Kai hadn't been paying super close attention when Finn had gone over the holds. E didn't exactly know what e was supposed to do but e reached out anyway, closing one hand over Siobhan's and letting eir bad arm rest behind Siobhan's shoulder blade. That was as low as e could make it go while it was still in the sling.

Laughter nearby. Kai couldn't help twisting a little to see what Jax and Oren were doing.

"That's more of an offset waltz hold, almost a foxtrot." Stick appeared beside Kai and Siobhan. "If you're going for a waltz, make sure you're facing each other. And chins up!"

Stick smiled encouragingly, totally in their element. Kai definitely wasn't. Stick had made it look so easy at the bonfire when they were dancing with Juliana, but

Kai's arms were already aching by the time e and Siobhan switched holds, trying out one called the Kilian.

Things only got more awkward when Finn showed them some dance steps and turned on the music. Kai constantly had to look down to avoid stepping on Siobhan's feet. E'd always thought e was pretty good at athletic stuff, but now Kai realized e'd only ever had to rely on eir own abilities. Moving this close to another person was a whole different type of skill.

More laughter.

Jax and Oren didn't seem to be struggling, but they didn't seem to be taking the class all that seriously, either. They made up their own steps, bumping hips, then shoulders, all grins.

Kai managed to keep eir expression neutral this time as Finn demonstrated a foxtrot hold with Stick. E tried the position for Siobhan's sake, but eir heart wasn't in it.

"All right, everyone. Great effort!" Finn called after what felt like an eternity. "I hope you had a good time learning some of the foundational elements of ballroom dance. Feel free to make use of this knowledge at Saturday's gala—or just freestyle it if you want. I won't be offended."

Finn tapped their phone and the music shifted from a waltz to a rap song. "I'll leave you with a little parting music as you head back to the cafeteria for lunch."

Kids from the other cabins headed toward the cafeteria in groups, ignoring the music. Stick, on the other hand, immediately found the beat and began dancing toward the lunchroom. A few other campers joined them, including Abigail, much to Kai's surprise. She was still near her partner and both were dancing a bit awkwardly, but Abigail's smile seemed genuine. As Siobhan jogged off to catch up with Ash and the other Blue campers, Kai trailed behind, near the back of the group.

"Hey, Kai?"

Kai twisted around and found emself face to face with Oren.

"Can we talk for a sec?" Oren asked. "Before we head back?"

"Sure."

They slowed, letting the group get farther ahead of them.

"So." Oren cleared his throat a little. "I heard that you might—I mean." He shoved his hands into his shorts pockets and bit his lip, and Kai's face got the good kind of warm just watching Oren search for the right words.

"It's okay," Kai said in the same reassuring tone e used when Abigail was worrying about something. "What's up?"

This approach seemed to help Oren, too. His shoulders relaxed as he looked over at Kai.

"Do you like me?"

Kai's heart stuttered, but e recovered quickly. "Of course I like you. I like most of the campers here. Everyone's pretty cool."

E picked at a loose thread on eir sling and then increased eir pace. It was mostly Yellow and Purple campers in front of them, plus the one kid from Red who'd been matched with Abigail. The other Crocheters were farther ahead. Some had already disappeared inside the main cabin.

"Not like that." Oren's eyebrows pinched toward the bridge of his nose. "I meant, do you *like* like me?"

Kai froze.

When e didn't respond, Oren took a half step closer. "Like, do you have a crush or think I'm cute, or . . . ?"

His tone was soft. To Kai, it sounded like pity.

Poor Kai, getting a crush on someone who couldn't possibly like em back. So pathetic.

The words echoed in eir head, in the same taunting tones two of eir classmates had used before shoving em up against a locker a few months ago.

"I . . ." Suddenly, it was Kai who couldn't look Oren in the eyes. Eir pulse pounded against the sides of eir head. "No."

The word sounded just as small as Kai felt. Pathetic.

Oren blinked, and Kai couldn't tell if his expression was one of disappointment or relief. Kai's gaze darted around the path. Eir cabinmates and the Yellow campers weren't too far ahead of them. Kai replayed what Oren had just asked, dissecting every word as e watched Abigail chat with the Red camper, still smiling.

Something clicked into place.

There was only one person Kai had told about eir crush. Suddenly, Abigail's smile didn't seem happy and carefree; it reminded Kai of eir classmates' expressions. The ones who had taunted em last year. Kai's pulse pounded painfully against eir temples as e turned back to Oren.

"Who told you that?"

"What? No one!"

"That's not what you said." Kai's tone was sharp. "You said 'I heard,' which means someone said it to you."

Oren shook his head, but his gaze moved in Abigail's direction.

"Figures." Kai's jaw clenched around the word.

"It wasn't her fault," Oren said quickly. "She was just trying to help."

Kai's face burned. Eir skin itched. Abigail had told Oren something she'd promised to keep secret. She was no better than eir old friends who'd said they supported em, then laughed at Kai behind eir back. Who hadn't done anything when those boys started pushing em.

"It doesn't matter, because she's wrong." E tugged at eir sling until the loose string ripped off. "I don't like you, or this stupid camp. My parents made me come here. Did you know that?"

E looked past Oren, toward the other campers. And there was Abigail, chattering and smiling and enjoying camp, and here was Kai feeling completely vulnerable and raw in front of Oren.

Oren shook his head, bewildered. "No, I—"

Kai didn't wait for him to finish. E turned and sped off.

"Kai, wait!" Oren called. "Where are you—"

But Kai had stopped listening.

Soon, Abigail spotted em. The smile lingered on her face, but then it wavered. Her dance partner from Red took a step back as though sensing trouble.

A rational Kai would've asked to talk to Abigail privately, like Oren had just done. Right now though, all Kai could think about was how deeply she had betrayed em.

"Did you tell Oren I liked him?"

That was all it took for the Red camper to beat a hasty retreat. In front of them, Cassidy, Bryn, and Stick stopped and looked back. Farther ahead, Jax and Juliana also turned around.

"Not—no . . ." Abigail's cheeks flushed. She glanced past Kai, probably to Oren. "K-kind of."

The words were slow and reluctant, like they'd been dragged out of her throat.

"But I didn't mean to." She looked back at Kai pleadingly. "It just came out."

Came out. That sounded a whole lot to Kai like *coming out*: something so many people said you should do. *Be your authentic self. Be loud and proud. Never back down.* And if people weren't supportive? *It gets better.* That's what Kai had read on so many online message boards. It was why e had decided to tell everyone about eir new name and pronouns in the first place. People made coming out seem like such a simple thing.

But what about the time after coming out, before it got better?

Like at school, where kids said they were cool with everything but didn't utter a word when those two classmates had bullied em. Or at home, where eir parents were trying to be supportive but they'd sent Kai to this camp instead of letting em go to parkour practice and be around kids who were actually eir friends.

And now, here at camp, where Kai had let eir guard down. E'd trusted someone and it had epically blown up in eir face.

"I should've known better," Kai muttered.

Their cabinmates stared at the two of them.

"I'm sorry," Abigail whispered.

She opened her mouth again but couldn't seem to find any words.

Kai had plenty.

"I never should've agreed to help you. I never should've trusted you to help my cabin win the competition, either. You got those extra points for your own cabin last week, and then you never helped me like you promised. You didn't even throw me that final trivia question, did you? I bet you just got nervous."

Kai realized what e'd done as soon as the words were out of eir mouth, but it was too late. Abigail's face went from red to pale as all the color drained from her face.

"You . . . and Kai?" Stick inched closer, looking between the two of them. "You mean you had your own alliance?"

Bryn's expression crumbled, a mix of confusion and hurt. "You were trying to let the Purple cabin win this whole time?"

"I knew it," Cassidy said, but she didn't look all that triumphant. She looked over at Stick and Bryn. "I figured there had to be a reason Abigail blew that trivia question."

"I don't . . . we just . . ." Abigail looked to Kai, then at the ground. She blinked fast, like she was trying to hold back tears.

Emotions flipped and twisted inside Kai, more complicated than any parkour pass e'd ever tried. E was still mad at Abigail for what she'd done, but e also wanted to hug her. Kai didn't know how to untangle one feeling from the other. But Oren was standing next to em now, giving em a look that made Kai want to disappear. Juliana and Jax were wide-eyed and watching too.

"But why?" Bryn's voice was quiet, gentle.

It seemed to set something off inside Abigail.

"Because I'm the WORST." The words burst out of her. "I needed Kai to help me learn how to be confident. I needed to make friends, and e really wanted to win the competition. So we made a pact to help each other."

Abigail's voice rose, her words racing until it was hard to keep up with what she was saying.

"I just wanted everything to be perfect, but it only took twenty-three minutes once I got here—literally just *twenty-three* minutes—for me to get a crush on Lena. Of all people." She tugged on her ponytail. "It was like Stacy's mom all over again. Or Laura Dern. Maybe it's more like *Jurassic Park*, but this wasn't supposed to happen. It *wasn't*."

Everyone stared. It was probably the most anyone had heard Abigail say at one time, Kai realized, except for em. Because the two of them were friends. Because they were supposed to support each other.

Kai thought that maybe e should say something—anything, honestly—to move the conversation away from Abigail's confession.

Before e could think of anything, a throat cleared behind them.

"My dear campers. You're on the verge of missing lunch."

Kai knew that voice. E recognized the mortification forming on Abigail's face, too.

It was Lena. And she had heard everything.

19

ABIGAIL

(SHE/HER/HERS)

EVERYTHING WAS TERRIBLE.

Everything.

Abigail had ruined her friendship with Kai. She hurt em just like Stacy and the girls at school had hurt *her*. E had trusted her with eir secret, and she'd opened her big mouth. Just like Stacy and the girls at school did to Abigail. They'd made Abigail admit her crush on Stacy's mom because she blushed and rambled in front of Mrs. Mackenzie, and everyone noticed. And then they'd gone and told the whole school because they thought it was funny.

It wasn't funny. Abigail had barely even come out to

herself yet, let alone anyone else. And suddenly everyone at school knew her most private secret.

Just like now Oren knew Kai's.

Abigail had been an awful friend.

Stacy had been an awful friend, too.

Stacy *was* an awful friend. Abigail had told Oren by accident! Abigail didn't mean to blab about Kai's crush. She was trying to help even if she messed it all up, but Stacy didn't do anything by accident!

Stacy never once tried to make anything better.

And Abigail didn't know *how* to make anything better.

Especially when it wasn't just Kai who she'd been a bad friend to. That night, all Abigail wanted to do was roll over in her bunk and disappear. Or at the very least sleep. Instead, her chest hurt from trying not to cry, or at least to cry as quietly as possible, especially as Cassidy said what everyone was probably thinking.

"You knew that *Jurassic Park* answer yesterday, didn't you?"

and

"You told me I didn't have to worry about Kai and Oren being sneaky about points. But it was you and Kai who were the ones being sneaky."

and

"You knew how important this was to me. Why was

Kai more important to you? I thought we were friends, Abigail."

Stick and Bryn hadn't said much of anything. While Cassidy dissected the entire week and a half of camp late into the night, Abigail had caught Bryn's eyes from his bottom bunk. He didn't look mad—but he kind of looked like Abigail's homeroom teacher when she'd asked what was going on when their class had spent all of homeroom laughing at Abigail, and Stacy had said, quite frankly, "We all just found out that Abigail is gay." Her teacher had looked disappointed, maybe, that the quiet student in the back of the classroom could cause such chaos.

(*But*, a voice in the back of Abigail's head was saying, *I didn't cause the chaos. Stacy did.*)

Bryn was the only one who'd talked to Abigail that afternoon after Kai yelled at her. The walk to lunch had felt like an execution walk. She had a mental image of Jesus walking with and through everyone to his crucifixion, and then felt really bad about that, because she sure as heck wasn't Jesus.

More like Judas, really.

She wanted to disappear into the Minnesota woods and become a myth herself, like Mx. Nutsford.

Now would be a great time to see Mx. Nutsford. Abigail sure needed that ridiculous squirrel.

But she sure as heck wasn't *worthy*.

Bryn, though, in the middle of Abigail's internal spiral, had stood close, like always. He quietly—so quietly that Abigail didn't think anyone else could hear him—said, "I don't like that you and Kai lied to us, but I'm sorry you felt so bad about having a crush on Lena. If you wanted to talk about that, or, like, whatever happened with your friend's mom? You could've talked to me about it. I just hope you know that."

Abigail hadn't responded. The pterodactyls were causing mayhem in her stomach.

Bryn was the first person in the history of the world besides Kai who hadn't made her feel bad for her crushes. He had a right to be mad at Abigail for a lot of things, but still, he hadn't made fun of her.

Stacy had. Stacy always had. And Stacy refused to stand too close to Abigail ever since they all found out Abigail was gay. She squealed anytime Abigail accidentally touched her. She narrowed her eyes and said, "I don't like you like that, Abigail!"

It was nice that Bryn always stood close to her. It was nice that he was still standing close, now.

You could've talked to me about it, Bryn had said, though. Past tense. Abigail was losing friends she didn't even fully realize she'd had until it was too late.

The pterodactyls got worse as she thought about

how badly she'd messed everything up. Her friends at home weren't her friends. They never were her friends.

She had real friends here, and she ruined it.

❧

The next morning, Abigail slowly followed everyone else to the main cabin for breakfast, the crowd of Yellows and Purples merging in front of her as she lagged behind, alone. Kai walked faster than everyone else, probably to keep as far away from her as possible. Oren slowed down a bit, not quite walking with Abigail, but not leaving her so far behind, either.

He turned around and whispered, "I didn't mean to tell Kai on you. I'm sorry."

Abigail wanted to tell him it wasn't his fault, and that it was okay, and that it was really nice that he was talking to her at all, but she was afraid if she opened her mouth she would just start crying.

When they got to the main cabin, there was no competition announcement sign on the bulletin board.

"Didn't they tally up the points yet?" Jax asked. "How are we supposed to know who's winning?"

"You guys probably are," Cassidy mumbled.

Juliana reached to grab for her hand. "It's just a silly competition," she said.

Abigail thought that was funny. If only Juliana knew how much both Cassidy and Kai wanted to win for her sake.

"Actually," Leticia said, coming up from behind the group with MJ, "after breakfast, my mom wants everyone to stay seated at their tables. She has an announcement to make before we plan the rest of our day."

Oh my God, Abigail thought, her stomach dropping. Lena wasn't going to announce to the entire camp that Abigail had a crush on her, was she?

Because that was one of the absolute worst things Abigail could think of. At least Stacy's mom, as far as Abigail knew, never *ever* learned about Abigail's crush. Stacy's mom hadn't found out why Abigail always offered to help with the dishes after dinner. She hadn't noticed how Abigail blushed every time she smiled at her. She hadn't been in the bedroom that night when Abigail admitted to everyone about her crush in the first place.

Lena *was* there yesterday.

Lena had heard *everything*.

Would she tell Abigail's parents? Did she now think that Abigail was a little freak? Would she ever smile at Abigail again, or place a hand on Abigail's shoulder?

Probably not, right? Because Lena would know that Abigail had a crush on her and wouldn't want to touch her at all, like Stacy and the girls at school didn't want to touch her.

As if they could catch lesbian cooties or something.

Which—that was awful of them, right? More and more Abigail was realizing that.

Why did Abigail even bother to lie to the girls back home about coming to camp in the first place? They would have found something to make fun of her about no matter how she spent her summer. They always did.

Abigail didn't eat breakfast. She pushed her eggs around on her plate. Leticia noticed, and tilted her head (and looked so much like her mom it *hurt*), saying, "Not hungry, hon?"

Abigail shook her head before tentatively saying, "Leticia?"

"Yeah?"

"I'm sorry," Abigail said. Because that's what she did after Stacy found out about her crush on her mom— Abigail apologized.

Leticia sighed. "Abigail—"

She didn't get to finish whatever she was going to say, which Abigail was actually grateful for, because she didn't know that she wanted to hear it anyway. The speaker system in the main cabin started squealing as Sol and MJ helped plug in the microphone. Lena was making her way up to the podium.

Oh no, Abigail thought. She wanted to sink into the floor, melt into it like quicksand and disappear forever.

"Good morning, everyone," Lena began, and the room took a bit to go from loud chatter to quiet murmurs to finally quiet. Abigail could even hear the bigger bugs—the cicadas and mosquitos—which made her think of Kai, which made her push her eggs even farther away from her.

"It has come to my attention"—*No no no please do not announce my crush on a loudspeaker in front of everyone!*—"that the competition we had hoped would bring the camp together this year, that would add some excitement and encourage teamwork and sportsmanship as we all worked toward a fun and important end goal of renaming our camp, has backfired."

Oh, Abigail thought. That wasn't what she was expecting.

"What do you think she's going to do?" Cassidy whispered.

"I dunno. Maybe set more ground rules so no one can cheat?" Jax said, his shoulders inching toward his ears before he turned to face Kai. "I didn't mean—I mean, sorry."

"The last thing I want is to give anyone here a reason to grow further apart from one another. This camp is supposed to be a safe place for you all to come together and be a community." Lena looked out around the room, and Abigail slinked back in her seat, not wanting Lena to see her. "I don't want to foster animosity or turn cabin against cabin. So, from this point on, the competition is over."

That got everyone loud again.

"Wait, what?"

"What does that mean?"

"Does that mean the points stay as is?"

"Does that mean the Purple cabin is the winner?"

"Do they still get to choose the camp name?"

Lena waited a beat before getting everyone's attention again. "We'll still be posting activities for you to do. But the point is just to have *fun*. The point is to be together and accept and support one another as you finish up your camp experience."

A few seats down, Juliana stood up in her chair.

"Juliana! Get down!" Leticia scolded.

Juliana did not get down. She raised her hand as high as she possibly could so that Lena could see her.

"Juliana, you may ask your question, but please do it from the safety of the floor instead of your chair," Lena said.

"What about the camp name?" Juliana asked. "Are we still changing it? Because that's still super important, Lena, way more important than a competition, and would bring us all more together as a community, like you said, and—"

"I promise you, Juliana, I would never back out on something like that," Lena interrupted Juliana's speech. She pointed along the wall, where the breakfast had been laid out moments ago. "You'll see we put up a new dry-erase board, with brand-new markers lined up along it. First, a caution: If anyone writes anything inappropriate, you'll face consequences; don't ruin this for everyone. We want everyone to make suggestions for the camp name. If you have an idea, write it on the board. If you like someone's suggestion, add a tally next to it so we can see. At the end of camp, I'll go through all the names and tallies and hopefully we'll have a name that everyone will be happy with."

Juliana sat back down, and everyone else at Abigail's table seemed to deflate. "That sucks," Jax said. "You know Lena and everyone else in charge will just pick whatever name they want now."

"We won't get a say at all," Cassidy added.

"Maybe we will," Bryn said. "Maybe we can come up with a suggestion we all like."

As everyone in the cafeteria got loud again and Lena stepped away from the microphone, Abigail tried to make herself disappear. No one at her table seemed very happy about the competition ending.

No one at the entire camp probably was.

And that was all Abigail's fault, too.

She glanced down to the other end of the table, accidentally catching Kai's eyes.

E looked as upset as she was.

KAI

(E/EM/EIR)

KAI'S PHONE VIBRATED WITH A SERIES OF TEXTS DURING the walk between the Benches and eir cabin. It was Friday afternoon, three whole days since Kai had yelled at Abigail and two days after Lena announced she was canceling the competition. No more earning points or competing against other cabins. They did arts and crafts and outdoors activities on Wednesday and Thursday, and it was all fine. Typical camp stuff.

Everything sucked.

Kai waited until the rest of eir cabinmates entered, then carefully climbed into eir bunk bed, one-handed. Across the room, Oren was on his bed looking at his phone and Jax had a pillow over his head on the bunk above him. Kai couldn't see Juliana directly below em but figured she was reading, like usual. Pulling out eir phone, e braced emself for Aziza's response to em deciding to stay at camp and miss her event.

Queen Aziza:
Noooooo how could u, I'm devastated

Jk jk, it's cool, we'll hang when you get back

Kai waited for relief to wash over em, but eir body remained tense. This could've been eir last day at camp if e hadn't told eir parents e wanted to stay through to the end. Now the Purple and Yellow campers were barely talking to each other. And whenever Kai caught sight of Abigail, e felt a confusing mix of emotions.

Kai was mad, obviously, because Abigail had told Oren eir secret. But more and more as the days dragged on, Kai had started feeling guilty. E'd revealed their pact *and* caused Abigail to get so flustered she'd blurted out having a crush on Lena in front of everyone.

At least Abigail hadn't told her cabinmates she didn't like them. Kai had.

Across the room, Oren hopped out of bed. Kai watched him rummage through his dresser, then choose clean clothes, plus a fresh kippah. It was purple, with silver embroidery.

As though sensing Kai's gaze, Oren turned. Their eyes met.

"Did you want to come with me to services tonight?" Oren asked.

The question sounded strained, like Oren was forcing himself to say it.

Kai's eyes dropped to the kippah in Oren's hands. The purple reminded em of eir cabin color. Except that barely meant anything anymore since the competition was over.

Kai shook eir head. "I'll just hang here tonight. I'm kinda tired."

Oren didn't say anything else. Maybe he felt relieved he wouldn't need to be alone with Kai. Kai's stomach turned over.

"I'll go," Jax called from his bunk. "If that's cool with you."

Oren nodded, even smiled a little. "That'd be cool. I'll shower now so I don't have to leave dinner early."

Kai blinked fast, then lay back in bed. Kids like Abigail cried when they felt bad. Eir sister, Lexi, did too. Not Kai.

"I'll shower, too," Jax said. "There's no way I'm missing Chef Kirstie's brownies."

Kai heard Jax drop from his bed to the floor. The door opened, but it didn't close immediately.

"She didn't mean to, you know." Oren's voice was soft but easy to hear, like he'd stepped closer to Kai's bed. "Abigail."

Heat crept into Kai's cheeks, but e stayed quiet. E couldn't even bring emself to turn and face Oren.

"She was just trying to find out if I could have a crush on a nonbinary kid. She never said your name. I just . . . guessed."

"Okay." Kai's throat got so tight, it was the only word e could manage.

A beat of silence. The door closed a few seconds later.

Suddenly, Kai actually did feel tired. E was *so* tired, of keeping up eir guard, of wondering who was safe to trust and who wasn't. At least with Oren and Jax gone, e could just rest for a few minutes.

Except e hadn't factored in Juliana.

"This sounds like a big misunderstanding to me." Her voice drifted up to Kai from the bed below.

Kai let out a heavy breath. Maybe if e ignored her, Juliana would get the message and leave em alone.

She didn't.

"I know a lot about misunderstandings." The bed frame creaked as she pushed up from her mattress. Her head appeared at the corner of Kai's vision. "Did you know I'm autistic?"

Kai rolled over to face her. "No?"

"Do you know what it means?"

"I mean, kinda? But not really. Isn't it like a mental illness?"

"No." Juliana shook her head. "It's something I was born with, and I experience the world differently than other kids because of it. I don't always get when people are joking. I sometimes don't notice when I'm talking too loudly, and I like to focus on one thing until it's done, instead of doing a bunch of things all at once. I don't just like to, actually. Sometimes it feels like it helps me to focus on one thing, and I get really upset when stuff changes unexpectedly."

"Yeah, I can see that."

Kai felt a stab of guilt. E was the reason they weren't doing the competition anymore. Lena's announcement and the activity schedule changes were probably really upsetting to Juliana.

"People don't automatically know I'm autistic, but I usually choose to tell them if we have a misunderstanding. Sometimes that helps us understand each other and work together better next time. Sometimes it doesn't."

"So . . ." Kai eyed her, not sure what point she was trying to make.

"So, I don't know." Juliana tucked strands of her hair behind one ear. "It just sounded like you and Abigail had a misunderstanding. Maybe you need to let her know why what she did upset you so she can understand you better. Maybe she'll get it or maybe she won't, but you haven't even given her a chance yet, have you?"

Juliana didn't wait for Kai to answer before disappearing back under the bunk. E flopped back against eir mattress. Abigail was the last person e wanted to talk to right now, except maybe for Oren. They both made Kai feel mad and guilty and awful all at once.

The boys returned, hair damp. Kai's gaze kept snagging on Oren's purple kippah whenever e glanced anywhere around the cabin.

Juliana stood up and reached for her bag. "Dinner?"

Jax and Oren nodded.

For a moment, Kai considered saying no and just staying in bed, but e figured Leticia might have something to say about that.

Without a word, Kai climbed down from eir bunk and followed eir cabinmates outside.

The short walk to the cafeteria dragged on forever. Awkward silence seemed to fill the space where there would usually be easy conversation.

It gave Kai time to think.

The more Kai thought about what Juliana had said, the more e realized about eir fight with Abigail.

Kai hadn't told Abigail what had happened to em at school last year. E hadn't told anyone at camp, actually. Aziza knew, and so did their parkour coach because Kai's parents had told him, but none of Kai's other teammates knew anything more than that Kai had been injured at school. It wasn't something Kai wanted to remember, let alone talk about. Eir shoulder hardly hurt anymore, but the memory of what had happened felt like a burn. It had left an invisible mark and made Kai question the motives of almost everyone around em.

Abigail didn't know any of this, Kai realized as e followed eir cabinmates into the cafeteria. She'd apologized for accidentally revealing eir crush but probably had no idea why e had started yelling at her in front of everyone. By the time the Purple campers sat down at their usual spot across from Yellow, Kai realized maybe it was time for em to explain emself. Time for em to apologize.

The only problem was how to talk to Abigail alone.

Maybe a napkin note would work. Except there was no way Kai would be able to slide it over to her without other people noticing. E also didn't have anything to write with.

Kai ultimately decided to drop eir fork below the table. E raised eir eyebrows at Abigail before leaning down to grab it.

Not only did Abigail fail to pick up on eir cue, a thick layer of hard, chewed-up gum was waiting for em on the underside of the table.

Chef Kirstie appeared at the end of dinner with a big brownie pan in each hand. A procession of volunteer Knitters followed along, each carrying their own smaller pans.

Everyone got up and took a spot in line. Cassidy, Juliana, and Stick reached the end of the line first. Abigail was standing a little off to one side by herself, but she was still too close to Bryn, Jax, and Oren for Kai to talk to her.

In front of em, Oren glanced at the wall clock, then turned to Jax. "I think we're going to have to eat dessert on the walk over if we don't want to be late."

"No worries." Jax already had a brownie in one hand, but he leaned over and grabbed another. "I'm good to go."

The two headed out, giving Kai a clear view of Abigail. She held a plate with her brownie and was waiting for the ice cream machine next to Bryn, Stick, and Cassidy.

Kai saw eir chance. E inched a little closer, then cleared eir throat.

Abigail didn't turn around.

"Are you done?"

Kai glanced down at a Weaver. Kai was blocking the brownie pan.

"Oh, sorry. Yeah."

Kai slunk the rest of the way over to the ice cream machine. Abigail's cheeks flushed when she spotted em, eyes darting around the cafeteria. Cassidy and Stick had already gotten their ice cream, but they lingered to talk to someone from the Green cabin. As Bryn reached for the soft serve lever, Kai stepped closer to Abigail.

"Hey," e whispered. "Can we talk privately?"

"Um." Her gaze flickered to her cabinmates.

"I swear I won't yell at you again."

Kai couldn't tell if Abigail believed em. Bryn finished filling his bowl, then looked over at Abigail with furrowed brows.

For one awful moment, Kai thought Abigail might say no. It'd be easy to shake her head and follow her cabinmates back to the table, leaving Kai alone.

"I have to go to the bathroom," Abigail half squeaked, half shouted.

All eyes turned to the two of them. Stick, Cassidy, Bryn, and Lin from Green all stared. Even some kids at the nearest table looked over.

"With . . . your brownie?" Stick tilted their head.

"Oh. I, um." Abigail's cheeks flushed a shade brighter.

"I'll take it back to the table for you," Bryn offered.

Abigail quickly passed off her plate. Cassidy's eyes narrowed at Kai, but she eventually followed the rest of the campers back to their table.

Abigail took off, not in the direction of the bathrooms but toward the doors that led outside. Kai waited just long enough to confirm Cassidy was focused on her conversation with Juliana before following Abigail out of the cafeteria.

E was greeted by the buzz of mosquitos, the soft light of dusk, and the sticky Minnesota humidity. It felt a lot like their first meeting. Except tonight, Abigail was standing, her back to the trees. And there were no tears, although she was hugging herself, like she was bracing for an explosion.

After eir outburst, Kai honestly couldn't blame her.

"I want to share something with you." E kept eir voice low and gentle. "It isn't really a secret but not a lot of people know about it."

Abigail looked up at em, arms relaxing a little.

That was all Kai needed.

"I came out as nonbinary last summer, right before school started. I told my parents and my little sister, Lexi, and they were confused at first but figured it out pretty fast. They were supportive. I also told my best friend, Cie-Cie. We were on the same gymnastics team, so I let my other teammates all know too. And they said they were cool with it, so I thought things would be fine when school started."

"But they weren't?" Abigail's cheeks flushed again. "Sorry, I didn't mean to interrupt."

"No, it's fine. You're right. Things weren't so great. Because people were constantly using the wrong name and pronouns for me. And whenever I pointed it out to Cie-Cie and my other friends, they'd just kind of blow it off, like it wasn't a big deal. Or they'd say, 'That's too hard to remember,' or 'I still think of you as your birth name.'"

Kai frowned. "Like that's even a good reason not to call someone what they've asked to be called."

Abigail nodded.

"Anyway, it got really hard for me to focus on gymnastics and I didn't like how all the apparatuses I was training on were specifically for girls anyway, so I quit and started doing parkour. And all my friends there are super cool. Sometimes they mess up my pronouns, but they always correct themselves. They don't make a big deal out of it.

"But things at school got worse. Cie-Cie got a boyfriend. He's a real jerk. He'd call me things like 'freak' and 'it' and would make jokes about no one ever wanting to date me, and Cie-Cie wouldn't say anything when she overheard. It hurt." Kai's chest ached. This was the first time e had admitted this to anyone. "It hurt *a lot*.

And he kept doing it. He'd follow me around between classes, saying the worst things. I kept telling myself it was dumb, to just ignore him. But I guess I couldn't. I even had dreams about people calling me those things. Like, all the time. It messed with my sleep."

Kai expected the memories to flood back to em now, each and every awful one, like they always did when e let emself think about the things that had been said to em. But the forest didn't morph into a school hallway. Cie-Cie's boyfriend didn't appear. It was just Kai talking to Abigail outside the Camp QUILTBAG cafeteria.

Kai made emself go on.

"One day, after lunch, that guy and one of his friends were following me down the hall. They were calling me the usual stupid stuff, but I just couldn't deal with it anymore. I told them to shut up."

"Wow." Abigail's eyes widened. "That was brave."

"Maybe." Kai shrugged with eir good shoulder. "Mostly, it just pissed them off. One of them—I don't even remember which—shoved me into a locker. I fell and I guess I landed the wrong way because I dislocated my shoulder."

Kai pressed eir lips together. Eir vision blurred with tears. "But the worst part was that Cie-Cie saw everything and she didn't tell them to stop or do literally anything."

"That's terrible." Abigail's mouth trembled, and she reminded Kai so much of Lexi that e stood a little taller, just like e would when Lexi got upset.

But e didn't blink back eir tears. For once, Kai accepted them as they came.

"It was terrible. And I think that's why I just lost it on you." Kai sniffled, making sure eir voice was steady enough for Abigail to understand what e was saying. "It's been really hard for me to trust people since that happened. My therapist's been getting me to realize Cie-Cie wasn't being a good friend to me, but it's still hard to believe not everyone is going to act that way when I share something important about myself."

"I get it," Abigail said. "I mean, not exactly. I just think I might know what it's like to have friends who sometimes aren't very good friends. But I'm still so sorry I let Oren find out about your crush. It sounds dumb now, maybe, but I really just wanted to help. Same for the competition. I never meant to earn all those points, and I thought throwing the last question on trivia night would make up for it, but it just made everything so much worse."

"It was kind of an obvious question for you to miss." Kai couldn't help smiling as e wiped away some tears. "We probably shouldn't have made the pact at all."

Abigail's face fell, and Kai rushed to explain. "I just

mean, we should've tried being friends. The pact made things complicated."

"Oh." Relief washed over Abigail's face. "Yeah, it did. But camp's almost over, at least? Hopefully that means people won't be mad at us for much longer . . ."

"I guess." Kai kicked a stone, thinking. "It probably also means that no one's going to want to be around us all that much at the gala. Or at least me, anyway." E looked up. "So. Want to go together?"

Abigail's brows rose.

"Not like on a date or anything," Kai said. "Just as friends. No pact or strings attached or anything like that."

"That'd be nice." She gave em a tentative smile, but it turned into a scowl a moment later as she reached down and slapped her leg. "These darn bugs. I ran out of the spray you gave me a few days ago."

"I'll make sure to get you some more before the gala," Kai promised. "I still have tons of it."

"Oh, thank God." Abigail took a small step back toward the cafeteria entrance. "Should we . . . ?"

"You go first," Kai said, knowing e still needed a moment to emself. "I'm going to see if I have enough signal to text my friend real quick. But see you at the gala tomorrow for our not-date!"

Abigail grinned.

As soon as Abigail was back inside, Kai pulled out eir phone. But before e could so much as unlock the screen, a rustling sound pulled eir attention up toward the nearest set of trees. E squinted. The rustling came again, and Kai followed the movement up to a branch.

E sucked in a breath.

White fur. Pink eyes. The squirrel looked down at em. Zie blinked once, then took off, scampering up the tree trunk. If the branch weren't still gently swaying, Kai might've thought e'd imagined Mx. Nutsford.

21

ABIGAIL

(SHE/HER/HERS)

ON SATURDAY, ABIGAIL MET KAI NEAR THE BATHROOMS after the rest of their cabins had already left for the gala. Abigail was wearing the "nice outfit" the Camp QUILTBAG orientation pamphlet had told her to pack.

It *was* a nice outfit, but still Abigail tugged at her skirt. She felt like she had gotten dressed up for church, except her mom wasn't there to tell her she shouldn't pull her hair back in a ponytail or she shouldn't wear sneakers, so she did both of those things.

Kai was dressed a little less formally, but e smiled when e saw Abigail approach. "You look nice," e said, then gestured to eir own outfit. "I didn't actually pack anything for this, but this shirt is the only not-wrinkled, not-dirty thing I have left."

"You look nice, too," Abigail said, and she meant it.

Kai sighed, a big deep sigh, and held out eir hand.

"You ready?" e asked.

No, not really.

But at least she wasn't alone. "I guess so."

They made their way to the Benches, except when they got there, it didn't look like the Benches at all. The benches themselves had been moved, leaving a big clearing that overlooked the lake. Fairy lights hung along the surrounding trees, creating a soft, twinkly glow. The moon reflected off the lake, and music played from the Bluetooth speakers. Everything was perfect.

Everything was overwhelming, too. Especially when Abigail noticed the dry-erase board with the camp name suggestions was out here, too. There were some good suggestions—Camp Pride, Camp Everyone, Camp Equality—and then also some not so good ones, like Campy McCamp Face.

Kai gave Abigail's hand a squeeze. "We'll have fun," e said, but Abigail wasn't entirely sure if e was talking to her or just to emself.

"Well don't you two clean up nicely."

They both whipped their heads around to find Leticia standing behind them. She was wearing a sparkly vest with flowing pants and high heels, and she looked amazing. Abigail felt her cheeks start to burn.

"Hi, Leticia," Kai said. "You look good, too."

That was an understatement if Abigail ever heard one.

She thought about saying as much, but then Leticia put her hand gently on Abigail's shoulder, and Abigail's stomach clenched right up. She looked down at her sneakers instead.

"I'm glad I caught you," Leticia said. "You've been really hard to catch, actually."

Abigail had worked exceptionally hard the past couple of days to lie low and keep small, and she was kind of pleased to hear she'd done a good job of it.

"I just wanted you to know, Abigail, that you don't need to feel weird around me, or apologize to me, or worry at all about anything. There's no need, no *reason*, for any of that," Leticia said.

Abigail looked up at her. She was kidding, right? There was a huge reason for all those things, and basically everyone at camp knew that by now.

Though, that might not *actually* be true. As far as Abigail knew, her crush on Lena hadn't spread past the Yellow and Purple cabins.

"Besides, I get it," Leticia said with a shrug. "My mom's hot."

"*Oh my God,*" Kai said, as if e was the one who should be mortified.

Leticia bumped em on eir good shoulder. "You two go on in and have fun, okay? And Abigail, maybe if I'm lucky, I'll get to have you in my cabin next year."

"Hey! You're already trying to poach my chickens!" MJ shouted, coming up behind them with Sol and a couple other counselors.

Leticia winked at Abigail and Kai and then left to head into the gala with the others.

Abigail didn't know what to make of the interaction. Her head was spinning, but she tried to shake it off when Kai gently tugged her hand to walk into the gala.

Now what? They stood in the clearing, music playing, all the campers chatting and running around and dancing. Stick was at the center of the clearing, trying to pull other campers in to dance.

Abigail was starting to sweat, so when Kai asked, "You want some punch or something?" Abigail nodded. "Okay, I'll go get some. Be right back."

And then she was alone.

Maybe the punch was a mistake.

Maybe she should trail behind Kai and stick to em like glue the rest of the night.

But then Ash and Siobhan from the Blue cabin skipped by her, waving and saying, "Hey, Abigail!" Across the clearing, Hannah from the Red cabin caught Abigail's gaze and they waved at each other, too.

"Abigail?" There was a tap on her shoulder, and Abigail jumped. "Oh! I'm sorry!" It was Bryn. He had on dress pants and a button-up shirt, complete with a tie that had little alligators all over it. "I didn't mean to scare you," he said. "I just . . . well, I wanted to tell you that you looked really pretty. Like, beautiful, I mean."

Abigail stared at him for a moment.

He tugged at his tie. "I brought like six ties because I couldn't decide, and then I couldn't even get it tied right. Stick did it for me. I wore my alligator one—alligators are kind of like dinosaurs, right? Though I guess I could have worn my rooster tie, too, because dinosaurs are supposed to be like birds, right?"

Abigail blinked at him. "What?"

"I'm not mad at you, Abigail," Bryn said. "You know that, right?"

"Really?"

Bryn nodded. He cleared his throat, taking a step closer to Abigail, close enough that if she wanted to, she could probably count his eyelashes. It didn't make her feel claustrophobic though. Bryn never did. Bryn's closeness always made Abigail feel warm and safe.

Just like it did now.

"I know you have a lot going on. And, I meant what I said the other day. You can talk to me about it."

Abigail exhaled deeply. "I think I'd like to tell you about it all."

"Good," Bryn said, smiling.

Stick suddenly came bouncing over to them, wrapping their long arms around them both. "Come dance with me! Let's get this GAYLA started!" They were shouting right in Abigail's ear.

"Me?" Abigail asked. "But I thought—"

"That we were all super mad at you?" It was Cassidy this time, coming up to stand with the rest of Abigail's cabin, her eyes sharp as she looked right at Abigail. She wore a blouse and dress pants and a pair of flats, and Abigail made a mental note to pack nice pants if she came back next year.

Not that she thought she'd be coming back next year. She'd barely survived this one.

"Well. Yes. That," Abigail said.

"We—I mean, me. I was mad. Well, hurt, kind of? I am a little still, I guess," Cassidy said. "But, we talked, well, Bryn and Juliana talked, and we listened, and well . . . we like you, Abigail. You made a mistake. And maybe . . . I know there's only tonight left, but . . ."

"But let's start fresh," Stick interrupted. They held out their hand. "I'm Stick, and I love to dance with my friends. So, can we all go dance, as friends, now please?"

Abigail looked at Cassidy. "I really am sorry. I know it was important to you. I should have told you what was going on."

Cassidy smiled. "Maybe next time if we all come up with diabolical plans to look good while winning a competition, we can all work together instead?"

"Deal," Abigail said.

"Great! Now please can we go dance now?" Stick begged.

They practically dragged everyone out to the center of the clearing, and almost the exact second that they did, the music switched to a slow song. Some of the kids groaned, but it didn't deter Stick, who grabbed Bryn by the hands. "Time to put those ballroom skills to use!" Stick said, though Bryn looked horrified.

Kai came back with the punch and handed one cup to Abigail, who drank it greedily. "You want to dance?" e asked.

After some awkward fumbling with their cups—Kai found a flat spot on the ground for them—Kai took the lead.

Neither one was very good at the ballroom stuff, and Abigail wasn't entirely sure how to work around Kai's sling, so Abigail and Kai kind of just swayed back and forth and in a small circle.

"It looked like you made up with your cabin?" Kai asked.

Abigail nodded. "I think so. I'm kind of . . . confused. It feels good, that they still want to be my friend. And also that Leticia I guess isn't mad at me? But it's weird, too."

"You weren't expecting it," Kai said, and e squinted for a moment, like eir mind was elsewhere, before focusing back on Abigail. "I was thinking about that. And about what you said about your friends back home. And, Abigail, of course Leticia isn't mad at you."

"But Stacy—"

"Is a jerk." Kai practically barked it at her. "She's no better than Cie-Cie was to me. You deserve better friends. You *have* better friends! You have me, and Bryn, and Cassidy, and Stick, and . . ." E paused for a moment before adding, "Oren. Juliana and Jax, too."

Abigail thought about that. She thought about Ash and Siobhan and Hannah, too. She thought about everyone at this camp who smiled or waved at her at meals, or while they swam in the lake, or while they all fell on top of each other during roller derby.

Maybe Kai was right. Maybe they hadn't needed a pact in the first place.

Maybe things really were okay.

"I don't mean to cut in here," a voice suddenly said.

Abigail turned from the safe cocoon of Kai to come face to face with Lena.

"But could I steal Abigail from you for a moment? I was hoping we could have a quick chat," Lena said.

Abigail immediately took it all back. Maybe things *weren't* okay after all.

❧

Abigail followed Lena to the far side of the clearing, as close as they could be to the lake without actually leaving the gala. Abigail stared at the water, the way the moon and the stars were so clear above it. *I should take a picture to post for Stacy to see*, she thought, before she remembered it didn't matter anyway.

Instead, Abigail took a mental picture. She didn't want to forget it.

She shivered. It was cooler away from the crowds, and her stomach was roiling with nerves. "Stupid pterodactyls," Abigail mumbled to herself.

"What's that?" Lena asked.

"The um. My stomach. When I get nervous, it's like there's a bunch of pterodactyls in there." She paused, shaking her head. "Never mind. Sorry. It's nothing."

"Don't be nervous," Lena said, and then she smiled. "Though, I may have to steal that from you. Much more fun than the butterflies I always say are in mine."

Abigail couldn't imagine Lena ever getting nervous enough for butterflies or pterodactyls or anything.

"I just wanted to make sure you were okay, Abigail," Lena said.

"Okay?" Abigail asked, looking up at Lena for the first time since she'd asked to speak with her. The soft breeze blew Lena's hair around her head. She was wearing a long, flowing dress with a myriad of mismatched patterns all over it, like a quilt. Abigail loved it and hated that she loved it.

She looked away, toward the lake, instead.

"I wasn't much older than you when I thought maybe I was gay," Lena said. Her voice was so soft, kind of like she was telling Abigail a bedtime story. "I don't think there were any camps like this back then. I didn't know what a Genders and Sexualities Alliance was, and my school certainly didn't have one. The only time I ever saw anything queer was when the local theater did a production of *Rent*. I felt really lonely."

"I'm sorry," Abigail said, glancing up at her.

Lena smiled. "All the girls in my class used to talk about the boys they had crushes on, or wanted to ask to school dances, or kiss under the bleachers during football games. I used to pick a boy at random who I'd say I had a crush on, too, so I wasn't left out. It was easier that way. Truth was, I didn't have any crushes on any of the kids at school. I didn't like boys that way, and I knew the girls wouldn't like me back, so it was easier to just not like anyone at all. Anything else seemed too scary."

Abigail understood that. "The girls at my school won't invite me to sleepovers anymore," she confessed. "Just in case."

When Abigail looked back at Lena, she was taking a deep breath through her nose. "I'm so sorry the girls at your school are so ignorant. I hope, if anything, you've learned that there is a community here for you who won't treat you like that. That's why I founded this camp, Abigail. For queer kids to learn that they should be accepted and supported and loved. To give them a community if they don't already know that. *I* didn't know that when I was younger. It didn't feel safe to crush on any of the girls in my grade . . . so my first crush I ever had? The first real crush I can remember? It was on my eighth-grade English teacher."

Abigail blinked at her. "What?"

Lena laughed. "She was *awesome*. She let us read whatever we wanted, even graphic novels, which were always my favorite. She had shiny dark hair and the longest eyelashes I've ever seen. She had a gap between her front teeth that sometimes the other kids made fun of behind her back, but it never stopped her from always smiling as big as she could anyway." Lena bumped Abigail against the shoulder. "You're the first person I've ever told this to."

"But . . . why?" Abigail asked.

"Because while no adult should ever take advantage of you regardless of your feelings for them, and it's important that you know it would have been absolutely not okay for my English teacher to cross any lines with me, how *I* felt *wasn't* wrong. You aren't the first queer kid with a crush on someone older than you, and you won't be the last, and anyone who makes you feel ashamed of that? *They're* wrong," Lena said firmly in a way that even if Abigail wanted to argue (and a small part of her still did), she wouldn't try. "You're a wonderful kid, Abigail. And I need you to try to believe that before you go home tomorrow."

Abigail turned to look at the gala carrying on behind them. At the splash of colors of everyone's clothes, rainbows draped everywhere, shining brightly under the fairy lights in the trees. At the shadows the pride flags made as they blew in the breeze. Abigail watched as everyone danced, laughing and enjoying their last night at Camp QUILTBAG together.

Those two weeks felt impossibly long.

Those two weeks also felt unbearably short.

She looked back at Lena, who Abigail realized was waiting for an answer. She took a deep breath, and tried to believe it. "Okay," Abigail said. "I'll try."

"Come on, then," Lena said, and she winked. Abigail, despite everything, felt her heart flutter. "Let's get back so you can dance with your friends."

My friends, Abigail thought, watching where Stick was still at the center of the clearing, making Jax laugh as they danced in circles around him. Cassidy and Juliana were dancing together, too, holding hands and staying close like they had been all camp. Bryn was standing off by himself, watching, and when he caught Abigail's eyes, he smiled even bigger and waved her over.

In the distance, she saw Kai talking with Oren. She closed her eyes and said a quick *please God thank you!* that their conversation was going well. Or at least not a disaster, because Kai deserved to be happy, too.

Abigail followed Lena back to the dance, only stopping when she heard a rustling sound coming from the dark trees behind them. She squinted, ready to grab Lena and scream if it was a bear or coyote or something.

Small eyes reflected at her in the dark.

She took a step forward, despite every instinct in her body telling her she would definitely be eaten by a T. rex if she did something like this at Jurassic Park, and the eyes got closer, too, as the creature crept forward, its white fur visible in the moonlight.

Abigail blinked.

She'd swear on her life the squirrel blinked back at her.

And then zie was gone, back through the trees, the leaves rustling.

"Abigail?" Lena called. "Everything okay?"

She opened her mouth to tell Lena, *Oh my God, I saw zem! I saw Mx. Nutsford,* really!

But she didn't. "Everything's okay," Abigail said, and followed Lena back to the clearing.

She wanted to keep this moment for herself.

KAI
(E/EM/EIR)

KAI WAS FINALLY TALKING TO OREN, WHICH WAS GREAT.
Except it was going terribly.

It wasn't that Oren was being mean or anything. The problem was simply that Kai couldn't bring emself to say what e actually wanted to say.

It was one thing to talk to Abigail about what had happened to em. Abigail was Kai's friend, but she also felt like a little sister, someone e could trust even when they sometimes butted heads.

Oren was different. More confident. Plus, he was friends with Jax. Maybe more than friends. Kai still couldn't tell. Not knowing was half the problem, because it felt like Jax was everything Kai was not. Not that e wanted to be a boy. If Oren only liked boys, Kai realized that was just something e'd have to accept, even if it would hurt.

So although Kai was sitting with Oren on a picnic bench at the edge of the gala space, they were only talking about safe things: the decorations (same as last year, according to Oren) and what kids were wearing (Ash had brought a top hat and decorated it during yesterday's art class, and Oren was wearing a special rainbow kippah).

"It's a really cool kippah," Kai said, not sure how to change topics.

"Right? I got it from this online shop that has a lot of awesome queer Jewish stuff," Oren said. "I can text the link to you, if you give me your phone."

Kai held eir phone out to Oren. While Oren added himself as a contact, Kai glanced at the nearby whiteboard. Campers would occasionally wander over to it, stopping to study the list of proposed camp names. A few kids added their ideas, then returned to dancing.

"Done." Oren passed Kai's phone back. "I texted myself so I'd have your number. I'll send you the link in a sec too."

"Cool..."

Music thrummed in Kai's chest as e took in the festivities. Kids were dancing and laughing and drinking punch. Eir gaze snagged on Abigail. She walked along the edge of the clearing, watching the dancers, careful to stay far enough away not to be pulled onto the dance floor. She seemed to notice Kai, too.

"All good?" Kai asked when she got close enough to hear em over the music.

"Yeah." She nodded but didn't fully stop, quickly glancing over at Oren. "I think I'm gonna go throw out our punch cups and let you two . . . well, um. Yeah."

Abigail gave Kai a not-very-subtle thumbs-up before sprinting off.

Kai's thoughts returned to the talk e'd had with Abigail yesterday. By the time eir phone buzzed with Oren's text, Kai knew how to start eir apology.

"Hey . . . thank you," e said.

"Yeah, no problem."

Oren shot em a half smile and it took Kai a second to realize he thought e was talking about the text.

"No, not that." Kai's chest fluttered with nerves. "Thanks for that too, obviously, but I also wanted—"

"Hey, you two."

Kai clamped eir mouth shut as Cassidy approached them. She waved with one hand, pulling along Juliana with the other. The rest of the Purple and Yellow campers trailed behind them. Even after they'd all come to a stop, Cassidy and Juliana continued to hold hands. Kai stared at their entwined fingers.

"Yeah, we're a thing now." Cassidy jutted out her chin.

"Officially an item," Juliana said. "Although *item* is kind of dehumanizing, now that I think about it. *Girlfriend* sounds better."

"Oh, cool," Oren said. "Congrats."

"Thanks." Cassidy beamed. "That's not why I wanted to talk to you, though."

Kai swallowed hard.

"Juliana and I were talking." Cassidy turned to her girlfriend. "And she—well, I'll just let her explain."

"Lena hasn't officially told us any of the criteria for choosing the new camp name," Juliana said, "but I was telling Cassidy there's a good chance that *overwhelming* support for a specific name might convince them to pick it."

Kai glanced over at the whiteboard. Lena had told kids to put tallies or checkmarks next to the names they liked the best, but none of the options had more than a few checks beside them. "You think if one of the choices got a ton of checks, they would go with that one?"

"Maybe, yes," Juliana said.

"So, here's what I was thinking," Cassidy said. "We let Juliana choose! Then we can all put checkmarks next to that option and try to convince some other kids to vote for it, too." She was practically vibrating with excitement. "Since Juliana's the whole reason we're even getting to suggest new names, it makes sense that she should get to pick, right?"

"Makes sense to me," Stick said.

Jax seemed to agree. "Yeah, sounds fair."

Abigail and Bryn nodded; so did Kai and Oren. It wasn't as perfect as the Purple cabin winning the competition and letting Juliana choose, in Kai's opinion, but it accomplished the same goal.

"That is very sweet of you." Juliana squeezed Cassidy's hand. "But no thanks."

Cassidy blinked. Her smile stayed in place a second longer, then dropped from her face. "Why not?"

"Because I don't have a clue what the new name should be," Juliana said. "I obviously want it to be inclusive so everyone feels like they belong here, but I think it will be now that Lena knows what we want. That's the only thing that matters to me.

"And speaking of inclusivity"—Juliana turned to Oren before anyone could say anything—"I spoke to Lena earlier today and informed her she really should have given you a point on Saturday and considered it an excused absence. This camp isn't inclusive if it puts someone at a disadvantage just for being who they are. Lena said she's not sure if they'll be having a competition next year but if they are, she will *definitely* do that."

"That's totally awesome." Oren smiled at her.

Brows pinched, Cassidy still looked like she was processing everything Juliana had said—especially the part about not caring who got to suggest a new name for the camp.

"Juli gets things done," Jax said. "But she's also cool with letting others have their turn at stuff."

"Yeah." Kai nodded. "So, I guess my part of the pact with Abigail was kind of silly, because I wanted our cabin to win so Juliana could pick the name."

And also to impress Oren, but there was no way Kai was sharing that.

"And . . . I was actually hoping to do really well in the competition to impress you for the same reason," Cassidy admitted, turning to Juliana. "Since we had an alliance, as long as one of us won, I thought we'd make you happy."

"Sounds like a misunderstanding." Juliana glanced at Kai. "Seems like there has been a lot of that going on lately."

"You think?" Jax burst out laughing, then sucked in air so fast he snorted, which made others laugh.

Eventually, Cassidy and Juliana headed back to the

dance floor, with Stick and Jax close behind. Bryn leaned into Abigail and said something that Kai couldn't hear.

"Is it okay if I go dance with Bryn?" Abigail asked. When Kai nodded, she fluttered her fingers at em. "Okay! Then I'll be right back, promise."

Kai couldn't help chuckling. "Take your time! Not like I'm going anywhere."

Oren turned to Kai. "Well, at least Cassidy isn't mad anymore. And things seem better between you and Abigail, too."

"That's actually what I wanted to thank you for," Kai said. "You were right about Abigail. We talked at dinner last night, and we're good now."

"That's great."

"Yeah . . ." Kai gripped the edges of the picnic bench, then took a breath.

"I'm sorry about everything I said to you, too. It's really hard for me to trust people after last year—it just wasn't great for me at school after I came out. But I should never have said I don't like you and the others, even if I was upset. That definitely wasn't true. Nothing I said was." Kai couldn't quite bring emself to confess eir crush on Oren. "So . . . are we good too?"

"Yeah, we're good." Oren smiled.

Kai's grip on the bench loosened.

"Honestly, I figured something else might've been going on, something that didn't have anything to do with Abigail," Oren continued. "You didn't seem like you were really seeing her when you said those things. Or me. It was like you were somewhere else."

"Right . . ." Kai chewed on the inside of eir lip.

"You don't have to tell me anything you don't want to," Oren said. "I just wanted you to know that I get it. Maybe not the exact *it*, but I get the part about feeling like you don't know who you can trust. Things change after you come out, even if people say they're supportive."

"Yeah, they seriously do."

If Oren could relate to this, Kai thought, maybe other campers could, too. There was immediate relief that e wasn't alone in feeling like this, but Kai also felt sad knowing that others had gone through what e had at school, like Abigail with Stacy. And maybe Oren would tell Kai his story someday. Maybe Kai would tell Oren eir story. The idea didn't feel quite as scary anymore after telling Abigail yesterday.

A pop song faded out. The next song was slower. Oren looked at Kai, then over to the dance area.

"I kind of think I should dance since it feels like I'm basically the only one who hasn't yet."

Kai shrugged a little, trying to act cool. "I mean, I've only danced a little so far, and it was with Abigail."

"I saw." Oren's smile returned. "Lucky her."

The fluttering in Kai's chest picked up.

Kai held eir breath, but the song cut out midway through, before Oren said anything else. Campers stopped dancing. Kids looked over from the punch table.

"All right, everyone." Lena waved from the center of the clearing. "This'll just be a brief interruption. Then you can all get back to your celebration."

Kai silently stewed beside Oren. Lena had the worst timing *ever*.

"In about five minutes, we'll be rolling the whiteboard away," Lena said. "So if anyone has a name suggestion you haven't written down yet, now would be the time to do so. Thank you all for the thought you've put into this. I'll be discussing each of these names with the board of directors later this summer."

Sol and Leticia moved to stand on either side of the whiteboard, right as Oren's hand brushed against Kai's. Kai tensed, waiting for Oren to jerk away, but his hand stayed where it was.

"How will we know what the new name's going to be?" a camper from the Orange cabin called out.

"You'll have to come back next year to find out." Lena winked. "Rest assured, though, we will focus on the name's meaning *and* aim for something that will be inclusive of all campers."

At the edge of the dance floor, Kai saw Juliana nod eagerly. Beyond that, all e could focus on was the sensation of Oren's fingers against the side of eir hand. The electric spark it sent from eir arm into eir chest.

"That's all from me, folks." Lena smiled, all dimples. "Enjoy the rest of your night!"

The music picked up where it had left off, and kids who had moved to the edge of the dance area scampered back to the center.

Oren looked over at Kai. "Do you want to . . . ?"

Kai swallowed. "Dance?"

Oren nodded.

"Sure, yeah."

E followed Oren to an open space a little apart from the other dancers and stood as straight as e could, shoulders back, pretending to be confident. Oren lifted his hands first, and Kai copied him with eir good arm. It took a moment for them to figure out what hand went on which shoulder, but eventually Oren's palm settled gently over the strap of Kai's sling.

It was everything Kai had wanted. At least, everything e thought e'd wanted. Because now that they were dancing, Kai had no idea where to look. Eir eyes focused on the spot over Oren's shoulder, to where Stick was teaching Cassidy and Juliana a complicated set of dance moves.

"So," Oren said. "I just realized something about that whole mess with Abigail."

Kai turned eir attention to Oren. "What?"

"You never actually asked me about my answer to Abigail's question."

Kai was so close to Oren, e could see flecks of green within the more familiar blue of his eyes. They sparkled, reflecting the fairy lights.

In that moment, Kai's mind went completely blank.

"Um, what question?"

"You know . . ." Oren looked down and his curls fell over his forehead. "She asked if I could have a crush on a nonbinary kid."

"Oh, right." Kai's cheeks heated up. "I guess I just thought you couldn't, because you said you're gay. And it's fine. I get that, I really do."

Oren slowed their dance to a gentle sway, even as the playlist changed to a bouncier song. He looked back up at Kai. Their eyes met.

"I am gay," Oren said. "I know that for sure."

Kai nodded. Out of the corner of one eye, e saw Stick move on from Cassidy and Juliana over to Jax, who was twirling Siobhan around with one hand.

"I also thought I only got crushes on boys, but I guess not always."

Kai stared at him.

"Like, there's this really cute kid at camp, and e's definitely not a boy, so I guess my definition of *gay* is more than just liking guys . . ."

Maybe it was just the dim lighting, but it looked like Oren's cheeks were also a brighter shade than normal. This was everything Kai had hoped for. The spark in Kai's chest felt like it could turn into fireworks at any second.

E caught a glimpse of another camper over Oren's shoulder.

"What about Jax?" Kai blurted out, then immediately wanted to kick emself.

Oren went still. "What about him?"

It was probably not physically possible for Kai's face to get any hotter, but that was exactly how it felt as the heat intensified, then spread down eir neck and into eir chest.

But this was something e had been wondering since almost the start of camp. If Kai didn't ask now, e might never get the chance.

"I thought you two maybe liked each other."

Oren tilted his head.

"*Like*," Kai tried again, "as in 'more than just friends.'"

"Oh." Oren's eyes widened. His hand slipped off Kai's shoulder as he took a step back. The spark in Kai's chest started to fizzle out.

Oren started laughing.

Kai looked at him, confused. Shoulders rounding, eir confidence wilted.

It took Oren a moment to get ahold of himself. When he next spoke, his grin stayed in place. "Jax has a girlfriend, Kai."

"He . . . *what*?" Kai's eyes darted from Oren to Jax, then back to Oren. "I thought . . . I mean, wait, so he's—"

"—bisexual."

"But he kissed you!"

"Just on my cheek." Oren shot Kai an amused look.

But Kai still remembered how e had felt when e'd seen Jax lean in and kiss Oren.

It was only after e frowned that Oren's expression shifted to something more serious.

"Jax has always been super kissy and into hugs and stuff, but I promise we're just friends. He's actually planning to come out to his girlfriend once he gets home because he really wants her to be okay with who he is."

Kai's mind was racing, turning eir thoughts back to what Oren had said earlier. "So, wait, when you said you liked someone at camp, you meant . . . ?"

"Yeah." Oren's eyes crinkled at the corners. "And when you told me that none of the stuff you said to me after I told you about Abigail was true, does that mean you also like . . . um, you know . . ."

"Yeah . . ."

Oren stepped closer to Kai. "Then is it okay if I kiss you?"

The world felt like it stopped, all the laughter and music, the dancing and chatter from other campers. It faded away, leaving Kai and Oren alone in the clearing.

Kai took a breath, then nodded.

They leaned in toward each other. Kai closed eir eyes, then felt the lightest brush of Oren's lips. The start of a kiss.

It felt wonderful, and right, and just a little bit awkward, because this was the first time Kai had ever kissed anyone. E didn't know if brushing eir fingers through Oren's hair was the right thing to do but it felt natural, like something e was meant to.

"*Finally!*"

The world unfroze. Kai and Oren pulled apart, eyes falling on Jax, who was pumping his fist in the air. Behind him, Kai spotted Abigail and Bryn. Abigail was bouncing up and down while Bryn clapped.

"Do you have *any* idea how long some of us have been waiting for you two to get together?" Jax called. "That seriously took forever."

Oren rolled his eyes as he placed his hand back on Kai's shoulder. "We've known each other less than two weeks, you drama queen."

"For. Ever." Jax blew a kiss their way, then switched partners with Ash. As the two of them started dancing, Siobhan partnered up with Lin. A few other campers also switched up, except for Cassidy and Juliana.

Kai and Oren stayed together as well.

A part of Kai knew this wouldn't last as e and Oren continued to sway together. Eir parents would pick em up and they'd drive home tomorrow. Oren would fly back to Brooklyn. Jax, Juliana, Stick, and Oren were all too old to come back to camp next year. Some of the others like Abigail and Bryn might return, though Kai wasn't convinced e would be among them.

But Kai had made friends who liked em for who e was this summer. More than friends when it came to Oren.

Although Kai had another year at the same school this fall, it seemed like less of a problem now. In this moment, dancing with a boy e really liked who liked em back, surrounded by new friends, Kai felt e could finally put eir trust in something beyond emself.

ABIGAIL
(SHE/HER/HERS)

ABIGAIL MADE HER WAY THROUGH THE AIRPORT, following the airport attendant like a baby duckling trying not to get left behind.

It was all jarring: the beeping and grinding noises from the security machines and conveyor belts, the way everyone on line shuffled forward, the suitcases surrounding Abigail like small boulders on wheels. The view of the concrete runways, the planes pulling into their gates, made Abigail miss the sight of trees; and the stink of a bajillion people and disinfectant spray made her miss the smell of the air around Shakopee Lake.

Camp QUILTBAG was over. She was headed home.

As she stood on line to get through security, she gripped her plane ticket and her ID in one hand and her cell phone in her other. She scrolled through her phone aimlessly, just to have something to make herself look busy so that her assigned flight attendant wouldn't keep trying to make small talk.

That proved to be a worse idea. As Abigail slowly moved through the line, she found herself scrolling through all the pictures and videos Stacy had posted in the last two weeks, all the summer plans the girls from school had made and done without her. Abigail had missed out on so much. Beach days and trips to the boardwalk and at least three big movies that everyone but her would be talking about.

Oh God.

Abigail was going *home*.

Abigail was leaving the safety of Camp QUILTBAG, the community that Lena had made for her, all her new friends, and going back to New Jersey, back to *Stacy*, back to everything she had left behind in the first place.

The flight attendant helped Abigail put her backpack into the bin on the conveyor belt, along with Abigail's phone, but she couldn't get those images of home out of her head. The damage had been done.

"Don't forget to take off your shoes," the attendant said. Abigail kicked them off, added them to the bin, and made her way through the X-ray machine, wondering if the TSA guard scanning her body could see the pterodactyls inside her stomach, if they could see how her insides were twisting up because everything she had gained at camp, everything she had wanted from camp, she now had to leave behind.

Abigail tripped over her own sock-clad feet as she made it through security and grabbed her belongings. She sat down to put her shoes back on, struggling to tie them because her hands were sweaty.

She was going home, and nothing would be different. She wouldn't have friends at school; everyone would still make fun of her. Maybe she should run away and live in the Minnesota woods and become best friends with Mx. Nutsford and—

Her phone buzzed in her hand.

It was a text from a number she didn't recognize. The area code was 952, which she didn't recognize, either.

Hey! It's Kai, so now you have my number, too! Have a safe flight! Text me when you land so I know you've made it!

It was exactly like something Abigail's mom would say.

It was exactly like something Abigail imagined a big sibling would say, too.

Abigail held the phone close to her chest. It settled the pterodactyls a little bit to think that at least she still had Kai. She could text em when Stacy was being extra *Stacy*, or she could text em an emoji when Sister Patricia gave them extra religion homework and she wanted to roll her eyes, or she could text em when she wanted a friend to text before bed, because she used to stay up hiding the light from her phone under her covers to text Stacy, and she could do that with Kai, instead.

She could text em when she landed to let em know that she made it home safe, instead of immediately turning her phone off airplane mode and hoping, ridiculously, to have missed texts from Stacy. She could—

"Abigail!"

She turned toward the voice and blinked to make sure she was seeing what she was seeing. There, in the waiting area chairs right under Gate 38, Jax and Oren were waving.

She looked back down at her ticket as her attendant placed a guiding hand on her low back to keep her walking toward where her friends were sitting. She was Gate 38, too.

She practically ran over to the boys, her attendant at her heels. Both Jax and Oren were dressed in sweats, same as Abigail, as they hugged their bags. Oren had on a shining silver kippah—a word she had officially learned from Kai.

"What are you two doing here?" Abigail asked. "I thought I was the only unaccompanied minor flying to JFK."

Jax threw his head back and sighed loudly, pointing his thumb in the direction of a man with shoulder-length dreadlocks pulled back neatly behind his head and wearing dark-rimmed glasses. The man looked up from his magazine and waved. "That's my dad," Jax said. "He was in Minneapolis for some academic conference, then got a rental car and drove up to pick up me and Oren so he could fly home with us. He thinks I'd be a handful for the poor flight attendants on my own."

Oren laughed. Abigail did, too. The boys shifted their bags over to make room for her to sit with them. "You're not unaccompanied anymore," Oren said. "We can all go home together."

Together. Abigail liked the sound of that.

"Hey, what's your phone number?" Jax said, pulling out his phone. "I'll add you to our camp group chat."

"It's how we stayed in touch after last year's camp," Oren added. "And we make plans for, like, video chats and stuff, too. Or even sometimes we try to make plans to visit each other."

"Thank God for technology!" Jax said.

As Abigail gave her number to Jax, she had to agree.

"Especially since we're too old to go back next year now," Jax said, his shoulders slumping. "Though maybe I'll apply to be a counselor when I'm old enough. That would be so cool! I could—what would MJ say? Lead my little chickies to success!"

"Are you gonna go back next year, Abigail?" Oren asked.

Abigail paused to think about it. It wouldn't be the same without Oren, and Jax, and Juliana, and Stick, and Cassidy, and all the other kids who were too old to come back again.

But Bryn would be there. And some of the other kids she had gotten to know. And Lena would be there, too—a crush was still a crush, after all.

And Abigail was still Abigail, and Lena had said that was perfectly okay. (Abigail was trying to believe that.)

Maybe new kids would come next year. Maybe she would have new cabinmates.

Maybe she would find someone new to trust enough to make a pact with. (Maybe she would just be their friend this time, instead.)

Maybe Mx. Nutsford would still be there, too, and Abigail would hang her Laura Dern poster proudly on the wall next to her bunk instead of keeping it rolled up in her suitcase.

Abigail looked at Jax and Oren, who were waiting for her answer.

"Yeah," she said, smiling, as the gate attendant announced they were going to start boarding.

"I'm definitely coming back next year."

AUTHORS' NOTE

Friendships can form when you least expect them. Nicole and Andrew first met online in 2018, quickly forming a bond through emails and text messages.

A year later we had the idea to co-write a book. We played around with some story ideas, but nothing felt like it had a spark—a special hook that makes you sit up and say, "Hey, this idea should definitely be a book!"—until we each contributed a short story to *This Is Our Rainbow: 16 Stories of Her, Him, Them, and Us*, an anthology centering queer characters that Nicole co-edited with Katherine Locke.

Through a wonderful coincidence, Abigail and Kai, the characters in our stories, ended up right next to each other on *Rainbow*'s cover. They were even looking at each other!

That was the first little spark.

But Abigail and Kai are very different kids, and we worried their differences might be too much. They live halfway across the country from each other, were raised in different faith traditions, and have unique interests.

The same goes for Nicole and Andrew. Nicole was born, raised, and still lives in New Jersey, while Andrew's family moved states every few years. Nicole teaches creative writing and is a member of a roller derby team. Andrew went to law school and is a longtime figure skater.

Despite being very different people, we are both queer, and many of our conversations focus on identity and how to navigate queerness in our day-to-day lives. That, we finally realized, was also the common thread between Abigail and Kai.

A starting point.

Neither of us can quite remember how we chose summer camp as our setting. Inclusive camps that welcome queer kids didn't exist when we were kids. But it turned out to be the perfect opportunity not only for Abigail and Kai to meet, but also for us to develop other queer characters and portray many different queer identities. Camp QUILTBAG is a space where kids are allowed to have fun while being who they are. It's a place where friendships are made (also sometimes tested) and identities can be explored safely, with the support of knowledgeable adult counselors. It's a place where kids who might not otherwise have ever met can become life-long friends.

Our friendship feels a lot like that, too. We might not have met if it wasn't for our shared love of writing about queer identities. And for nearly four years, our interactions were confined to texts and email.

In June 2022, we met in person for the first time. Just like the Camp QUILTBAG kids on their first day at camp, we were excited and a little nervous to meet up.

We ultimately ended up having a wonderful, whirlwind few days together on that visit. Now we can't wait to see each other again and are grateful we'll always have Camp QUILTBAG to connect us.

So, keep an open mind as you search for your own friends and understanding. You might find both in the most unlikely of places, just like we have.

ACKNOWLEDGMENTS

It still feels like a dream that we got to write this book together, so first and foremost, Nicole and Andrew would like to thank each other. Co-writing a book sounded fun from the outset, but we couldn't have imagined what a joy bringing Camp QUILTBAG to life would be until we started drafting. Each stage of this novel's creation has brought us closer and made us more grateful we had the opportunity to work together.

Nicole and Andrew would also like to thank our spouses, Liz and Deven. We wouldn't be where we are today without their support. Same for our families, who have cheered us on from the start. On the other hand, we'd probably have written this book much faster without our cats demanding attention, but thanks for at least being cute and fluffy, Gillian, Amo, and Alistair.

Thank you to our agents, Jim McCarthy and Jordan Hamessley, and the teams at Dystel, Goderich & Bourret and New Leaf Literary. Your enthusiasm for this project when it was only a handful of chapters encouraged us to make it even queerer and campier.

The team at Algonquin Young Readers has been a dream to work with. Thank you, Krestyna Lypen, for loving our camper kids as much as we do and for your insightful editorial guidance. Thank you to illustrator Violet Tobacco and designer Carla Weise for bringing Abigail, Kai, and Camp QUILTBAG to life in such beautiful detail. Thank you to production editor Ashley Mason and copyeditor Sue Wilkins for guiding us toward the finish line with edits, and to Rebecca Carlisle, Moira Kerrigan, Shaelyn McDaniel, Meghan O'Shaughnessy, Chloe Puton, and every other member of the AYR team who has helped us get our story into readers' hands. Thank you to AYR publisher Stacy Lellos for your commitment to publishing the best books for all young readers. We are honored to be part of the AYR family.

Finally, thank you to all the booksellers, bloggers, librarians, educators, and parents who are committed to getting books like ours into the hands of readers who may need them.